A Killing Agree

Hampshire Crime - DI Charlotte Steele
Book 1

Christine Pattle

COPYRIGHT

Chapter 1

Fliss Edmondson quietly sneaked a peek at her watch. Would it be rude of her to leave the party early? Her job stressed her enough with its long hours and constant pressure, without her career impeding on her social life as well. This poor excuse of a party didn't count as a social life, not with attendance forced upon her as part of her job.

After well over a year of negotiating, writing reports, and presenting them at committee meetings, she finally got the contract signed off late last year.

Not that they had much to show for it so far. Tenurewise was contracted to provide the council with 200 properties over the course of two years, to be used as temporary accommodation for homeless families.

Finally, many months later than promised, the company managed to procure the first suitable property. To celebrate, Tenurewise organised a small party at the inaugural house before they handed over the property.

Fliss nodded at the man speaking to her, pretending to be interested. Truthfully, she didn't have a clue what he'd been talking about. She glanced at his name badge. Stephen Pollock, the company's property acquisitions manager. She remembered him from some of the meetings. Funny how, when everything takes place online these days, it makes remembering people's names and faces harder. Meet them in real life and they always appeared younger and better looking, to the extent that she barely recognised them.

"What's the new timeline for procuring the full two hundred properties?" Fliss asked, realising he was talking business and hoping the probing question would divert his attention from the fact that she hadn't been listening.

"It's difficult to say at this stage. We have several properties in the pipeline, and we're confident we can pick up momentum and still achieve the contract outcome within two years."

Fliss stifled a yawn, wondering if they would still be having this same conversation another year down the line. The two-year time span wasn't supposed to be reset every few months to hide the fact that the company lagged embarrassingly behind the original schedule.

"Of course, adjusting the contract price would help things tremendously. We did bid rather low, which is making it harder to find suitable properties." Stephen gave an apologetic smile.

Fliss translated the words in her head. What he really meant was that Tenurewise wasn't making nearly as much profit as they'd hoped. Too bad. They should have checked their calculations more thoroughly before they submitted the bid. She hoped the contract would be sustainable. A breakdown in the arrangement would be embarrassing for her, as she was only too aware of her failure to check out the company's credentials thoroughly before they finalised the deal. She'd been blinded by the stellar amount of money she would save the cash-strapped council. Even so, increasing the contract price wouldn't be an easy undertaking and, at this stage, she simply wouldn't entertain the idea.

"Spending public money comes with a fiduciary duty to our residents, and therefore we must stick to the agreed price, I'm afraid." What sort of pushover did he take her for? They signed a binding contract. Besides, it wasn't in her power to agree to a price increase. A change like that would require a detailed report, which would be subject to severe scrutiny from councillors, following which, they would probably vote against the proposal. No way would she send such a report to the Cabinet. She'd sweated blood to gain the initial approval in the face of some extremely vocal opposition from the more conservative councillors. Her bold and innovative move to save the council millions by leasing these properties to replace expensive hotel usage to house homeless families was seen as reckless by some.

Did Tenurewise organise this party solely to butter her up before asking for extra money? She wondered again how soon she'd be able to get away.

To be fair, they'd done a good job with the party. Especially the top-notch canapés, which Fliss devoured by the dozen in lieu of a proper meal, and plenty of rather good champagne, although she'd only drunk one glass. She regretted driving here because a few more glasses of champers might have made the evening more agreeable.

Kate Lovell, the contractor who'd helped with negotiations and the financial modelling of the potential outcomes of the contract, sneaked up beside her.

"I'm going home," she said. "Tomorrow's a workday. I don't want to be out too late."

Fliss looked up. Only Alicia Gardner, Tenurewise's chief executive, and Stephen Pollock remained. She hadn't noticed the others leaving.

"I'll come with you." She didn't want to walk to her car on her own in the dark. "We'd better say goodbye to Alicia first."

The walk back to where they'd parked seemed further in the dark than it had when she'd arrived in daylight. Neither Kate nor Fliss had brought a torch with them, so they resorted to their phones. With no streetlamps along this stretch of road, the thin streams of light from their phones barely made a difference to the pitch blackness.

"I hope the new tenant doesn't need to walk anywhere at this time of night," Kate said.

"She's got three young children. I doubt she'll go out much in the evenings." The family was due to move in next week. Fliss wondered if the moving date could be hurried along before the prospective tenant realised the disadvantages of the area and demanded to be housed elsewhere.

"Do you have children?"

Fliss stopped dead. She liked to keep her private life separate from her work, so she wasn't expecting the question and considered it presumptuous of Kate to ask. That was the downside of socialising with your work colleagues. It blurred the lines. This wasn't the first time Kate had asked personal questions, all of which Fliss carefully skirted around with the skill of an expert politician, always avoiding an actual answer. She didn't want to be Kate's friend. She probably should say something to her. Instead, she brushed the question off with a laugh. "God, no! I'm a hardened career woman. I've got a cat instead. What about you?" She hoped that turning the focus onto Kate might stop her nosiness because she could almost predict the next question, and she had no intention of explaining the state of her marriage to this woman.

"Not yet."

Fliss waited for the follow-up, the inquisition about her husband, which she would have to deflect, but Kate had taken the hint and shut up.

Kate's car was parked closer than Fliss's, despite Fliss arriving at the party earlier. The two women said good night, leaving Fliss to carry on toward her own car, miffed that Kate didn't offer her a lift for the final few hundred yards, to save her from walking alone in the dark. She wished she hadn't worn high-heeled boots. They weren't the most comfortable for walking and if she had to make a run for it, they would slow her down.

Fliss still didn't know what to do about Max. This week, they were meant to celebrate their fifteenth wedding anniversary, but instead of buying her a present and taking her out to dinner, they'd had a blazing row, something that seemed to be a regular occurrence lately.

As soon as Fliss got into the car and locked the doors, she relaxed. She rummaged in her handbag for her glasses, which she needed to drive, cursing when she failed to find them. Where on earth were they? She turned on the internal light and tipped the contents of her bag onto the passenger seat.

No glasses.

Then she remembered. She'd taken them out when she'd gone upstairs in the house to inspect a chipped tile, which she'd immediately asked Alicia Gardner to get fixed to avoid the council getting a bill for the damage at a later date.

Damn. She would have to go back and get them.

She walked faster this time, to spend as little time as possible alone in the darkness. For a moment, she wished Max were here. But that wasn't going to happen. Funny how much of her working life revolved around discussing property repairs, yet she wasn't capable of plastering over her rapidly crumbling marriage.

Max had inconveniently absented himself for the last couple of days, leaving her with no idea of when, or if, he might be back. The divorce petition she'd received in the post bluntly answered that question for her.

She'd changed the locks yesterday, giving him no chance to change his mind. A clean break would be less painful for both of them. She'd already accepted that, drifting easily into a routine of microwave meals for one, then cuddling up on the sofa with Mr Muggle, crying herself to sleep. Even that might not last. Max would probably try to claim custody of the cat simply to be vindictive.

She found the front door still unlocked when she arrived back at the party. Quietly, she pushed it open, planning to sneak back upstairs, grab her glasses, and be out again before anyone spotted her. At all costs, she wanted to avoid getting trapped in conversation for another hour.

The door to the open-plan kitchen and living room, where they'd held the party, was firmly shut. Raised voices came from beyond the door, but Fliss didn't dare linger long enough to make out any details of the conversation or to identify the speakers, although she assumed it must be Alicia and Stephen. Perhaps she ought to stop and listen. The more time she'd spent talking to the key company employees tonight, the deeper her misgivings became. She should have pulled the plug on this contract months ago. Something didn't sit right, apart from the total lack of performance, taking an inordinate amount of time to purchase a single property for them. But the council had left it far too late to pull out now. They'd already signed the contract, so she would somehow have to make the relationship with Tenurewise work because she'd be the first to be fired if the contract failed and the council lost money.

She tiptoed up the stairs, ignoring the pile of blue plastic shoe covers scrunched up on the bottom stair. They'd been asked to use them for the guided tour of the property earlier, reminding Fliss of a crime scene. She'd probably seen far too many detective series on TV, her main guilty pleasure when she wanted to unwind after a long day's work. She let out a soft chuckle. Other people listened to music to relax or opened a bottle of wine. She binge-watched murder mysteries on Netflix.

In reality, the plastic shoe covers were a ploy by Tenurewise to avoid having to clean the whole house again after the partygoers tramped through it. But they'd need to clean the house now anyway. With the couple of snagging issues they'd discovered, the chipped tile and a broken window catch, they'd need to get repairs contractors in to fix them before officially handing the property over.

To Fliss's relief, she found her glasses sitting on the bathroom windowsill. She swooped them up and put them on. A creak on the staircase startled her, and she felt like a trespasser creeping back into the house like this. *Stop being so stupid.* She pulled herself together and picked up her handbag, keen to get out of the house before anyone waylaid her.

The bathroom door opened fully before she reached for the handle.

"You?" Fliss wasn't sure who she'd been expecting.

"I need to show you something."

Fliss walked towards the bathroom window as directed. A hand clamped over her mouth, and she was pushed against the sink, trapping her arms. Immediately, she was twisted sideways. The hand across her mouth shifted downwards, grabbing her arm roughly instead. She tried to scream, but her head was slammed forwards against something hard before any sound came out. As she collapsed towards the bath, Fliss finally realised what had been worrying her so much tonight.

Chapter 2

Charlotte Steele reversed into a parking space at the side of the road. It must be a ten-minute walk to the police station from here, but she might still arrive on time, and walking would give her time to clear her head and think about how she was going to handle things. Besides, she didn't have access to the staff car park yet, which didn't give her much choice.

She walked quickly, not wanting to be late on her first day. She'd moved down from London a couple of days ago for this job, her first as a detective inspector, so it was vital for her to make a good first impression.

It felt odd starting a new job on a Wednesday. She supposed it was due to it being the first of the month, although starting the job on April Fool's Day didn't bode well.

The silence struck her more than anything else. Was this really the main road in this town? Already, she missed the hustle and bustle of London. Only three cars had driven past so far. But perhaps a slower pace of life would be a good thing for her first DI post. And if Hampshire proved too quiet, with nothing more than missing cats and stolen bicycles, she would search for a DI position in London pretty damn quick.

Within minutes of Charlie entering the building, a slim, blond woman came to fetch her from the reception area.

"I'm DC Sally Geeson." She held out her hand. "I've got instructions to take you straight up to the DCI's office."

"Thank you." Charlie shook her hand briefly. "How long have you worked here?" If this woman belonged to her team, she might be able to find out something about her experience without being too obvious.

"It will be ten years next Monday," Sally said.

Charlie followed her up the stairs. Ten years and still a DC. Did that mean she wasn't much good, or did she lack ambition? Charlie had got to DI in that time.

"Is this town always so quiet?"

Sally laughed. "You're from the Met, aren't you?"

"That's right."

"We're not a bunch of country hicks here. Hampshire's a huge county. I'm sure you'll find more than enough major crime to keep you busy." Sally held the door open for her.

Charlie followed her to the end of the corridor, wondering if she should apologise, but unsure what for. Before she reached a decision, Sally stopped and knocked on one of the office doors, then opened it as soon as a response came from inside.

"DI Charlotte Steele, sir." She held the door open as Charlie passed her.

Charlie recognised DCI Talbot from the job interview panel. "Everyone calls me Charlie."

"Welcome to Hampshire & Isle of Wight Constabulary, DI Steele." Talbot held out his hand. "Unfortunately, I've been called away to an urgent meeting, but DC Gleeson will take you to meet your team, and we'll catch up later."

"Yes, sir." Charlie shook his hand with mixed emotions. Whilst she would prefer to get acquainted with her team as soon as possible, she was expecting a longer chat with the DCI first to get some background on them and bring her up to speed with any ongoing issues in the county. Never mind. She would find out soon enough.

The large incident room buzzed with chatter, all of which stopped the moment she entered.

Sally introduced her. "Everyone, this is DI Charlotte Steele."

"Charlie." She realised a moment too late that it might prove easier to manage the team and gain respect if she remained more formal. But she hadn't answered to her full name since the age of nine. Best to stay true to herself, and if her team getting too familiar caused a problem, she would deal with it.

Sally introduced the small team. "This is DC Tyrone Wilson."

Charlie held out her hand to the muscular Black DC. He gripped it firmly before shaking it. He looked young, barely in his twenties, but she guessed he spent much of his spare time working out, and she'd put her faith in him if she needed someone to watch her back in a dangerous situation.

A phone rang across the room. "Do you mind if I get that, ma'am?" Tyrone was already heading towards it.

"This is Zack Hollands," Sally introduced the remaining man in the room. "He's our civilian techie. He's a genius with computers."

The young man seemed nervous. She shook his hand and wasn't surprised to find it slightly clammy.

Charlie noticed the team lacked a DS and was about to comment on that when Tyrone interrupted from across the room.

"A dead body's been reported on the other side of Eastleigh, ma'am." He put the phone down.

For a couple of seconds, Charlie froze, then quickly came to her senses. "We need to get over there. Sally, can you drive me? Tyrone, will you follow on, please?"

"Yes, ma'am." Tyrone picked up a set of car keys from his desk.

Charlie cringed. Ma'am made her sound like an old lady, and she wasn't sure if she liked it. But she'd fought hard to earn the title. She guessed she would soon get used to it.

Her mind buzzed as she followed Sally out to the car park. She would be the senior investigating officer on this case, a prospect all at once exciting and overwhelming. She swallowed any feelings of doubt and reminded herself she knew what to do. After all, she'd attended crime scenes dozens of times before and watched her old DI take charge. She'd got this.

They were about to get into what Charlie assumed must be one of the pool cars when someone ran towards them, carrying a big box. He stopped dead when he spotted Charlie.

"Rick, this is our new DI, Charlotte Steele," Sally said. "Richard Henderson is our DS."

Charlie locked eyes with him.

"Sorry I'm late. The plane got delayed, and then they re-routed us to Glasgow. We spent all night trying to get home, then I had to drop off Janette and Mia."

"Rick, I mean, DS Henderson, has been on holiday for two weeks," Sally explained.

"I brought doughnuts." Rick lifted up the box while continuing to stare at Charlie.

It seemed like forever before Charlie found her voice. "We've got a murder."

"You can come with us," Sally offered.

Charlie cut her off. "Get another car. We may need to go in different directions after we assess the murder scene." The last thing she needed was her brother breathing down her neck on her first case as SIO. How could she not have known he worked here? She'd barely seen him in the last ten years. Of course she was vaguely aware of him being a police officer, but it never occurred to her that he might be based at the same station, much less on the same team.

"We need to get moving," Charlie said, turning away.

Sally called back to Rick. "I'll text you the address."

Chapter 3

"You and Rick know each other, ma'am?" Sally glanced across at Charlie as she pulled out of the car park.

"You could say that."

"Friends, or...?" Sally left the question hanging.

Charlie sighed with annoyance. She ought to be concentrating on the murder case. She would prefer some quiet time to go through procedures in her head, to ensure she didn't miss anything obvious in the heat of the moment when she arrived at the scene. But Sally clearly didn't intend to let this go. She ought to shut her down with a sharp word or two, but that wouldn't stop Sally from thinking about it or gossiping with her colleagues. And she didn't like the direction in which Sally's thoughts were travelling.

"He's my brother."

The surprise on Sally's face indicated a completely different scenario going through her head. "But you didn't seem to be expecting him."

"Are we nearly there yet?" Charlie needed to get her head in the game. Sally mentioned earlier that the crime scene was on the other side of Eastleigh. Surely they must be close by now.

"Five minutes. So don't you guys speak to each other?"

"Do you always ask so many questions?" Charlie almost laughed at herself. Of course she would ask questions. Sally Gleeson might be a decent detective after all. She'd picked up on the tension between her and Rick, then followed it up by getting an answer out of her, an answer she hadn't really wanted to give. Added to that, Charlie was beginning to find her infuriatingly likeable.

"Well, do you? Speak to each other, I mean."

"Let's concentrate on the case." Screwing up wasn't an option, not on her first time as SIO. And explaining why she'd drifted apart from her brother would take far too long and was none of Sally's damn business.

Tyrone arrived at the scene before them and stood talking to a middle-aged man dressed in smart green overalls. A black van with *Houseworks* painted on the side in big white lettering stood parked in the driveway.

Charlie made a beeline for one of the two police constables standing outside the house. "PC Barnes." Charlie read the constable's name from his badge. "Can you log everyone in and out of the crime scene, please?"

"And who are you?" PC Barnes stood across the path, his broad shoulders blocking Charlie's way.

"DI Charlotte Steele." Charlie put her hand in her pocket for her warrant card before remembering they'd been called out here before she'd been issued with her ID.

Barnes didn't budge. Charlie looked around for Sally, who was talking to the other PC in front of the neighbouring house.

"I only started this morning. We got called out a few minutes after I arrived at the station."

"Sorry, ma'am, but I need to see your ID before I can allow you to go any further."

Charlie called Sally over. "Please, can you tell this jobsworth who I am. I didn't get a chance to pick up my warrant card this morning." She realised the constable was simply doing his job, and she'd be the first to bawl him out if he let anyone into the crime scene without identification, but that didn't stop her from being annoyed. Five minutes as SIO and she already looked like an idiot.

"It's okay, Barnsey, DI Steele is the new DI."

Barnes moved aside. "Sorry, ma'am."

Sally immediately brought her up to speed. "The repairs contractor found the body. He came to do a couple of odd jobs. He's in a bit of a state, so Tyrone is looking after him."

"Does the contractor know the victim?"

"No, ma'am."

Charlie wanted to see the body but was so worried about doing the wrong thing, she remained glued to the spot. "Are the CSIs on their way?" She would be happier when the crime scene investigators showed up.

"They've been held up. They'll be about twenty minutes," Sally said.

Charlie didn't want to wait that long. They'd probably already missed the golden hour—that first hour after the crime was committed, the chance to gather fresh evidence. Every minute they waited meant the crime scene became older, and the delay gave the murderer more time to cover their tracks. "Do you have gloves and shoe covers?" She didn't like being caught unawares. She was accustomed to having everything she needed with her, but she didn't feel prepared for this, with the case being thrown at her within minutes of entering the police station this morning. This would be a real baptism of fire. She only hoped she wouldn't crash and burn.

Sally produced the required items from her pocket. "I've only got one set. You'd better take them. I'll get a statement from the repairs guy while I'm waiting."

Charlie would have hoped that Tyrone had already done that. She glanced around outside the house to see if there was anything obvious she needed to consider. Another car pulled up on the road in front of the house, and the driver got out. Rick. Charlie pulled on the gloves and shoe covers and entered the house quickly to avoid him.

As soon as she stepped inside, Charlie realised no one had informed her where to find the murder victim. She made a quick check of the ground floor before heading upstairs.

She didn't need to search far. The bathroom door at the top of the stairs stood wide open, and she spotted the body in the bath before she even reached the top step. As she got closer, she hesitated. The scenario didn't make for a pretty sight. The woman was lying in a small pool of blood. Charlie carefully moved closer. Both wrists were expertly slit lengthwise along the arm, not across the wrist, which most people would choose to do. By the looks of things, she'd bled out quickly. The plug was preventing her blood from draining away. Even so, there was much less blood than she would have expected.

Footsteps sounded on the stairs. Rick joined her.

"Suicide?"

Charlie shook her head. "No. Where's the knife?"

"Might be under all that blood."

"There's not enough blood to cover it." There may have been four or five pints of blood at most. Not enough to cover even the bottom of the bath. "The knife would more likely be on top of the body, close to the wrists. With these wounds, there would be no strength left in her arms to move the knife, even a few inches." Was Charlie arguing with Rick because she always wanted the last word? Except this time, she almost wanted him to be right. Suicide was bad enough, but at least it would be what the woman wanted. The alternative, a vicious, frightening attack, would have been far worse.

"The CSIs will soon tell us," Rick said. "They're very good here."

Another set of footsteps on the stairs interrupted them. Charlie turned around, and a moment later, a tall, well-muscled man filled the bathroom doorway.

"Who the hell are you?"

Charlie stood up straight to make the most of her five-foot-ten height, even though this man still dwarfed her. She stared at him, refusing to be intimidated, despite the large scar stretching from the middle of his forehead, down his cheek as far as his jawbone. "DI Charlotte Steele." She automatically put a hand in her pocket for her warrant card before remembering for the second time that morning that she didn't yet have one. "It's my first day on the job here."

Rick stepped into view from behind the bathroom door. "It's okay. Ollie. She's with me." He moved to stand next to Charlie. "This is Oliver Flanders, our senior CSI."

"Yes, and I'd like to get on with the job, so will you both get your sorry asses out of my crime scene. And you'd better not have contaminated anything."

"I can assure you we followed the correct procedures." Charlie didn't want to start her first day by antagonising anyone, but this obnoxious man needed putting in his place. She wondered who he'd upset to obtain the scar. No doubt there were people queuing around the block to give him another one.

"We'll leave you to it. We've got plenty of other things to do." Rick tried to usher Charlie out of the bathroom as Flanders stepped aside to let them pass.

"We need to identify the victim as soon as possible." She instinctively reached into her pocket to hand him her business card before realising that was another item she hadn't yet organised. She didn't have a work phone either, and she certainly didn't want to hand out her personal number to this man. It threw her for a moment, although she recovered quickly. "Please phone DS Henderson as soon as you find some ID for the victim."

"We need to find out who owns the property," Charlie said as soon as they left the house.

"Already done that, Sis. I got the details from the repairman on my way in."

Charlie scowled at him. "Don't call me sis, not when we're at work." It wasn't professional.

Rick didn't offer an apology. "It's a company called Tenurewise, based in Southampton."

"Can you drive me there?" She instantly regretted asking him. Perhaps she should go with one of her DCs instead. On the other hand, Rick was family, despite their differences. If she did anything wrong, he ought to have her back. At least she assumed so. She hoped she wouldn't have to put that to the test. If she screwed up in front of Rick, he would never let her forget it.

"Sure. We should talk to the repair guy first. He found the body."

"I'm about to do that." And she would be sure to allocate some tasks to the DCs before she left the scene. She needed to take charge.

Chapter 4

Tyrone was still with the repairs contractor when Charlie and Rick approached them.

"I'm DI Steele. This is DS Henderson." Charlie held out her hand to the man, who was perched on a low wall.

He stood up and shook her hand briefly. "George Goss, maintenance engineer for Homeworks."

"You found the body?"

"Ay. And it was a shock, I'll tell you. I only came to do a couple of repairs. They wanted them done urgently, so I started early. I've got a busy schedule today." He glanced at his watch. "I'm never going to fit everything in now."

"Did you notice anybody else when you got here?"

"No. It's a quiet road. I got straight to work, mending the broken window catch in the downstairs toilet. Looked like someone forced it with a screwdriver."

"And you finished the repair before you found the body?" Charlie guessed the broken window might be how the killer got into the house. And the evidence was already destroyed.

"Yes. I replaced the handle and the lock on the window. Whoever broke in made a right mess of it. I've got the before and after photos."

"Can we see those, please?" At least they might have some evidence.

George took out his phone, then quickly brought up the photo gallery. "See how that handle is hanging." He pointed to the top part of the photo. "The window lock is completely broken."

"Would it have been possible for someone to open it from the outside?"

"The window opens outwards, so you'd need a screwdriver or something to put under the edge and lever it open. But if you weren't aware of the broken window, you wouldn't even try. It would have appeared perfectly secure from the outside."

"Can I forward this photo to my phone?"

George handed her his phone. "Do you think that's how the murderer got in?"

Charlie ignored him. "We need to take your fingerprints for elimination purposes. DC Wilson will arrange it. As soon as we've eliminated you from the enquiry, your fingerprints will be deleted from the police system."

"You mean I'm a suspect?" George's face paled. "I didn't kill her. No way."

"Whoever broke in may have left fingerprints. If we can disregard your fingerprints, then whatever is left will help us to track down the killer. There's nothing for you to worry about." Charlie hoped that would reassure him. The last thing she needed was to start the investigation with an uncooperative witness.

"What do you reckon?" Rick asked as soon as they were in the car.

Charlie ignored the question. "Can we swing by the police station on the way to visit Tenurewise? I need a warrant card, some business cards, a phone, and a decent cup of coffee." And a pass that let her into the staff car park would be good, too.

Rick laughed. "I'm sure I can sort out some of that. A decent coffee might be more difficult. There's a Starbucks in Southampton."

"Why do police stations never have good coffee?" As soon as she got home, she intended to order a coffee machine online. With luck, it might ingratiate her with her new team, as well as satisfy her own caffeine addiction.

Rick ignored the question. "So what do you think? About the case, I mean."

Charlie sighed. "Difficult without even knowing who the victim is." If the CSI didn't come up with an identity by the time she'd sorted out her new employee admin in the office, they should probably delay visiting Tenurewise. They'd get more out of the visit if they could question them about the victim. On the other hand, George Goss might have already phoned the company, so the longer they waited to visit, the more chance for the Tenurewise employees to get their stories straight. She needed to snap out of this indecisiveness. She'd investigated murders before as a DS. And she was good at it. Being thrown in at the deep end as SIO on her first day as a DI didn't change that.

"I reckon someone must have known about that broken window. Probably the person who broke it." Rick slowed down and made a right turn.

"I agree. We need to find out who had access and what that woman was doing in an empty house."

Rick smiled briefly at her. "It's nice to see you again, Sis. I didn't think you'd want to work in Hampshire."

"There was a DI job going here." She didn't want him to think she'd come here specifically because of her family roots.

"Well, whatever the reason, it's still nice to see you. Welcome to Hampshire and Isle of Wight Constabulary."

Charlie smiled. Perhaps working with Rick wouldn't be so bad. He was clearly making an effort. "Thank you. I must admit, I didn't expect a murder on my first day."

"Murder?" Rick looked across at her for long enough that Charlie started to worry he might crash the car. "Still looks like suicide to me until the pathologist says different."

"There's no knife and no water in the bath."

"What's that got to do with anything? She slit her wrists. End of."

Charlie recognised the police station ahead. They'd arrived back in no time. Charlie guessed they hadn't driven much more than a mile. "It's a fact that people who slit their wrists in the bath always fill it with water first." An experienced coroner who had dealt with dozens of such cases had told her that. Every single one filled the bath with water first, as if they'd all read the same manual on how to do the job.

"Really? Why?"

"No idea." She'd asked the coroner exactly the same question and got the same answer. "They just do."

"Doesn't prove it's not suicide. Maybe this one's a maverick. Perhaps she wanted to do things differently."

Charlie sighed. This was more like the Rick she knew, always arguing with her. "It's possible, but it doesn't feel right. Also, everyone cuts across the wrists. That way, they cut through everything, with no risk of missing the vital artery. But did you notice this one sliced lengthways along her arms, in exactly the right place to open up the artery so she'd bleed out quicker?"

"She probably read how to do it on the internet." Rick always had an answer to everything.

"It's not easy to do on the first arm. Can you imagine how much more difficult it is to make that same cut on the second arm, with your first arm in that state? And people always naturally use their dominant hand for preference, so she'd be doing it left-handed. It's virtually impossible." Charlie wasn't certain it was completely impossible, but it most definitely would be extremely difficult. With the tendon sliced through, the fingers probably wouldn't work at all. "And don't forget we didn't find a knife." She wanted to win the argument with Rick at all costs. She wouldn't let him forget anything. How did he expect the poor woman to hide the knife afterwards with her wrists in that state?

Rick turned the car into the car park.

"I'm telling you, this is a murder." The questions Charlie needed answered were what was the woman doing in an empty house, and who was she?

Rick's phone interrupted him before he got the chance to reply. He pulled into a parking space and answered it.

"The victim's name is Felicity Edmondson," he said, stuffing the phone back into his pocket. "Ollie found her handbag hidden behind the bath panel."

Charlie immediately picked up on that detail. "Why would she hide her bag if she was about to commit suicide?" No way did the victim take her own life. Not that being proved right gave her any satisfaction in this case. "Do we have an address?"

"Not yet, but Sally's onto it."

"That's great. Can I get my warrant card before we visit Tenurewise?" Unless they discovered the victim's next of kin before then, it seemed like the most sensible thing to do. Perhaps the owners of the house would be able to explain why Felicity Edmondson was in their bath.

Twenty minutes later, Charlie was on her way to Southampton, armed with a warrant card, a phone, some business cards, and some spare pairs of nitrile gloves. She felt much more prepared than earlier, although she still needed to sort out access to the staff car park.

"What's Sally's story? She seems competent. I'm surprised she hasn't made DS yet." Charlie decided to use the journey to the Tenurewise offices to grill Rick about her new team.

Rick laughed. "She *is* a DS. At least she was until recently. She got demoted."

"Why?"

"You'll have to wait for her to tell you that."

"Is she trouble? Should I be worried?" This job wasn't giving her an easy ride so far. First, a murder, and now possible staff problems.

"Sally's good. You're lucky to have her on the team."

Clearly, Rick didn't intend to enlighten her. But if it was going to cause her a problem, she needed to know. She hoped she would have time to get to know her new team properly soon. It would be better to know their strengths and weaknesses before they launched into a murder enquiry.

"When are you going to visit Mum?" Rick asked.

Charlie swallowed the lump in her throat. "I doubt I'll get much free time until this murder investigation is over." She expected to be working long hours, with few days off. After not seeing Mum for so long, visiting her would be an ordeal. Charlie welcomed any excuse to put it off for as long as possible.

"You should make time. She'd like to see you."

Charlie wasn't sure if the feeling was mutual.

Chapter 5

The Tenurewise offices were on the second floor of a smart-looking shared office block on the edge of the main shopping centre in Southampton.

"I'm Alicia Gardner." The woman who approached them in reception held out her hand. "Chief Executive of Tenurewise." If the cost of her designer clothes and perfectly styled hair were anything to go by, Tenurewise must be doing well for itself.

Charlie introduced herself and Rick, relieved to have a warrant card to show. "Your company owns a house on Highfield Road."

"That's right. Number seventeen. It's our most recent purchase. Is anything wrong?" A note of concern came through in Alicia's voice, but otherwise, she seemed extremely confident.

"Perhaps we should discuss this in your office." She and Rick might need to interview other employees as well, so an office would be useful.

Alicia hesitated. "I'm quite busy this morning. Could you at least tell me what it's about?"

"Mrs Gardner, it really would be best to discuss this in private." Rick nodded towards the receptionist, who immediately turned away and pretended to be occupied.

Alicia's office was as stylish as the woman herself, although the remainder of the premises seemed strictly functional. The plain white walls were punctuated with photos of beautifully renovated homes, presumably belonging to Tenurewise. Charlie's gaze rested lustfully on the shiny, state-of-the-art coffee machine that took pride of place on a set of cupboards on one side of the spacious room. A glass coffee table surrounded by five comfortable chairs overlooked a panoramic view of the city. Alicia pulled out one of the chairs and signalled to them to sit opposite her.

"What's this about?" A flicker of worry shadowed her perfectly made-up face.

"We understand the property is empty." Charlie didn't want to play her hand too soon.

"Yes, we're handing it over to the council in a couple of days."

"Who has keys to the property?" Charlie would have to break the news to her that she wouldn't be doing anything with the house until they'd finished with the crime scene.

"The keys are kept in this office, so only myself and the property manager have access to them. But we also gave a set of keys to the company that does our repairs. They're sending someone there today." Alicia's expression turned to worry. "Has something happened?"

"I'm afraid someone has been found dead on the property." Charlie watched Alicia carefully to gauge her reaction.

"Dead? Who?" She looked towards the closed office door as if she might be able to see through it and check off an attendance register of who might be missing this morning.

"Does the name Felicity Edmondson mean anything to you?"

Alicia looked blank for a moment. "Fliss?" Her expression turned to shock.

"You know her?"

"She's the housing director at the council. They're planning to use the property to house one of their homeless families. What was she doing there?"

"That's what we were about to ask you. When did you last see Felicity?"

"Yesterday evening. It's the first property that Tenurewise is providing to the council. We held a party at the house to celebrate.

But I don't understand how you found her inside the property. She left before I did."

"I'm going to need the names of all the attendees at the party," Charlie said. At least that would give her a list of suspects.

"Yes, of course." Alicia got up to fetch a pen and a pad of paper from her desk. She returned to her seat and started to write. "There's me, of course. Stephen Pollock. He's our property acquisitions manager. Danny Owen is the company lawyer. They're both in the office now." She paused speaking to jot down the list. "Then there's Zoe Neale. She's a contractor we use sometimes to do the catering for events. I'll get you her contact details."

"What about on the council side? How many of their employees were at the party?" Rick asked.

"Fliss, of course. Then there was her tenancy manager, Tracey Gulliver. And Kate Lovell. She's been involved in a lot of the negotiations. She doesn't work directly for the council. She's an external consultant. And Diana Horn, one of the local councillors. Her portfolio is temporary accommodation, so she takes a keen interest in this contract." Alicia tore the sheet of paper from her pad and handed it to Charlie.

"Is that all?" Eight people, including the caterer. Not much of a party. Hardly worth getting a caterer for it.

"Yes, we wanted to thank the key people in the council who have supported our company."

"When did each person leave the party?" With such a small group, Charlie hoped she would remember with a fair degree of accuracy.

"The caterer, Zoe, left first. She spent some time packing up and made a couple of trips to her van, so I'm not absolutely sure what time. Then Councillor Horn left. It may have been about eight p.m. Everyone was quite pleased to get shot of her. All she did was moan about everything."

"Did she moan to Fliss about anything in particular?" Perhaps they argued.

"Not that I particularly noticed."

"So who left next?" The order of leaving might be important. It might not be. If Fliss left the party, she must have come back or been brought back. Any one of the others may have done the same.

"I'm pretty sure it was Fliss and Kate. They left together."

They would need to talk to Kate Lovell as soon as possible. She may have been the last person to see Felicity Edmondson alive. "What time was that?" She wanted to establish a timeline. It would help them when the pathologist gave them the time of death.

"Nine-ish."

She didn't sound sure. "Okay, so who was next to leave?" She glanced over at Rick, who was writing everything down.

"Tracey Gulliver and Danny Owen. Danny offered Tracey a lift. They must have gone about twenty minutes after Fliss and Kate. That left myself and Stephen Pollock. We cleared up the leftover food and drink and shared it out to take home."

"Did you leave together?"

"Pretty much. I phoned for a taxi because I'd been drinking. Stephen waited with me until the taxi arrived, then I left him to lock up."

"What time was that?"

Alicia paused for a few moments as if trying to work out which answer would incriminate her less. "Perhaps another twenty minutes later."

"So nine forty p.m.?"

"That's right."

"Did anyone argue with Fliss at the party?"

Alicia answered immediately. "No. Fliss was a nice woman. Why would anyone want to argue with her?"

Charlie found that hard to accept. Not whether she was nice, but about her never arguing. The woman held a position of high office in the council. As director of housing, she must spend much of her time arguing, or did they call it debating these days? Unless she was a total pushover, part of her job description was surely making difficult decisions that may upset some people.

"Did you pick up on any tension at all?"

"Inspector, everyone drank at least one glass of champagne. It was a party atmosphere."

"How long have you known Felicity Edmondson?"

"It's coming up to three years. Things move excruciatingly slowly in the public sector."

"And what is the nature of the contract between the council and Tenurewise?"

"We're contracted to provide two hundred properties to the council over the next two years. We buy the properties and lease them to the council on ten-year leases. They use them as temporary accommodation to house homeless families."

"Two hundred properties. That must be lucrative for Tenurewise. What's the total value of the contract?"

"It depends on the size of the properties we purchase, but the total rental value of the leases, when we've completed the purchase programme, is likely to be at least three and a half million a year."

Rick interrupted. "Is there a break clause in the contract? If the council wanted to back out now, is it legally possible?"

Charlie had been about to ask the same question. If Felicity got cold feet and wanted to terminate the contract, that would be a huge motive for murder.

"The council is very happy. They don't want to terminate anything." Alicia smiled, although to Charlie's mind, her expression seemed forced.

"That wasn't what we asked."

"Sorry. Yes, there is a break clause if certain conditions are met within the first year. It's complicated."

"Can we have a copy of the contract, please?"

"I'll get someone to print it for you."

"Can you email it to me?" Charlie realised she didn't know her new email address. She rectified the mistake quickly. "DS Henderson will give you an email address to send it to, then we'd like to speak to Stephen Pollock and Danny Owen."

Chapter 6

Stephen Pollock was out viewing a property, so Alicia showed them to Danny Owen's office.

As soon as they entered the office, it became clear where the company's entire interior design budget had been spent. Although clean and tidy, Danny's office possessed none of the style of Alicia's workspace and seemed cramped by comparison.

"Is this going to take long? I've got a lot of work to do." Owen shuffled some papers on his desk.

"If you give us your full attention, I'm sure it won't take long." Charlie didn't need attitude. She'd already got the measure of Danny Owen. Good-looking, believed he was God's gift to everyone, and didn't give a toss about anyone except himself. "A woman has been murdered," she said, injecting a good amount of gravity into her voice.

Owen looked up abruptly. "Murdered? Who?"

Charlie assumed Alicia Gardner would have already passed on that vital piece of information. "Felicity Edmondson was found in one of your houses, 17 Highfield Avenue, this morning."

"What?"

They held his full attention now.

"Did anyone argue with Felicity Edmondson at the party last night?" She didn't consider Owen empathetic enough to pick up on any bad vibes between anyone else, but with only seven people at the party, eight if you counted the caterer, he might have noticed something.

"Not really."

Charlie waited for him to continue. Most people were unable to resist filling a silence. Danny Owen turned out not to be most people. He stared at her blankly.

"Who argued with Fliss Edmondson?"

"No one." Owen stared at his desk, avoiding eye contact.

"*Not really* doesn't mean there was no argument. Who was the argument with?"

"I didn't mean *not really*. I meant *no*." Owen backpedalled.

"May I remind you this is a murder enquiry?" Charlie took a deep breath. The pathologist hadn't confirmed that yet. Rick's suicide theory had better be wrong. "Everyone at that party is potentially a suspect, so you'd better start telling the truth."

Owen blanched. "She did have a discussion with Stephen. Not really an argument."

"What was the *discussion* about?"

Owen glanced towards the closed office door, perhaps checking that his boss wasn't about to eavesdrop on the conversation. "We needed to increase the contract price. It took over two and a half years to get the contract up and running, and in that time, property prices have gone up. Our profit margin now will be minimal, and we'll have to wait until we can sell the properties when the leases expire to make any money. Stephen thought he could get through to her."

"And what did Mrs Edmondson have to say about that request?"

"She gave Stephen a hard no. I warned him she would never agree to it. We've already signed the contract, so, legally, we're screwed. I told them that. But Alicia assumed she could butter Fliss up with a few glasses of champagne. That's why she organised the party. Unfortunately for her, Fliss drove to the party, so she didn't drink much."

Charlie wondered if Alicia Gardner or Stephen Pollock might have killed Felicity Edmondson to clear the way for price negotiations with someone more cooperative. They were allegedly the last people to leave the house. She made a mental note to check Gardner's and Pollock's salaries and whether they owned shares in the company. If Tenurewise ended up filing for bankruptcy, they stood to lose a lot of money.

"What time did Felicity Edmondson leave the party?"

"I don't know. She was still there when I left."

That differed from what Alicia Gardner told them. "Are you sure?"

"Of course I'm sure. Alicia gave me hell this morning for leaving too early. Apparently, she expected me to stay until the bitter end. But Tracey wanted to go home and was worried about walking to the bus stop on her own in the dark, so I offered her a lift home. To be honest, I used it as an excuse to get away early."

"Tracey Gulliver?"

Owen nodded.

"What time did you leave the party?"

Owen automatically glanced at his watch as if that might give him the answer. "It must have been shortly after nine p.m."

"Where does Tracey live?"

Owen shrugged. "Somewhere out towards Southampton. As soon as I realised it meant going out of my way, I decided to drop her off at the bus stop."

Very chivalrous. Charlie wondered if Owen had hoped to get lucky, and Tracey Gulliver turned him down. "Did you go straight home after that?" He could easily have gone back to the house.

"Of course."

"And what time did you get home?"

"It must have been about nine thirty or nine forty. I live in Winchester."

Rick made a note of Owen's address. They would check the timings later.

"Can anyone confirm what time you arrived home?"

Owen hesitated. "No."

Charlie wasn't sure if he was telling the truth, but she didn't really like him for the murder. They could always check the facts more thoroughly if necessary. She stood up.

"Thank you. That will be all for now, but we may have to come back at some stage." She handed him one of her still pristine business cards. "If you remember anything else, please call me."

"Of course. I still can't believe..."

"We need to talk to your colleague Stephen Pollock. Would you please check if he's back in the office yet?"

He wasn't. After eliciting a promise from Danny Owen to ask Pollock to call her and arrange an appointment, she and Rick headed back to the car.

"I need coffee," she announced, still miffed that neither Gardner nor Owen offered them anything to drink.

Rick was busy checking his phone. "No chance." He put his phone back in his pocket. "The DCI wants us back at the station immediately."

Chapter 7

Charlie didn't need to wait long to find out what the DCI wanted. She hadn't even stepped into the main office when a voice thundered along the corridor behind her.

"Steele. My office, now."

She followed DCI Talbot in silence, like a small child being summoned to the headmaster's office, only from the tone of his voice, this would be more than a minor reprimand. She quickly reviewed the morning's events in her head, trying to work out what she might have done wrong.

"Close the door."

He didn't tell her to sit, and she wouldn't take that liberty in case it upset him even more. This wasn't the brilliant start to her new job she had hoped for.

"Where have you been?"

Charlie willed herself to remain calm. "We visited the Tenurewise offices in Southampton. They own the property where Felicity Edmondson was found dead." Surely he couldn't find fault with that. They'd made progress on the case already.

"And I suppose you told them that Felicity Edmondson was dead."

"Yes, but I didn't give them any details. I found out some useful information about the victim." She wondered if he knew that Rick went with her, but it wouldn't matter. The buck stopped with her now.

"Are you completely incompetent?" Talbot roared at her.

Charlie's automatic instinct was to step back, but she stopped herself in the nick of time. She opened her mouth to speak, but the DCI didn't hesitate long enough for her to get a word in.

"The victim's husband phoned earlier, threatening to sue because he found out about his wife's death on Facebook. Didn't it occur to you to start with the next of kin? Not only should you have informed him as soon as possible, but he might be a prime suspect. He's hardly going to cooperate with the police now, is he?"

"Sorry, sir." Charlie couldn't imagine how awful it must be for someone to learn of his wife's death on social media. "But at the time, we didn't even have an ID for the victim. I considered it to be the best use of our time, and I hoped someone at Tenurewise would be able to tell us who the victim might be."

"But you found out the victim's name before you got to the company's offices?"

"Yes, DC Gleeson phoned."

"And yet you still ploughed ahead and visited the property owner."

"We were almost there at that point."

"It doesn't matter. You should have changed your plan."

"Sorry, sir," Charlie repeated, wondering if she would ever be able to apologise enough for her career to recover from this terrible start. Her employment contract included a three-month probation period. She couldn't afford any more mistakes or they wouldn't make her permanent. "I'll visit the husband now and apologise in person."

"Make sure that you do. I don't know how you did things at your last station, but here, we do things by the book."

"Yes, sir."

"I understand you were in the army before you joined the police."

Charlie felt herself standing to attention automatically. Old habits died hard. "Yes, sir. Ten years, sir. I was a sergeant."

"You'll be used to following orders then."

"Yes, sir." Charlie felt about ten inches tall. This wasn't how she'd envisioned her first proper conversation with the DCI.

Talbot dismissed her.

Charlie wasn't looking forward to visiting Mr Edmondson. She needed to sort out a pool car because she sure as hell wasn't taking

Rick to this interview. If she was forced to eat humble pie, she didn't want her brother to witness it.

Chapter 8

Charlie took a deep breath. She needed to check in with her team for an update on any new information from the pathologist or the crime scene investigators. But she didn't want to face them while she felt so utterly deflated. She still hadn't managed to get a coffee. She'd seen a machine on the way to the DCI's office. The coffee would probably taste like shit, but anything that gave her a caffeine hit would be better than nothing.

"How's it going?"

Charlie recognised Sally's voice behind her and turned around. "It would be going a lot better if I could get a proper cup of coffee."

Sally smiled at her. "Follow me. The CSI team has a decent coffee machine. I'm sure I can persuade them to let you use it, seeing as it's your first day. Besides, the office will probably be empty. They're all still at the crime scene."

Charlie tagged behind her down a flight of stairs. "How do I get a car? I can't keep relying on lifts from other people." If she got desperate, she would use her own car, but that would be a last resort. She didn't want the local criminal fraternity finding out what car she drove. It made things too easy if someone bore her a grudge in the future and wanted to track her down.

"Let's get a coffee first, then I'll sort you out. It must be a bit of a shock having to jump straight into a case like this."

"It's what I'm here for, although it would have been nice to have a couple of hours to get acquainted with the team first." Charlie wondered what Sally's story was and why Rick refused to fill in the details. She decided it would be antagonistic to ask Sally now. After her bollocking from Talbot, she needed her team to be on her side. "Did anything come up from interviewing the neighbours earlier?"

"Most of them were out. We found one man who complained about a lot of coming and going last night."

Charlie realised she hadn't briefed the team about their visit to Tenurewise this morning. That reminded her she also needed to start the murder board and the murder book, to keep a record of their investigation. "The owners of the house held a party there last night. How much coming and going did he mean? There were only eight people at the party."

"It might mean anything. He didn't seem particularly reliable."

The CSI office was empty. Sally refilled the coffee machine and turned it on. "It only takes ten minutes." She found two mugs and a spoon. "What are you going to do next?"

"I need to visit the next of kin, Max Edmundson." Charlie's heart sank even thinking about it. Would Max Edmondson's complaint end her career?

"Well, you can't do that yet. He's at a conference in Edinburgh. He's on his way home, but he won't be here until at least mid-afternoon."

Immediately, Charlie's spirits lifted. DCI Talbot completely failed to mention that Max Edmondson had been 350 miles away. So Charlie couldn't have visited the husband earlier this morning even if they'd tracked down his name and address sooner. She'd been feeling guilty about nothing. The DCI couldn't have known the full facts.

"In that case, do you want to come with me to the council offices? We need to interview the people who attended the party last night and find out more about the victim. I'll send Rick back to the crime scene to check on progress."

Charlie still hadn't found time to sort out a car, so Sally drove to the council offices in Southampton.

"Who do we need to speak to?" Sally slowed for a set of traffic lights, which conveniently turned green before she got there.

"Definitely Tracey Gulliver, the tenancy manager, and Kate Lovell. Both of them were at the party last night. It might be helpful to talk to anyone who worked closely with the victim. The more we can find out about her, the better. And if she had any issues related to her job, that might provide a motive for someone." People were always complaining to the council. The chances were that a great many people were queueing up with complaints for Felicity Edmondson. But not many of the complaints would be worth murdering for.

It was Charlie's second journey of the day into Southampton, so she recognised parts of the route. Hampshire was one of the largest counties in the UK. It would take her a considerable length of time to learn her way around all of it. She would undoubtedly be relying on satnav for several months at least.

Charlie showed her warrant card to the receptionist at the town hall. "We need to talk to Felicity Edmondson's PA." Her personal assistant would be the person who knew most about Felicity's business at the council. She would also be good at getting things done and could help organise interviews with the other people they needed to speak to.

The PA came out to the reception within a couple of minutes. Angela Grier was a tiny woman, barely five feet tall, and looked close to retirement age.

"What's this about? Is there a problem with one of our tenants?" Mrs Grier bore an air of impatience as if she had far more important things to do.

"Is there somewhere we can talk in private?" Charlie and Sally followed her along a corridor on the ground floor. She led them into an office at the end.

"We can use Felicity's office for now. She hasn't come in today, but if she shows up, we'll have to move."

"Shall we sit down?" Charlie pulled a chair out, placing herself opposite the desk, and waited for Angela to sit.

"I'm afraid we have some bad news." Charlie wondered how she would take the news about her boss. Did she adore the woman she worked for or hate her guts? "Felicity Edmondson is dead." She waited a few moments for the news to sink in.

"Was she in an accident?" Angela asked tentatively. "There was a pileup on the M27 earlier, but I didn't think that would involve her."

"We can't give any details at this stage, but she was found in Eastleigh this morning. When did you last see Felicity?"

"Eastleigh? That's nowhere near where she lives. I haven't seen her since I left the office at five p.m. yesterday. She was in the middle of writing a report, then she planned on attending a work event in the evening. That was in Eastleigh, something organised by one of our temporary accommodation providers." She fumbled in her sleeve for a tissue and wiped her eyes. "Poor Fliss. Are you sure it's her?"

Sally spoke up. "We found her driving licence, so we were able to identify her from the photo."

"Did she have any problems at work? Issues with colleagues or complaints from tenants?" Charlie asked.

"We get plenty of complaints. It's the nature of the business." Angela wiped her eyes again. "Wait a minute. Do you think someone killed her?"

"Has anybody made any threats towards her?" Charlie asked, without directly answering the question.

"Not as far as I'm aware."

"And what about her colleagues? Or ex-colleagues? Has she sacked anyone recently?" That might be motive enough for murder, although, given the murder location, the most likely suspects were the seven other people at the party, simply because they had the opportunity.

"I can't imagine any of her colleagues wanting to hurt Fliss. Everybody really liked her." Angela looked as if she might burst into floods of tears at any moment. "She did frequently get into some pretty heated arguments with councillors in cabinet meetings. Fliss was passionate about what she did."

"Was there anyone in particular?" Charlie wondered if Councillor Horn had been on the other side of any of those passionate arguments.

"I'm not sure. I never attended those meetings. They're always held in the council chamber in the evenings."

"We do need to interview Councillor Diana Horn. Can you give us her address, please?"

"I'll have to ask a different department for that, but I can get it for you." Angela was beginning to return to her efficient PA persona. Charlie guessed she would be grateful to have something to keep her busy.

"Will you please email me her address as soon as you get it?" She passed Angela her business card. "We also need to talk to Kate Lovell and Tracey Gulliver."

"Tracey spends a lot of time out of the office, but I saw Kate earlier this morning. They both work on the third floor. I can take you up there if you would like."

"Yes, please. And is there anyone else who worked closely with Felicity who might know her well, someone she might have confided in?"

"You should probably talk to one of our assistant directors, Tom Walker, although I'm sure Fliss wouldn't confide much to him. She liked to keep work separate from her private life. Have you spoken to her husband, Max?"

"We'll be seeing him shortly," Charlie said. "In the meantime, perhaps you would take us to see Kate Lovell."

Angela headed straight to an empty desk in a large open-plan office on the third floor. The computer was switched off.

The young man sitting at the adjacent desk looked over at her. "Kate went out about ten minutes ago."

"Thanks. Did she say how long she would be?"

"She said she'd see me tomorrow, so I guess that means she's not coming back."

Charlie scowled. "What about Tracey Gulliver?" she said quietly to Angela.

There was obviously nothing wrong with the young man's hearing. "Tracey's out all afternoon at a tenants' meeting."

Charlie ignored him and addressed Angela. "Can you please get hold of both of them and tell them we need to talk to them as soon as possible? We can come back first thing tomorrow morning, or they can come into the police station at Eastleigh." She'd be tied up for the rest of this afternoon anyway, visiting Max Edmondson and catching up with the forensic team. Poor Angela looked as if she wanted to go somewhere private and have a good cry, but she appeared professional enough to organise the meetings first. She seemed even smaller now and, in different circumstances, Charlie would have wanted to give her a hug. She reminded herself she had a job to do, and she needed to get it right.

Charlie and Sally returned to the police station. Max Edmondson wasn't due to return home for another hour. It would give time for Charlie to get a coffee and plan her approach to the investigation.

DCI Talbot was waiting for the lift when they got back.

"Have you visited Max Edmondson yet?"

Charlie followed him into the lift. "No, sir. He's been in Edinburgh at a conference and is on his way back now. I'm due to meet him in an hour. So I couldn't have..."

"Don't give me excuses, DI Steele. You should have located him earlier and asked the police in Edinburgh to break the news to him."

"Yes, sir." Charlie wished she hadn't got into the lift with Talbot. The awkward silence lasted until the lift doors opened on her floor. The DCI was right. She had screwed up. She wouldn't make that mistake again. She only hoped Talbot wouldn't continue to be this difficult to work with.

Chapter 9

Sally pulled up the car at the side of the road. "This is it." She pointed to a rather nice-looking detached family home. Concrete paving, arranged in an eye-catching diamond pattern, covered most of the large front garden.

A nearly new Mercedes stood in the driveway. The Edmondsons obviously weren't short of money. As Charlie and Sally walked towards the house, the car door opened and a man got out.

"You must be DI Steele." He extended his hand towards Sally, positively exuding charm.

"I'm DI Steele." Charlie held out her warrant card, ignoring his hand. "This is DC Gleeson."

"Max Edmondson." He smiled at them both, accentuating the wrinkles around his piercing blue eyes. If he'd been angry when he'd made his complaint, he'd certainly calmed down now. He didn't appear particularly grief-stricken either.

"I'm sorry for your loss, Mr Edmondson."

Max nodded but didn't make a move towards the house.

"Shall we go inside?" Charlie suggested, still looking for any signs of a grieving widower. That smile seemed genuine, a cheeky grin that lit up his bright blue eyes, making them sparkle like polished sapphires.

"Now, here's the thing. I seem to have lost my house keys. I was wondering if you found Fliss's keys." He flashed Charlie a sheepish smile. "Otherwise, I'll have to call a locksmith."

Charlie considered the request for a moment. Fliss's keys would be locked in the evidence store by now. They may be vital evidence. It wasn't possible to hand them over at this early stage. "I'm afraid you'll have to call a locksmith," she said. She would like to search the house in case there were any clues as to who Felicity Edmondson may have upset. She wondered if now might be the right time to broach the subject. If Max turned down the request, she would need to apply for a warrant.

Max looked annoyed. "I travelled all the way back from Scotland this morning and now I can't even sit down with a cup of coffee."

It was the first proper emotion Charlie had seen from Max Edmondson. Even then, it was annoyance rather than grief. "I'm sorry. We'll make this as quick as possible." Even if she was prepared to bend the rules to help him, it would mean driving back to the station to collect the keys. It might actually be quicker for him to call a locksmith. But she didn't want to help him, not now that his attitude had elevated him to the top of the suspect list.

"When did you last see your wife?" Charlie asked.

Max counted on his fingers. "Two days ago. I've been at a conference in Edinburgh."

"I'll need details of the conference and the hotel you stayed in, please."

"Are you suggesting I killed my wife?"

"No, of course not, but we have to rule you out. It's standard procedure. The sooner we do that, the sooner we can get on with finding out who killed Felicity." Charlie noted that Max didn't actually say he didn't kill her, not in so many words, but the omission probably wasn't significant.

"What was the conference about?"

"Zero-carbon homes. I'm an architect. The industry is moving towards making every new building as eco-friendly as possible. Without sufficient sustainability incorporated into the design, there's little hope of obtaining planning permission these days."

"Did any of your colleagues attend the conference with you?" That would give him a solid alibi.

"No. It's a small practice, so I planned to disseminate the information to my colleagues when I got back."

"You must have known plenty of people at the conference. Can any of them confirm you were there?" Edmondson would probably have been networking with fellow professionals or simply using the conference as an opportunity to have a drink with some old mates.

"I didn't know anyone there. Most of the attendees came from Scotland and the north of England."

That made some sense, although Charlie doubted it was completely true. Surely, if he had been in the business for a long time, he must have made a vast number of contacts. She let it go. They would ask the conference organisers for an attendance list if need be.

"You haven't even told me how Fliss died. What happened?" Max asked.

At last, he was taking an interest in his wife's death. "We aren't able to release that information yet, sir. When you saw her last, how was she? Did she have any concerns about anything?" Charlie was convinced that Felicity Edmondson's death was murder, not suicide. But until the pathologist confirmed her theory, she would have to cover all bases. She'd deliberately phrased her questions to cover both possibilities, murder or suicide.

"She was fine," Max responded a little too quickly. "Where did she die? I assume it wasn't here, or the house would be swarming with police officers by now."

"No, it wasn't here." Charlie didn't like the way Max changed the subject so abruptly. Two could play at that game. "So when you saw her, would you say she was in her normal state of mind?"

"Yes. I didn't do anything to upset her, if that's what you're getting at. And you still haven't told me where she died."

"She attended an evening event connected to her job." It wouldn't do any harm to give him that information. If Felicity's death was linked to her work, her husband might be able to shed some light on things.

"A council meeting?"

"No, a social event. Didn't she tell you she was going?" Perhaps they didn't phone each other every day when they were apart. Two busy people leading largely separate lives.

"I must have forgotten."

Charlie still couldn't detect any obvious signs of grief. If Max Edmondson loved his wife, he was keeping it well hidden. "Is there anyone who might want to harm your wife?"

"No. I mean, she upset plenty of people as part of her job. I watched one of the council meetings online once. It was a bloodbath. Some of the councillors were having a real go at her because her budget was overspent. It wasn't even her fault. They can't turn people away if they're genuinely homeless. The council has a legal obligation to house them."

Charlie hadn't missed his unfortunate turn of phrase. Had the word *bloodbath* sprung to mind because he'd murdered his wife and still carried the image in his head, or was it simply a coincidence? "Did she ever mention anyone who might hold a grudge against her?"

"Not that I remember. If someone killed her, you will find them, won't you?"

"We'll do our best, sir." Charlie intended to pull out all the stops to solve this case, but she refused to make promises, especially this early in the investigation.

Chapter 10

"Dad." Mia ran up to her father, skidding to a halt before jumping in the air.

Rick caught her and swung her around, making her scream with delight. At nearly ten years old, Mia was starting to get too heavy to catch like that. He put her down, carefully avoiding Duke, their little brown dachshund, who had joined in the welcoming party.

"Don't get her too wound up, love. She's about to go to bed." Janette gave Rick a quick kiss. "How's the new boss?"

"Dad, can we watch TV together?" Mia interrupted.

"It's your bedtime, young lady." Rick glanced at Janette. His wife liked Mia to stick to her routine. He knew better than to undermine that.

"Daaaaaddd!"

"How about you go upstairs and get ready for bed, then I'll come and read you a story?" That trick usually worked, and he always made her read the story to him so she got some extra reading practice.

Mia reluctantly agreed and headed up the stairs. Duke followed her, his short legs making surprisingly light work of scampering up the stairs, despite each step being as tall as he was.

"So what's your new boss like?" Janette asked again.

Rick sat down next to her. "It's Charlie. The new boss is Charlie."

"Your sister, Charlie?"

"Yep. It was a surprise to me too."

"Of all the people... I didn't even know she was a DI."

"Apparently, this is her first DI job." She must have taken her exam at the same time as him. Rick was told before he went on holiday that he hadn't got the job, but it was a kick in the teeth for him when his sister showed up this morning.

"Do you think you can work together without arguing?" Janette appeared concerned at the prospect.

"I'm gonna have to. We managed okay today, and I'll try to partner up with Sally or Tyrone when I can. That way, I won't see too much of her."

"Well, if you're going to try to get on, you'd better invite her over for dinner."

Rick gave his wife a hug. "I will, but not yet, love." He needed time to get used to the idea of having his sister around again.

Chapter 11

Charlie was first into the office on Thursday morning. She ran through her list of what they needed to do today. The post-mortem was due to start at nine and she planned to attend it personally. After that, she needed to interview Stephen Pollock, who hadn't been in the office when they visited Tenurewise yesterday.

She would task her two DCs, Sally and Tyrone, with completing the house-to-house interviews in Highfield Road. Someone may have seen something. Rick could help Zack put together some background information on Max Edmondson. So far, he was their only suspect, but they had no evidence, and a simple gut feeling due to his lack of real grief wouldn't be enough.

By the time the rest of the team arrived, Charlie had updated the murder board and made a plan for the day.

The first part of Charlie's plan, once she had briefed the team, involved visiting the CSI lab. She wanted an update on anything they had found at the crime scene yesterday, although, she admitted to herself, their coffee machine played its part in drawing her towards that area of the building. As she opened the door to the lab, a waft of freshly brewed coffee heightened her craving for caffeine.

"What do you want? I'm about to go out." Oliver Flanders was no more charming in his workplace than he had been at the crime scene yesterday.

"Do you have time to give me an update on what you found yesterday?"

"Not really." His scar stood out more prominently in the bright lighting inside the lab.

"Then perhaps I can visit the crime scene myself." Charlie stood her ground. She outranked Flanders, who was only a civilian employee. There was a limit to how much rudeness she would tolerate.

"We haven't finished processing it yet," he snapped. "The rest of the team is there now."

Charlie looked at him questioningly. It was an empty house. Surely it wouldn't take that long.

"I like to be thorough," he said, despite her not asking for an explanation.

"You found Felicity's handbag."

"That's right. It was hidden behind the bath panel."

"Was there anything useful in it?" The average woman's handbag was a treasure trove of interesting items. It would probably tell Charlie more about the victim than anything else they had found.

"Just the usual: purse, phone, lipstick, glasses case, but no glasses, tissues, umbrella. Probably a dozen other things. They'll all be listed in the report."

"Is there anything you can give me now?" She didn't want to wait for the official report. She needed to get a head start on this case as soon as possible.

"I'll let you know when I finish the full report." He headed towards the door. "You can see yourself out."

The door slammed shut behind him, leaving Charlie wondering what had just happened.

The coffee machine tempted her. With the whole team at the scene of the crime, she could pour herself a cup and no one would even know. It would only go to waste. But it would feel like stealing, even though Sally had done the exact same thing yesterday. But Sally had an existing relationship with the CSI team. She obviously knew she would get away with it. Charlie couldn't afford for them to make a complaint against her to the DCI, not after yesterday's fiasco with

Max Edmondson. She breathed in the heady aroma of coffee. It smelt fantastic. But she had to do the right thing. Ignoring her craving, she left the room. She had a post-mortem to attend. Hopefully, the pathologist would be a good deal more helpful and charming than Ollie Flanders.

Chapter 12

Tabitha Newbury, the pathologist, wasn't what Charlie had expected. As she marched towards her, Charlie's gaze fixed on the huge pink bow in Tabitha's hair.

Charlie introduced herself.

"There's a viewing gallery, if you'd like to observe from there." Tabitha pointed to her left.

"If you don't mind, I'd rather be in the room with you." Charlie had gained a great deal of information on previous cases from being closer to the body and getting the full experience, so to speak. "I promise I'll keep out of your way." It also made it easier to ask questions as they went along. Overall, the advantages far outweighed the unpleasant smell.

"You've done this plenty of times before then."

Charlie nodded.

"That's good because I'm not big enough to be picking you up off the floor if you faint."

Charlie smiled. The petite woman wouldn't even make eight stone with her clothes on. She wondered how Tabitha manhandled some of the bodies she had to deal with.

Tabitha looked over Charlie's shoulder. "My assistant has arrived. We can begin." She introduced Frank Dawson, who must be twice her size. They made an unlikely team but complemented each other perfectly. She guessed he did any necessary manhandling.

Tabitha directed Charlie to a chair in the corner of the room. "It's not the most comfortable, but you might prefer it to standing up for the whole procedure."

Charlie looked at the chair. Like everything else in the mortuary, it was stainless steel, although the seat was contoured, as if it had been moulded around someone's buttocks. She decided to stand.

Tabitha spoke into a microphone hanging from the ceiling. "The victim is a woman, Felicity Edmondson, appearance consistent with the stated age of forty-six years." She turned towards Charlie. "I like to work through a methodical procedure. That's the best way to make sure nothing is forgotten. But in this case, I'll comment on the wounds on her wrists now, so you can pop out for a coffee and come back later if you want to."

"I'd rather stay." Charlie didn't want to miss anything significant. It was important to her to nail this case as soon as possible.

"Well, aren't you a toughie? Most detectives jump at the chance to take a break."

"I'm not most detectives." Charlie guessed Tabitha Newbury didn't fit into the category of *most pathologists* either.

Tabitha smiled. "About the wounds on Felicity's wrists. They're unusual."

Charlie was pleased the pathologist had used the victim's name. Some of them simply referred to *the victim*. "Lengthways instead of crossways."

Tabitha stared at her in astonishment. "Excellent," she said. "Can you guess how many times I've seen people who have slit their wrists this way?"

Charlie had no idea how long Tabitha had been a pathologist. She looked like she was still in her twenties. "Not many," she replied.

Tabitha laughed. "None," she said. "I've been a pathologist for seventeen years, and I've never seen this. It's virtually impossible to do it yourself, especially on the second wrist, and this is particularly well done. Very precise."

Charlie allowed herself a moment of pride and intended to relay this conversation to Rick at the earliest opportunity. "So she must have been unconscious. She may have been drugged."

Tabitha picked up a scalpel, holding it out towards Charlie. "Do you want my job?"

Charlie couldn't imagine anything worse. "No, thank you." She noted Tabitha hadn't answered her question. Asking the same thing again would be pointless. Until the tox screen was done, any answer would be pure speculation.

Tabitha moved around the table to the other side of the body to make the large incision that would enable her to open it up.

Charlie immediately noticed her shoes. Tabitha was wearing leopard-print stilettos. Those heels must be four inches high. Charlie spent most of her time in trainers. She couldn't imagine being able to walk in shoes like that. It was a miracle she didn't slip on the polished floor. For a moment, she imagined Tabitha flying across the shiny surface and ending up in a heap of human organs.

"Lovely shoes." Charlie actually did quite like them, even if she would never wear them herself. "Aren't they uncomfortable to wear all day?"

"Not really. I'm used to them. I'm barely five feet tall on tiptoes. I don't take these off for anybody." She cut out an organ and placed it on the electronic scales. "Good, healthy-looking heart," she commented. "And before you get all *health-and-safety* on me, I've got rubber soles on these shoes so they don't slip."

"Any idea about the time of death yet?"

"Difficult to say. There was a sharp spring frost overnight, and the heating wasn't on in the house, so that would have affected the state of the body by the time I got there in the morning." Tabitha considered for a moment. "I'd say between nine thirty and ten thirty p.m."

Tabitha moved down the body.

"Are there any signs of sexual assault?" Charlie wasn't expecting it. If the attack had taken place while Alicia and Stephen were still in the house, they would have heard something. It would have to have been quiet and quick.

"No signs of any bruising there. The only signs of bruising are on her arms and back and are consistent with falling into the bath. I'll swab for semen, but she might have had sex with her husband before she went out, so it won't necessarily prove anything."

"Her husband hasn't seen her for two days," Charlie pointed out.

"It won't show up then, which makes any results more clear-cut. She has had a baby at some point. You can see where the pelvis is wider." Tabitha explained some of the other signs of childbirth. "But sexual assault looks unlikely."

Charlie gave an involuntary shiver, thinking of her own experience of giving birth. Her most painful, but also her happiest, moments ever, until the elation had been dashed eleven days later when baby Louise gave up her fight for life.

Charlie pulled herself together and concentrated while Tabitha went through some of the routine stuff that would probably reveal nothing important. She checked the clock on the wall. With luck, the PM would be finished before lunch, giving Charlie time to check up on her team, then head over to the Tenurewise offices to interview Stephen Pollock.

"Aye, aye, what have we here?"

Charlie immediately looked up. "What have you found?"

"There's a nasty head injury. It looks like she was bashed on the top of her head."

"Does that mean the attacker was tall?" Charlie tried to remember how tall the other people at the party were, the ones she had met so far.

"It could mean she was bashed against the wall or the bathroom sink. Check the CSI reports. If her head hit anything, it will have blood and hair on it."

A head injury would explain the precise cuts on her wrists. She must have been unconscious when they were done. "Did the head injury kill her?"

"No. There was too much blood. If she'd been dead when her wrists were slit, her heart would have stopped beating, so there would be far less blood." Tabitha signalled to Frank to take photos of the head wound. "She was definitely alive when that was done but almost certainly unconscious or she would have struggled. The cuts are too neat for that."

She would also have screamed the place down, Charlie guessed, then perhaps she would still be alive.

Chapter 13

Charlie phoned Tenurewise as soon as the post-mortem finished. Stephen Pollock agreed to meet her at the offices in half an hour, so she grabbed Sally, who had returned a few minutes earlier, and drove straight there.

Pollock showed them into a pokey little office with only two chairs. "Apologies for the lack of space. I spend a lot of time out of the office, so I don't really need much room." Pollock seated himself in the comfortable chair behind the desk.

Charlie noted the selfish gesture. The hint of annoyance in his voice suggested that the size of the room was a bone of contention for him. She directed Sally to the remaining chair. It would be easier for her to take notes sitting down.

Charlie took the lead. "Talk me through the night of the party. What time did you arrive?"

"Alicia insisted that Danny and I got there at a quarter to five. She wanted the Tenurewise people there before anyone else arrived. We needn't have bothered. No one else showed up for another hour."

"Who was the first to show?"

"Fliss arrived first. But Kate Lovell arrived soon afterwards, followed by Councillor Horn."

Charlie wondered if Felicity had got there early, in the hope of leaving first. "What about Tracey Gulliver?"

"Tracey arrived much later. She got lost. She came by bus, then walked the last bit. It's quite dark once you get off the main road. I don't think she enjoyed the walk at all."

Charlie nodded. That tallied with what she'd already been told. "Did you speak to Fliss much during the evening?"

"I spoke to all of them. Alicia wanted us to be friendly and keep the conversation going. She insisted we must mingle."

"So what did you talk to Fliss about?"

Stephen looked at her blankly. "All sorts of stuff. Obviously, we discussed our future plans for the contract and how nice the house was. Everybody admired it. We made a particular effort with this first one. That was the reason Alicia wanted to show it off, to make sure the council was still on board with the project."

That implied standards would go downhill with any subsequent properties the company provided. "What else did you talk about?"

"Just this and that. The weather. Kids, although that didn't last long as Fliss didn't have any. Food. We provided a variety of upmarket canapés. Fliss seemed to appreciate them. She was stuffing her face all evening."

Charlie noted Pollock's comment about Felicity having no children. She would have to confirm that with Max. Perhaps Tabitha had got it wrong. "Did you notice anyone arguing with Fliss during the evening?" In a relatively small house, any raised voices would be obvious to everyone there.

Stephen shook his head. "Not that I can remember."

"Did you argue with her?"

"No, of course not. We had strict instructions from Alicia to be nice to our guests."

"But you asked her if you could increase the contract price? Surely that must have turned into an argument." It rang alarm bells for Charlie that Stephen Pollock hadn't even mentioned that conversation.

"That wasn't an argument. I asked her. She said no. End of. Then we changed the subject." Pollock wiped a streak of sweat from his brow.

Charlie didn't completely believe him, but he obviously wasn't going to go back on his story now. "What time did people start to leave?"

Stephen considered for a moment. "It must have been around eight p.m. The councillor left first. After that, things started to fizzle out."

"Why? Was she the life and soul of the party?"

"Not at all. If anything, Alicia took that role. It's just that, as soon as one person leaves, everyone else gets the same idea, and they're all wondering if it would be rude for them to go next."

Charlie nodded, understanding what he meant. "So who did leave next?"

"Tracey said she needed to get home, but she was a bit nervous about walking back to the bus stop in the dark, so Danny offered to give her a lift. I expect he wanted an excuse to leave as much as the rest of us."

That confirmed Danny Owen's account of events but contrasted with how Alicia Gardener remembered things. She specifically said that Fliss and Kate left before Tracey and Danny. "Are you sure?" Charlie asked.

"Of course I'm sure. It was a small party. I wouldn't get that wrong. Kate and Fliss left together shortly after that. Then I ended up helping Alicia clear up."

"What time did you both leave?"

"About a quarter past ten. We were talking for a long time, and Alicia had to wait for a taxi because she'd been drinking heavily."

That matched with what Alicia had said, although if Stephen was right about the amount she'd been drinking, her account may not be reliable. "Did you check the house was empty before you locked up?" Tabitha's estimated time of death didn't leave time for someone to break in after everyone had left, then get Felicity inside and kill her. Besides, the front door would need to be unlocked with a key, and she couldn't imagine Felicity Edmondson being persuaded to climb through a window. No, Felicity had been killed while Stephen and Alicia were inside the house.

"No. Why would I? I'd seen everyone leave. Besides, if anyone was still inside, I would have heard them. I wanted to get home to my daughter because I'd left my mother babysitting, and she doesn't like to stay out late. I wish I'd got in before Danny and offered Tracey a lift home."

Perhaps if Pollock had been more conscientious and made a final check of the house before he left, Felicity would still be alive. Or was she already dead by then? "How close to the house was your car parked?"

"It was right outside. That was the only advantage of getting here early. I bagged the prime parking space."

"Did you notice anyone hanging around when you went out to the car?"

Stephen shook his head. "All I wanted to do was get home."

Charlie handed over her business card. "If you remember anything else—"

"I'll call you."

Alicia Gardner was coming out of her office as Charlie walked past.

"Can I have a quick word?" Charlie wanted to ask her again about the order in which people left the party, since her account conflicted with Stephen's and Danny's. "It won't take long."

"Of course." Alicia ushered Charlie into her office. "What's the problem?"

Charlie didn't bother to sit. "How much did you have to drink on Tuesday evening?"

Alicia smiled. "Enough to put me over the limit to drive, but otherwise not that much. I sipped slowly, so I always had a glass in my hand to appear sociable, but honestly, the council contract will be worth millions to Tenurewise over the next few years. I couldn't afford to get drunk and screw things up."

That made sense to Charlie and fitted with the shrewd businesswoman image Alicia had previously portrayed. "Can you clarify the order in which everyone left the party?"

"I'll try to remember. Diana Horn left first. Then it was Fliss and Kate. Zoe Neale was in and out of the house, packing up her stuff. Danny and Tracey left next. Then I left a bit later in a taxi, leaving Stephen to lock up."

"Thank you." At least she was consistent, but why did she still differ from Danny's and Stephen's accounts? Which of them was lying?

Chapter 14

As soon as Charlie got back to the police station, Rick came to her office to tell her that Ollie Flanders wanted to see her.

"Also, I've read the contract between Tenurewise and the council." Rick displayed a look of triumph. "There was a non-delivery clause in it. If fewer than fifty properties are delivered within the year, the council can rescind the contract and either hand back any properties they are already leasing or keep the existing properties, but refuse to take any more."

"And what does that mean for Tenurewise? When is the first year up?"

"The contract was officially signed on 1st June last year."

"So Tenurewise has less than two months to buy another forty-nine properties." Charlie let out a whistle. That would prove impossible. "Were there any signs that the council wanted to rescind the contract?"

"I wondered if Tracey Gulliver would know."

"It's possible. We still need to interview her." If she didn't know, Charlie would ask the council's chief executive about the contract. Felicity may have discussed a decision of such importance with him, to get his approval before she went ahead with putting the decision to the councillors for a vote. "I'm going to the council offices later. I'll ask Tracey about it. Hold off broaching the subject with anyone at Tenurewise until we hear what Tracey has to say about it."

"And I visited Felicity's mother," Rick said.

"Did you ask her about the baby?" According to the post-mortem, Felicity had given birth at some time in the past. She'd phoned Rick, asking him to check it out.

"Her mother flatly denied it. Even when I asked if Felicity could have hidden a pregnancy from her and gone away for a few months when it started showing, she was adamant that it couldn't have happened."

Charlie headed to the CSI lab. Could Tabitha have been wrong about Felicity giving birth? She seemed extremely competent, but everyone made mistakes sometimes, didn't they? She wondered if she dared broach the subject with the pathologist and decided it wasn't worth making an enemy of her yet. She would wait and see if any other evidence came up.

Ollie Flanders waved her across to his desk. "We've finished the report on the Highfield Road house."

Flanders seemed as prickly as the last time she met him. "That's good. Is there anything significant in it?" Why couldn't he have emailed the report to her? Now she would have to be nice to him.

"Yes, actually. We found blood on the wall next to the bath. It's been wiped clean, so nothing obvious showed on the tiles, but traces of blood remained on the grouting. Testing with Luminol showed a significant amount of blood on the tiles about four feet from the floor. The blood is a match to Felicity Edmondson."

"Is it splatter from the wrist wounds or from the head injury?" Charlie asked.

"Undoubtedly the head injury. Arterial blood from the wrists would have covered a larger area. And someone would have needed to hold her upright for the blood to end up at that height on the wall. We performed a reconstruction. Our theory is that she was bending forward over the bath, and someone rammed her head into the wall. She drops unconscious into the bath. The killer then tidies up her arms and legs to make it look as if she got in by herself. Then they put the plug in the bath and slit her wrists. A quick wipe down of the tiles—job done." Flanders looked pleased with himself.

Charlie tried not to be annoyed by his smugness. If Felicity fell into the bath, it would explain the bruises Tabitha found. "Would the killer have been splattered with blood?"

"Possibly. They could have avoided it if they were careful."

"So we should be searching for a knife and the blood-stained cloth that the killer used to clean up."

"Good luck with that. The cloth or sponge is probably long gone by now."

"But the knife might not be." They needed to search again. "One more question."

Flanders looked at her expectantly.

"Was the killer a man or a woman?"

"Could be either. Easy enough to slam someone against the wall if they're already in position and slightly off balance."

It wasn't the answer she wanted. If the murder had required brute strength, it would have ruled out half of their suspects and made her job much easier.

Chapter 15

Reject52 sat on a bench in one of Southampton's Central Parks. She had a good view of the Titanic Engineers Memorial from here, where she had arranged to meet ChessDevil501.

She was taking a risk meeting him, but at least she'd chosen a place that was public enough to be safe, yet quiet enough to be able to talk freely without being overheard. She'd asked him to wear a red baseball cap and carry a copy of Alice Feeney's book *Rock, Paper, Scissors*. The latter demand amused her. Would ChessDevil realise the book was a metaphor for the impossible situation they both found themselves in? She needed more than a one-in-three chance of coming out on top, but she could see no obvious winning solution.

Once she identified ChessDevil, she would decide if she wanted to approach him.

Of course, ChessDevil had made his own requests. She was supposed to wear a red bow in her hair and carry a newspaper. She'd ignored his demands. Better that she had the upper hand. She would know who he was, but he would have no way of identifying her. That way, she would be in control, not him.

A man wearing a red baseball cap approached the memorial from the left. The cap wasn't really red. It looked old and had faded to a deep shade of pink. Was he ChessDevil? If he couldn't be bothered to get simple details right, like the colour of a baseball cap, perhaps he wouldn't be capable of doing what she wanted.

He stood in front of the memorial, looking around him. She was too far away and, with the baseball cap pulled down over his eyes, his face wasn't clearly visible. Perhaps she should walk by nonchalantly to get a better look at him. After all, he had no way of knowing who she was, so she would be perfectly safe. Already, she was getting cold feet. It was one thing chatting online, but was she putting herself in danger by meeting with ChessDevil in person?

The man in the baseball cap looked at his watch, fidgeting restlessly as if he might not wait much longer. It was now or never. She had no choice because she needed one more thing from him. He wanted something from her, too, and if he insisted that she delivered, then she was in trouble. But she had a plan to get around that problem. She would remain in control.

She took a deep breath and marched up to him.

ChessDevil had turned around to read the inscription on the base of the memorial.

Reject52 tapped him gently on the shoulder. "ChessDevil?"

She sensed something was wrong before he swung around.

"You?" His eyes were fearful. "You're Reject52?" His voice sounded incredulous.

Reject took a step back. This had been a bad idea. She wasn't sure what she'd expected, but it hadn't been him. She hadn't expected ChessDevil to be someone she already knew. Suddenly, she felt much less in control.

"Did you know it was me all this time? Did you use me?" Chess Devil demanded angrily.

Reject glanced around her, her gaze darting from left to right, but this area of the park was deserted now. "No. I had no idea." She was genuinely as shocked as he was.

For a few moments, she froze to the spot, unable to speak. He knew who she was. There was no going back now. And if there was no going back, then the only way was forward.

"I need you to do one more thing for me," Reject said.

Chapter 16

Max Edmondson flicked off the TV in his hotel room and threw the remote onto the bed. He hadn't been thinking straight. It must be the shock of hearing about Fliss's death. And it had been a huge shock, almost making him feel sorry for her. He'd actually shed a tear and mourned her loss. That was why he'd booked into a hotel for tonight, even though Lisa would have welcomed him with open arms. He'd cried real tears over Fliss until he realised the bitch had changed the lock on their front door. *His* front door. It riled him even more that the police wouldn't hand over Fliss's keys. She hadn't been killed in their house, so why would they need to keep the keys? Why did they tell him to find somewhere else to stay for a few days? A few days! Now he was relegated to a cheap hotel without a clean change of clothes. Right now, he was too pissed off for any more regrets about what had happened to Fliss.

But once he stopped feeling sorry for himself, he finally realised that the police would want to search his house. And he needed to get there first.

It was dark by the time he reached the house. He started to turn into the driveway, then reconsidered and parked his car in the shadow of a large hedge in the adjoining road.

If his hunch was right, that Fliss was too penny-pinching to change the locks on the back door as well, he could slip in and out in no time at all. Max moved one of the wheelie bins up to the side gate that led to the back garden, then pulled himself up onto it by the solid gatepost. Climbing over the top of the gate proved easy. Too easy. He'd have to do something about security as soon as the police officially allowed him back into the house.

He jumped off the gate, bending his knees as he hit the concrete path. It wasn't enough to absorb the momentum. He stifled a small yell as he fell back onto his arse. Thank God no one witnessed his loss of dignity. He brushed himself off and moved quickly towards the back door.

Max fumbled with the key in the dark. It didn't work. He cursed himself for underestimating his wife, sure she wouldn't have bothered to change the lock on the back door as well. He was here now, and he still needed to get in and pick up some stuff.

Hastily, he made a plan: break the kitchen window and climb in. He remembered the assortment of stones at the end of the garden, Fliss's attempts to build a rock garden where the ground sloped upwards immediately before the boundary fence. He hurried across the grass, his eyes now accustomed to the dark, and selected a couple of large, rough rocks to do the job.

The lights were on in the neighbours' house. It would be best if their friends next door didn't get involved. He took off his coat and used it to muffle the sound of the rock smashing into the glass.

As soon as Max had cleared a small area of broken glass, he reached through and found the window key hidden under a plant pot on the windowsill. It didn't take long to climb through the window once he'd opened it.

He clambered off the draining board, jumping down onto the floor. A sharp pain shot through his right hand where he embedded a piece of glass into his palm as he reached out to balance himself. He should have worn gloves, but there hadn't seemed any point. After all, he lived here until a couple of days ago. His fingerprints would be all over the house.

He stood still for a minute, waiting for his eyes to adjust to the dark. It would only draw attention if he turned on the light. Something brushed against his lower leg, making him jump back sharply. He looked down, relieved to see the shadowy outline of Mr

Muggle slinking across the floor. The cat meowed loudly and Max realised no one would have fed him for at least twenty-four hours. He opened the cupboard where they kept the cat food and pulled out a pouch and a packet of dried food. He held up the pouch towards the sliver of moonlight shining through the window. Tuna. That would do nicely. He spooned it into the cat's bowl and topped it up with plenty of the dry nuggets. Hopefully, that would be enough to last until the police searched the house, or he was able to move back in, although he was no longer sure he wanted to.

Max placed the bowl of food on the kitchen floor, then refilled the cat's water bowl. He'd wasted enough time on this. Now he needed to find what he came for.

He had no idea where to start searching. It was impossible to find anything in the dark. He'd have to risk turning the lights on. If any of the neighbours called the police, he would use the excuse of needing to feed the cat.

He started his search in the main bedroom. Fliss didn't sleep well with the light pollution from the streetlamp outside and an occasional car driving past during the night, so the window was fitted with blackout curtains. He groped his way up the stairs in the dark and shut the curtains before turning on the bedroom light. No one would see the light through the curtains.

Max found a sports bag and flung a few clean clothes inside before he started searching. That was his other excuse for coming here: he needed a change of clothes.

Fliss used one particular drawer in the bedside table on her side of the bed to store anything important. If what he wanted was in the bedroom, it would be in that drawer. He pulled the drawer out and tipped the contents onto the bed.

A metal box contained important documents, split between two envelopes: Fliss's envelope held her birth certificate and passport, her degree certificate, and household insurance details. Max had wanted to get a proper safe, but Fliss insisted they didn't have anything valuable enough to warrant that. All they needed was something that would be fireproof. She didn't even bother to lock the box.

The drawer also contained a whole host of less valuable paperwork. The letter must be among them, although Max was miffed that Fliss hadn't accorded this enough importance to store it in the metal box.

He searched methodically through the piles of papers. There were numerous old photos, a couple of love letters from when they'd first met, and guarantees for several electrical appliances, most of which were out of date. He sifted through everything twice. The letter from his solicitor wasn't there.

If the letter wasn't in the bedroom drawer, Max didn't have the slightest idea where to look. Perhaps she'd thrown it away. He went downstairs to look in the kitchen bin. That seemed the most likely place to find it. He imagined Fliss discarding it in anger, deciding to refuse his request for a divorce. That was just the sort of thing she'd do.

He couldn't find any trace of the letter in the bin, not even shredded into confetti. He made a cursory search of the living room, but there were so many potential hiding places, he stood no chance. He was rubbish at finding things, always having to ask Fliss to locate anything important he had lost. There was no point in looking any further. If it wasn't in the obvious places, it probably wasn't here at all. And if it wasn't here, the police wouldn't find it. He would go back to the hotel and forget about it.

Chapter 17

Charlie fumbled with the keys on Felicity Edmondson's keyring. There were five of them. One obviously belonged to her car. They still needed to locate that. She selected the most likely looking key to unlock the front door of the Edmondsons' house. It slotted in perfectly.

She pushed the door open, giving the bunch of keys to Sally. "Can you find out what these other three keys belong to? And don't forget, we need to find Felicity's missing glasses." The CSI team hadn't found them at the crime scene, only the empty case in her handbag. She may have left them at home, unless the killer had taken them as a trophy.

She returned to the car to help Trina Lucas with her equipment, leaving Sally in the house to start searching. She had requested a CSI to come with them, and thankfully, Ollie Flanders had assigned her someone much friendlier than himself. Even though this house wasn't the primary crime scene, it might still yield clues to their victim's murder. She would have liked to get into the house yesterday, but Max Edmondson losing his keys made it more difficult.

Trina handed her a metal case. "If you wouldn't mind carrying that, I can take the rest myself. I've got a trolley."

Charlie looked at the house while she waited for Trina to finish loading her trolley. She wanted to get an overall impression, although to some extent, she had already done so when she'd visited yesterday. The first thing that jumped out at her was the curtains. They were drawn shut, both upstairs and downstairs. Charlie swore they'd been open yesterday. Had someone been in the house since then? She'd made it clear to Mr Edmondson that the house was a potential crime scene and he wasn't to return there until they finished searching it. As he'd lost his keys, she assumed that would be the end of it. He obviously didn't call out a locksmith to change the locks because Felicity's key fitted the front door perfectly. She wondered if the Edmondsons used a cleaner. That would certainly explain the curtains, although it would be a disaster if she'd destroyed any forensic evidence with a thorough cleaning session.

She tried not to worry about it as she pulled on some gloves. This wasn't the crime scene, and in any case, both Felicity's and Max's fingerprints and DNA would be everywhere. Their visit would be more useful to give them a feel for Felicity as a person, and, if they were lucky, to discover what her last movements might have been before she went to the party.

Charlie headed straight for the kitchen. If the husband was responsible for murdering Fliss, he may have taken a knife from home. They still hadn't found the murder weapon, but it might give them something to match it to when they did, assuming the knife was part of a set.

She stopped dead as soon as she opened the kitchen door. A cold draught hit her, and she immediately noticed broken glass on the draining board.

"Trina," she called out. "You'd better start in here." If someone had broken in, she needed to find out who and why. Was this connected to Felicity Edmondson's murder?

Trina poked her head around the door. "What's up?"

"Broken window. Someone must've got in here last night."

Trina parked her trolley outside the kitchen and began opening drawers in the plastic cabinet that was strapped to the trolley frame. She seemed to remember exactly where everything was stored as she took out various bits and pieces, lining them up neatly on a piece of plastic laid out on the floor.

Sally came into the kitchen and tried a key in the back door. "What happened here?" She pointed at the broken window.

"Someone's been in here. Can you visit the neighbours? Ask them if they saw anything last night?"

"Sure." Sally handed her the bunch of keys. "This one's for the back door." She pointed out a large silver key. "The Yale key fits the side gate into the garden. I'm guessing the other one will unlock the garden shed."

Charlie had a quick scout around the ground floor, looking for signs of an alarm system, but found nothing. She left Trina to carry on and unlocked the back door.

The door opened out onto a large patio. Overall, the garden was disappointingly small compared to the size of the house. Most of the space was grassed over, with the lawn neatly mown. The shed Sally referred to stood in the far corner. The only sign of proper gardening was an amateurish attempt at a rock garden in front of the rear fence.

Charlie headed straight towards the shed, sorting through the bunch of keys for the right one. She needn't have bothered. The padlock lay on the ground next to a heavy stone. Someone had smashed the lock with the stone and slid off the padlock.

She opened the door. Most of the interior was filled with garden furniture, which must have been stored for the winter. A lawn mower and a few gardening tools completed the inventory. If the shed had contained anything valuable, whoever had broken the lock must have stolen it.

She looked back towards the house. A narrow passage alongside the house led to a tall, solid gate. A ladder leaned against the gate. Charlie went to take a closer look. This must have been where the intruder got out. Perhaps they broke into the shed to get the ladder so they could make their escape. It might be worth Trina fingerprinting the ladder, but Charlie didn't hold out much hope of a useful result.

She went back inside to tell Trina about the shed and the ladder. "We'll need Max Edmondson to check if anything's missing from the house."

"Let's have a proper look round first," Trina suggested. "We don't want him interfering with any evidence." She pointed at the draining board underneath the broken window. "There's a small amount of blood here. It's likely the person who got in cut themselves on the broken glass as they climbed through the window."

Charlie moved closer to take a look. It wasn't much, but it might help identify whoever broke in, assuming they already had a police record. Perhaps one of the local petty criminals heard about Felicity's death and decided the house would make easy pickings. They definitely needed Max Edmondson to confirm if anything was missing.

Chapter 18

The Edmondsons' neighbour's door was answered by a youngish woman with a toddler hoisted on her hip. Sally showed her warrant card. "Can I come in for a quick chat? It's about the Edmondsons."

The woman put down the toddler and ushered Sally inside. "Is everything okay?" She grasped the child's hand and led him into the living room, then lifted him into a playpen before switching on the TV. "Be a good boy and stay put." She turned to Sally. "We'll go into the kitchen. I'm dying for a cup of tea."

The woman filled the kettle, then repeated, "Is everything all right?"

Sally still didn't answer, instead asking the woman her name.

"I'm Abi Hargreaves."

Sally smiled at her. "Someone broke into the Edmondsons' house, probably yesterday." They weren't even certain when the break-in took place as Max Edmondson was away for a couple of days. It may have happened at any time in the last thirty-six hours. "Have you noticed anything unusual?"

Abi took a packet of teabags out of the cupboard above the kettle.

"Not really, but I suppose that explains why Max was messing around in the back garden yesterday evening."

"Max?" The boss told him to stay away from the house until they were finished with it. "Are you sure it was him?"

Abi handed her a steaming mug of tea. "Of course I'm sure. We've been neighbours for five years, and we socialise a lot together. At least we did until I had the baby. I'd recognise either of them anywhere, even in the dark."

"What time did you see him?"

"It must have been about seven thirty. My husband was late getting home, and I heard a noise, so I ran upstairs to look out the window. Max was walking across his back garden."

"Can you show me?" Sally didn't want to drag herself away from the tea, but it was still too hot to drink.

Abi led the way upstairs. "This is my son's bedroom. It overlooks the back gardens." She pointed to the left. The window gave her a great view of the Edmondsons' back garden. "I saw Max right in the middle of the lawn."

Sally took a couple of photos on her phone before they returned downstairs.

She took a sip of tea while she waited for Abi to sit down. "When did you last see the Edmondsons?"

"It must have been Sunday. We generally only see them at weekends. They both work long hours during the week, although Max drops in occasionally if he gets home from work early. He likes playing with Noah."

Sally assumed Noah was the child, not the husband. "How did they seem last time you saw them?"

Abi gave her a puzzled look. "I'm not sure what you mean."

Sally was reluctant to elaborate in case she led the witness, but she supposed she would have to. "Did they seem happy together? Any tension? Any worries? Any difference to their normal behaviour?"

"To be honest, I didn't notice. Noah had a touch of colic and wouldn't stop crying. My husband thought they'd had a row, and I suppose they were snapping at each other a bit. Fliss couldn't wait to get away, and I don't blame her. Why are you asking? Is it about the break-in? Did someone want to hurt them?"

Sally waited for Abi to place her hot mug of tea back on the table. "I'm afraid I have some bad news. Felicity Edmondson was found dead on Wednesday morning."

"Dead? But that's impossible. Fliss was fit and healthy."

"I'm afraid so. Can you think of anyone who might want to hurt her?"

"Are you saying someone killed her? But she was really nice. Why would anybody?"

The post-mortem confirmed it was murder, so someone definitely didn't like Felicity Edmondson. "We aren't sure yet, but we will find out."

Abi looked like she was about to cry. "Did someone break into the house and kill her?"

"No, it didn't happen here." Sally immediately noticed Abi relax slightly. She drained her mug of tea. She needed to get back to the DI.

Abi lifted Noah out of the playpen, hugging him tightly, more to give herself comfort, rather than him. She wondered if she should have mentioned the incident with the woman to the police officer. She hadn't even thought about it—her head had been spinning with the dreadful news about Fliss. But it was nothing. And it was several weeks ago now. The woman had simply stopped to admire Noah in his pushchair as she'd been coming out of the Edmondsons' drive. She'd only dropped in on her way to the park to post something through the letterbox. The postman was always delivering things to the wrong address. She'd got the impression the woman thought she was Fliss, although she'd dismissed that idea pretty quickly. Fliss was, after all, nearly twenty years older than her. She'd thought nothing of it at the time. Except that when she got home, she caught a fleeting glimpse of the same woman loitering across the road from the house. Had she been watching Fliss?

Abi reached for the card the police officer had left, then immediately put it back on the table. What if the woman had killed

Fliss? She'd got a good look at Abi and Noah. She even knew where they lived. Would she guess if Abi reported her to the police? Would she come back and kill her too? She couldn't risk anything happening to Noah. It wasn't as if she had anything useful to tell the detective. Abi barely remembered what the woman looked like. It only took a few minutes to convince herself she would be wasting the officer's time.

Chapter 19

Trina came to find Charlie as she was walking down the stairs, having failed to find anything useful in the bedrooms. "You need to read this." She waved a piece of paper at her, snatching it away before Charlie could grab it. "Gloves."

Charlie pulled on a pair of gloves. She should have left her gloves on when she finished upstairs.

"Max Edmondson asked for a divorce." Trina handed over the sheet of paper.

Charlie quickly skimmed through the letter from Max's solicitor to Felicity. It was dated four days ago.

"Do you reckon the husband did it? He would benefit financially."

"This certainly gives him a motive." Charlie would get Zack to examine Max Edmondson's finances. If he was in any kind of financial trouble, it would strengthen the motive to murder his wife. "Have you found anything else?"

"Plenty of fingerprints, although most of them probably belong to the Edmondsons. And they've got a cat."

"A cat?" Who was looking after it while the house was empty? Another thing to discuss with Max Edmondson. She needed to find Sally and get back to the office.

Chapter 20

The incident room was quiet when Charlie and Sally got back. Charlie filled the coffee machine she had brought in earlier this morning. She'd been tempted to keep it in her own office, but she needed to ingratiate herself with her new team, and this was as good a way to start as any, so she'd found somewhere in the large incident room to plug it in.

"Where is everyone?" Charlie asked Zack, interrupting the frantic tapping of his keyboard.

Zack jumped at the sound of Charlie's voice before composing himself. "Rick's around somewhere. Tyrone is still doing house-to-house interviews near the crime scene. I'm doing background checks on the people who attended the party."

"That's great. Can you add Max Edmondson to that? He's Felicity's husband. I'm particularly interested in his finances."

Zack nodded and resumed typing.

"Have you found anything useful so far?" Charlie asked.

"A bit. Alicia Gardener comes from a well-known Hampshire crime family, the Castles. Gardener is her married name. Andrew Castle, her oldest brother, is in prison for GBH."

"Could be relevant. Can you check her finances, too? Find out where she got the funding to start Tenurewise. Did it come from the proceeds of the family's criminal activities? And are any other family members involved in the company?" If Tenurewise planned to purchase 200 properties for the council, they must have some serious funding behind them. They would never get loans for the entire amount they would need, not as a start-up company.

"And Danny Owen's father is an archdeacon. He's hotly tipped to be the next Bishop of Leeds when the present incumbent retires."

Charlie laughed. "That might be useful when we catch the murderer. He can pray for his soul." She bit her tongue, hoping Zack wasn't religious. She didn't want to upset any of her new team in her first week.

Zack didn't seem to be offended. "I've sorted out a car for you to use. You simply need to fill in a form and show them your driving licence."

Charlie's spirits immediately lifted. That would make her job so much easier. She was about to go and organise it when Rick showed up.

"I've been with the CSIs. They're still waiting on some test results."

Charlie had planned to check in with them, but she needed to visit Max Edmondson to ask him about his request for a divorce and what he was doing at the marital home last night and who was feeding the cat. Talking to the CSIs would wait until tomorrow if they hadn't found anything yet. There was so much still to do. She needed to get better at delegating, although that didn't come easily to her. She preferred to take control of everything herself.

"Can you check on Tyrone, please?" she asked Rick. "He's doing more house-to-house near the crime scene. He may have found out things that need following up on."

"Sally's perfectly capable of managing that."

Charlie silently agreed with Rick. But she'd asked him to do it. She needed to start as she meant to go on and assert her authority, not let Rick dictate to her what she did. "I'm well aware of that. Get Sally to help. There may be more people to interview than we realised. There's a block of flats opposite the house, as well as the neighbours on either side. We need to contact anyone who may have seen or heard anything before they forget."

Charlie marched out of the room before Rick got a chance to answer back. She wasn't being controlling, not really. She was simply doing her job.

Chapter 21

Max wasn't answering his mobile and wasn't at his office when Charlie phoned to check, so she drove straight to the Town Hall in Southampton. They still hadn't interviewed Kate Lovell.

Kate appeared flustered when she came down the stairs to meet Charlie in reception. She looked at her watch. "I've got a meeting, so I can only spare you ten minutes. I don't want to be late."

"I'll try to be as quick as possible. Is there somewhere we can talk in private?"

Kate led her along a corridor and showed her into a small room.

Charlie got straight to the point. "How long have you known Felicity Edmondson?"

"Less than a year. I only met her when I started working here."

"Did you work closely with her?"

"I suppose so. I'm in charge of getting the Tenurewise contract up and running, making sure all our procedures are in order so that we can find suitable tenants for the properties as quickly as possible. I was updating Fliss regularly on progress, or lack of it. We're ready, but the company isn't providing the properties they promised."

"Did Felicity ever talk about life outside of work?"

Kate shook her head. "Not really. I tried to engage her in conversation sometimes, but she preferred to talk about work."

Kate wasn't the first person to say this. Charlie was painting a picture of Felicity Edmondson as someone who wouldn't let anyone get close to her. "So you didn't pick up on any worries she might have had at home?"

Kate shrugged. "No, I wouldn't know about that."

"What about the people at Tenurewise? Did Felicity clash with anybody there?"

"Fliss clashed with everybody, but in a nice way. She challenged everything. If anyone from Tenurewise told her anything, she bombarded them with questions about how they were going to do it, or what they were doing to mitigate any risks, or whether there would be any extra cost to the council."

"Did anyone at Tenurewise bear any grudges for that?"

"Not that I noticed. It's part and parcel of doing business. They expect questions."

"Tell me about the party. Did Felicity argue with anyone?"

Kate glanced at her watch before answering. "She was a little more relaxed than usual. Although she still gave Stephen Pollock a piece of her mind when he suggested increasing the contract price. Fliss wasn't having any of that, said they were bloody cheeky to ask after the council had already signed the contract."

"Did you speak to Felicity at the party?" Charlie fired her questions rapidly, hoping to wrap up the interview before Kate's ten-minute deadline was up. She wasn't confident she would be able to stop her from leaving if they hadn't finished by then.

"Only a little. We were told to mingle with the Tenurewise people."

"What did you talk to her about?"

"Nothing much. Just general stuff. The delicious canapés, whether she had kids, that sort of stuff."

"And did she?" Tabitha Newbury seemed to think so. It reminded Charlie she still needed to broach the subject with Max. Strange that Kate wouldn't already know, after a year of working together, if Felicity Edmondson had children. Perhaps Felicity really did like to keep her private life separate from work.

"No. Probably just as well. She would have made a lousy mother."

"Why do you think that?" Charlie was keen to get any insights into Felicity's personality.

"She was too wrapped up in her work to have time for children. They would have felt totally neglected." Kate looked at her watch again. "I really have to go."

"Just one more question. Who was still at the party when you left?"

Kate thought for a moment. "Alicia, definitely. I really don't remember who else."

"I still need to see Tracey Gulliver. Where can I find her?"

Kate was already walking away, clearly on a mission to get to her meeting. She glanced over her shoulder. "Tracey's on the third floor. Anybody up there will show you to her desk."

Charlie watched Kate Lovell disappear along the corridor, her brown hair catching the light from the harsh fluorescent strips in the ceiling. Kate had certainly given the impression that Felicity Edmondson was a very private person. Private people often had secrets. She needed to find out what Felicity's secret had been.

Chapter 22

Charlie found the stairs easily. She never got enough time to work on her fitness, so she ran up to the third floor.

The small lobby at the top of the stairs led through another door into a large open-plan office. Kate Lovell was walking towards her from the opposite end of the office. Charlie wondered why she wasn't in the meeting she'd been so desperate to attend and how she'd got up here so quickly. Had she lied about the meeting to put an end to the interview? Charlie walked towards her. Lovell could damn well introduce her to Tracey Gulliver.

As she got closer, it was obvious that this woman wasn't Kate Lovell. There were definite similarities—brown hair and a heart-shaped face that Charlie, with her square jaw, envied. They were even wearing similar clothes: black trousers, teamed with a pale-coloured blouse, although Kate's blouse had been white, whereas this woman wore pale pink. But this definitely wasn't Kate Lovell.

"I'm looking for Tracey Gulliver." Charlie held out her warrant.

"That's me." Tracey's face took on a serious demeanour, etching the joyful heart shape with worry lines. "I suppose you want to ask about Fliss."

"Is there somewhere private we can talk?"

Tracey led her into a glass-fronted office and sat down. "What do you want to know? I keep going through everything in my head, and I can't make any sense of it."

"Why don't we start with how long you've known Felicity Edmondson?"

"I suppose about five years. She'd just got the director's job, and she was on the panel that interviewed me for my current post. We bonded over a chocolate creme egg. I showed up slightly early, and she'd just stuffed one into her mouth and could hardly speak. I was disappointed she didn't offer me one, but she offered me the job instead, so I guess that was a better result." Tracey laughed briefly before the worry lines returned.

"And did you have much to do with her in a normal week?"

"Yes, I'm one of six managers below her, so she's always meeting with us, either together or separately."

"Did she ever talk to you about any concerns outside of work or anyone threatening her?"

"She was very private. I didn't even know she was married until at least six months after I started working here."

That tallied with what Charlie had been told by everyone else who worked with Felicity Edmondson. She didn't like to talk about her private life with work colleagues. "Did you ever meet her husband, Max?" She knew as she asked that she was wasting her breath.

"No," Tracey confirmed, "but Fliss never met my husband either."

Charlie changed the subject. "Tell me about the contract with Tenurewise. I gather there's a reversion clause if they fail to deliver enough properties in the first year."

"That's right. The year is up at the end of May. Fliss and I discussed that recently. There's no way they can deliver a further forty-nine properties before then. It's impossible." Tracey threw her hands up in a gesture of hopelessness. "They would need to find suitable properties and get their offers accepted. Then go through the entire purchase process, with surveys and conveyancing. Then they need to refurbish the properties, which may entail simply giving them a lick of paint, or it may be substantial work: new bathroom, kitchen, flooring, maybe even structural repairs in some cases. There's no way that will happen in the next two months."

"What did Felicity think? Did she intend to invoke the reversion clause?" Losing so much business would be a plausible motive for someone at Tenurewise to murder Felicity Edmondson, except that, if she'd discussed it with other council employees, they might still carry on and revoke the contract anyway.

"She really didn't want to. I think she would have lost face if the contract failed. I'm not sure what will happen now. Fliss was the driving force behind this scheme. Without her, other people in the council may want an excuse to get out of it."

Charlie paused for a moment to think it through. It sounded as if Felicity's death had potentially made things much worse for Tenurewise, not better. She parked the theory and continued. "What happened at the party? Why did you leave with Danny Owen?"

"He offered me a lift. I'd had trouble finding the address on the way there. I'd been there once before, but that had been in daylight, and someone else had been driving, so I hadn't paid any attention. To be honest, I found it rather scary walking from the bus stop in the dark. There wasn't much street lighting and hardly anyone around. So I really wasn't looking forward to walking back afterwards."

"Where did Danny drop you off?"

"He let me out at the bus stop. I was a bit disappointed because initially, he offered me a lift home. I think he got cold feet when he realised I didn't live anywhere near him. I suppose I should be grateful I didn't have to make that horrible walk in the dark."

"How far is the bus stop from the Highfield Road house?"

"I'm not sure. It took me twenty minutes to walk it, but I did take a wrong turn at one point. It only took a couple of minutes to drive there."

"And you took the bus straight home after that?"

"Yes, I wasn't going to walk back to the house in the dark, if that's what you're getting at. I'd had enough of that the first time I did it." She fiddled with her hair nervously. "What happened to Fliss? I heard she killed herself, but she would never do that. She was a strong woman. You have to be to get to her position. If she'd had a problem, she would have tackled it head-on, not given up and topped herself."

Charlie took a deep breath. She hated breaking bad news. "We believe Felicity Edmondson was murdered."

Chapter 23

Rick finally managed to track down Max Edmondson, who had forgotten to tell them where he was staying. He'd booked into a small hotel on the outskirts of Winchester. He and Sally were lucky not to miss him. Max was about to go out when they caught up with him at the hotel.

"Can we have a word, please?" Rick identified himself and Sally.

"It's not really convenient. I have an appointment."

"This won't take long." Rick stood in front of him, blocking his exit.

"Oh, all right. I suppose I can spare five minutes."

Max took them into his room and shut the door. "What's this about? Have you found out what happened to my wife yet?"

"Not yet, sir. It's still early days. Can you please tell me where you were yesterday evening?" Rick spoke quickly to shut down further questions from Max. He didn't want to run out of time.

"Yesterday? I must have been here."

"Can anyone confirm that?" They already had a witness who placed him at his own house, but Rick wanted to hear it from him.

"Not really. I was in this room all evening. To be honest, I was a complete mess. I still can't get my head around what happened."

"We're very sorry for your loss, sir," Sally chipped in. "Are you sure you didn't leave this room at all?"

"Of course I'm sure."

Rick wondered why he was here in the first place. Didn't he have any family or friends? His wife had just died. Surely someone would take him in for a couple of days. "The thing is, sir, we have a witness who says you were at your house yesterday evening."

Max looked surprised but hid it quickly. "Oh yes. I had to fetch a few things. Clothes, toothbrush, that sort of thing."

"Didn't you already have all that stuff from your trip to the conference?" Sally asked.

"Yes, but I was in such a state when I received the bad news, I got straight into the car and drove home. I left everything at the hotel."

"We did tell you not to go into the house until our forensics team had finished." Rick intended to check with the hotel as soon as they got back to the station. He'd lay odds on Max Edmondson being a lying bastard.

"I didn't imagine it would matter. It's not as if Fliss died there."

"So you returned to the house. How did you get in?"

"Through the front door."

Rick shot Sally a look and got in first before she got the chance to speak. "Did you spot the kitchen window?" Clearly, Max had forgotten about his lost keys, and Rick wasn't going to remind him that he knew. Let him dig himself into a hole if he wanted to. The blood sample they had found wasn't on the police database and, although it was possible it belonged to a local house-breaker who hadn't yet been arrested, Rick's money was on it being a match to Max Edmondson.

"I didn't even go into the kitchen."

Now Rick was certain Max was lying. "Do you have a cat, Mr Edmondson?"

"Yes. He's Fliss's cat, really."

"He must have been hungry, what with no one being in the house for twenty-four hours by then."

"Yes, that was another reason I needed to go to the house, to feed the cat."

"So you fed the cat in the kitchen?"

"Yes." Max didn't seem to realise he'd directly contradicted himself.

"But you didn't notice the broken window?" Rick kept on applying pressure. He could feel Edmondson was about to break.

Max checked his watch. "I really need to go now."

"That's okay," Rick said. "But before you go, answer me one question. Why did you break into your own house yesterday evening?"

He didn't even try to deny it. "I remember now. I lost my keys."

"And you didn't consider calling a locksmith?"

"I'd just lost my wife. I wasn't thinking straight." Max was becoming more and more flustered. It was a far cry from the calm, emotionless man they'd met previously.

"Mr Edmondson, does your wife have any children?" Sally asked softly.

Max jerked his head towards Sally, staring at her in puzzlement at the curveball question she'd asked. He hesitated before answering. "No. She didn't like children. We were constantly arguing about it because I wanted kids and she didn't."

"Did you argue about it on Tuesday evening?" Sally asked sensitively, continuing with the sharp contrast to Rick's more aggressive approach.

"No. Of course not. I didn't kill Fliss."

"We may need to question you again," Rick said.

Max looked worried. "When can I go back to my house?"

"You should be able to return to your house later this afternoon. I'll phone you as soon as we've finished with it. Your cat will need feeding."

"He's definitely lying," Sally said as soon as they were both back in the car. "He's not even particularly good at it."

"Can you check out his alibi when we get back to the station? If he really spent a couple of days in Edinburgh, we can take him off the suspect list. Otherwise, we need to work out if he could have actually got access to the Tenurewise house to kill his wife." Rick sighed. He may not have had the opportunity, although it was likely he knew where his wife would be, despite having denied it.

"He broke into his own house," Sally pointed out. "So what about the broken window catch at the crime scene? He might have broken in there."

"It's possible, but we need to check the alibi, then find some concrete evidence to place him in that house or at least nearby. In the meantime, we need to keep an open mind. There were eight people at that party. Any one of the other seven had more opportunity than Max Edmondson."

Chapter 24

Zoe Neale lived in a big house on the outskirts of Southampton. Charlie had already explained the purpose of her visit on the phone earlier.

Zoe answered the door wearing an apron. "I'm in the middle of prep for an event I'm catering this evening. Dinner for ten at a private residence. Do you mind standing in the kitchen doorway, and we can talk while I keep working? I have to maintain strict hygiene standards to keep Environmental Health happy. If I let you into the kitchen, I'll have to clean everything again, and quite frankly, I don't have the time."

"So you work from your home kitchen? I assumed you must have a restaurant."

"Yes, this suits me better. It's more flexible than running a restaurant. My parents left me the house, and I found it easy to get a loan to refit the kitchen after I came fifth on MasterChef a few years ago." Zoe skilfully filleted a large fish. It took seconds.

Charlie could see she was talented. "Congratulations. So the event you catered for Tenurewise was a normal thing for you?"

"That was small fry. Canapés for eight people. I did a wedding party for two hundred last weekend. Mind you, I did get agency staff to help with that one."

"Did you meet any of the people at the Tenurewise party before Tuesday?"

"Only Alicia Gardener. I've catered a couple of other events for her in the past."

"How much did you talk to the party guests?" Charlie hoped they might have been less guarded with an outsider, may have let some important piece of information slip.

"Hardly at all. A little polite conversation when they praised the standard of the canapés. My job was to set out the food and hand it around, blend into the background and keep in my place. In between that, I was heating up some of the canapés and washing up as I went along. To be honest, I would normally send someone else to set up the food and waitress for a small event like this, but Alicia is a good customer, and she really wanted me to be there. She paid over the odds to ensure that. She likes to boast that I won MasterChef, which makes me cringe because it's not true. Fifth place is still a huge deal, but I don't think she gets that."

"You must have overheard a lot of conversations." Charlie remembered the house. Most of the ground floor was taken up with the large open-plan kitchen/living space. Zoe would have been in the same room as most of the party guests all evening. "Did anything stand out? Any arguments? Or anyone paying Felicity Edmondson extra attention?"

"The dark-haired man from Tenurewise paid her a fair bit of attention. I think his name was Danny. But he paid lots of attention to all the women, including me. He was flirting like crazy."

"How did Felicity respond to that?"

"She seemed to find it quite funny."

"You mean she was laughing at him, not *with* him?" Charlie imagined that Danny Owen would hate that.

"Hard to say, maybe a little of both."

"Did you spot any signs that they might have arranged to meet later?"

Zoe laughed. "You're barking up the wrong tree. Danny left with one of Felicity's colleagues. I don't know her name. A pretty brunette, but a bit common. If he did try to get it on with Felicity, she must have turned him down, but if you think he was angry with her for that, he really couldn't have cared less. He simply moved on to the next one."

Charlie was about to leave when Zoe remembered something vital.

"I nearly forgot, I lost one of my knives at the party. I meant to tell you earlier."

"Can you describe the knife?" Charlie asked. There was a good chance it might be the murder weapon.

"I can do better than that." Zoe opened a drawer in one of the kitchen units and took out a knife. The blade glinted in the light as she carried it over to where Charlie stood.

Charlie took the knife. It was about six inches long, with a black handle and a serrated blade. It looked expensive and very sharp.

"The knife I lost is exactly like that one, but with a straight blade, not a serrated one."

"Can I borrow this one?" Charlie needed to show it to Tabitha to confirm if a similar straight-bladed knife could have been used to slit Felicity Edmondson's wrists.

"If you must." Zoe sighed. "But I need it back as soon as possible."

Charlie agreed. "When did you notice the knife was missing?"

Zoe had returned to her food prep. "When I was packing up my stuff to leave. I looked everywhere for it. I even rummaged through the waste bin. The kitchen was virtually empty, apart from my stuff. There weren't many places it could have been."

"Did you search the rest of the house or outside?" It was possible Zoe had dropped it, or someone had borrowed it and left it upstairs.

"No. I assumed I must have dropped it in the kitchen. Do you think someone took it?"

Charlie wasn't sure what to think. If the missing knife was the murder weapon, it certainly pointed towards someone who had been at the party. But until they found it, she couldn't confirm anything.

Chapter 25

Sally had spent much of the day on the phone. There had been an eco-architecture conference in Edinburgh on the date Felicity was murdered, but Max Edmondson wasn't registered for it. It was possible he'd taken a colleague's place at the last minute, something she would need to check with him. But when she tried to locate the hotel he claimed to have stayed at, no such hotel existed in Edinburgh. The nearest Three Thistles hotel was over the border in Carlisle, 100 miles away. She phoned the Three Thistles hotel anyway. They didn't have an Edmondson staying this week. After failing to reach Max Edmondson on the phone to clarify the situation, Sally looked for hotels in Edinburgh with similar names, in case he had misremembered. She ended up phoning every single hotel in Edinburgh. They all came back with the same story. No booking under that name.

"Max Edmondson is a two-faced liar," she said to Rick after hanging up the phone for probably the fiftieth time.

"I think we already established that."

"I don't believe he was anywhere near Edinburgh." Sally decided to check his car on the ANPR system to be absolutely certain. "So where was he? He could have done it."

Rick grunted. "I know it's a cliché, but it's always the husband."

"Huh. Our job would be much easier if that were true."

"We need to interview Edmondson again."

"Yes, but I'm querying his registration number on ANPR first." When she asked him where he'd really been, she wanted to have the answers already, in case he lied again.

Chapter 26

Max still wasn't answering his phone. Sally had tried him several times and left messages for him to call back. She had also tried the hotel he was staying in, but he'd already checked out.

"Let's go to his house," Rick suggested.

"It might be a wasted journey." It was the most likely place to find him, but he may have finally gone to stay with family or friends, under the circumstances.

"Or it might take him by surprise. In any case, it won't be wasted. We can interview the neighbours again to ask if any of them saw him on the days he was supposed to be in Edinburgh."

To Sally's disappointment, there was no car in Max's driveway.

Abi was in her front garden. "You've just missed him," she shouted over the fence.

Rick pulled out his phone. "What's his number?" he asked Sally. "Let me try. He might answer if he doesn't recognise the number phoning him."

Rick dialled the number. After a few seconds, his expression of annoyance morphed into a beaming smile. "Max Edmondson?" He nodded at Sally. "My name is Detective Sergeant Richard Henderson. We need to speak to you."

Sally remained silent as Rick listened to the reply.

"Where are you? We can come to you."

Sally guessed that Rick only offered to go out of their way because he wanted to know where Max had gone.

"We're at your house. Can you come here?"

More silence. The smile vanished from Rick's face.

"Then you'd better come to the station. We'll expect you in half an hour." He hung up the call.

"He's got some explaining to do. He wouldn't tell me where he was. And he didn't want to come here because he says he still hasn't found his keys, so we can't get in. Why wouldn't he have got a locksmith by now? How is he feeding the cat?"

"I don't think he lost his keys at all." Sally led the way to the car. They needed to leave now to get back to the station before Max showed up. "He asked his wife for a divorce. What if she changed the locks? That's what I'd do."

"You might be right."

"As soon as we get back to the station, I'll check the ANPR again. It might show up where he's just been."

Chapter 27

Sally looked up from her computer screen. "Edmondson should be here soon."

"Assuming he's coming," Rick said.

"He can't be too far away. The ANPR clocked him on the M27 about half an hour ago, then it lost track of him. It looks like he might have been somewhere in the New Forest."

"Then we have no chance of tracking him. There aren't any cameras once he's out in the countryside." Rick answered his phone. "We're in luck. He's downstairs now. I'm going to fetch him before he changes his mind. I've already booked interview room two."

"I'll be there in five minutes," Sally said.

Sally closed the door of the interview room behind her and put a plastic cup of water on the table in front of Max Edmondson. Rick smiled faintly, glad she hadn't fetched Edmondson a coffee after the runaround he'd given them. She sat down opposite Max.

Next to her, Rick shuffled his stack of papers. There was nothing relevant on them, but he was convinced it looked important and frequently psyched the interviewee into being more cooperative.

"Where did you stay last night?" Rick asked. It was an innocuous opening gambit, not directly related to the case but designed to get Edmondson talking.

It didn't work.

"With a friend." Max took a sip of water, taking his time to swallow it, as if buying himself valuable extra seconds to come up with a better answer.

"That's good. What's your friend's name?"

"She doesn't need to be involved in this. Do I need a solicitor?"

So it was a female friend. "You are entitled to legal representation at any time. If you don't have your own solicitor, we can appoint the duty solicitor. You're not under arrest. Do *you* think you need legal representation?"

"No. I haven't done anything wrong. But you hear so many things about the police stitching people up for crimes they didn't commit."

Rick counted to ten quickly to stop himself from saying something he might regret. "That rarely happens. You've been watching too much TV."

Max remained silent, which Rick interpreted as not wishing to appoint legal representation.

"Where does your friend live?"

"That's completely irrelevant."

Rick disagreed and ignored the protest. "Did you stay with the same friend when you were allegedly supposed to be at a conference in Edinburgh?"

Max Edmondson had recently asked for a divorce. That made it extremely likely that the woman he was trying to keep secret was a lover rather than a friend. He'd put two and two together, and perhaps he'd come up with five. But it was more likely to add up to a big, fat four.

"I was at a conference." Max paled. He avoided eye contact and fidgeted with his cup of water.

"You weren't registered for the conference."

"I took over a colleague's place at the last minute." He seemed to have regained his confidence. "That's why my name won't be on their list."

"What's the name of this colleague?"

Max hesitated for a split second. "Colin Sampson."

"How did you travel to Edinburgh?" Sally asked.

"I drove."

"Are you sure?"

"Of course I'm sure."

"Because I checked your car on our Automatic Number Plate Recognition system. There's no sign of your car anywhere north of Eastleigh during those two days you were supposed to be in Scotland."

"I borrowed a friend's car."

"Is that the same friend you stayed with last night?" Rick interrupted.

Max jerked his head towards Rick. "Yes."

"What's the registration of the car you drove to Scotland?" Sally asked.

"I don't remember." Max seemed a little less confident, unsettled by the two-pronged attack from both detectives.

"Then we will need the name and address of your lady friend," Rick pressed.

Max stared at him. "I really don't want to involve her. She hasn't done anything wrong."

Was he implying that he had done something wrong? "Mr Edmondson, do you understand the seriousness of this? We can't verify your alibi for the time of your wife's murder. You're not registered for the conference you claim to have attended. The hotel you say you stayed at doesn't exist. No other hotel in Edinburgh has a record of you staying during that time. If you won't cooperate and give us your friends' details, we will have no choice but to arrest you."

Max stared down at the table, visibly shaken. "Her name's Lisa Grant."

Rick barely heard the whisper. "Please speak up for the recording."

"Lisa Grant. She lives in Brook. He reeled off the address.

Rick was familiar with the tiny village on the road towards Fordingbridge. "Thank you. Now, would you like to tell us where you really were when you claimed to be at the conference?"

Max took another sip of his water. He looked defeated. "I stayed with Lisa," he admitted.

"What is your relationship with Lisa Grant?"

"No comment."

He could refuse to comment all he liked. Rick didn't care. He intended to ask Lisa herself.

Chapter 28

Lisa Grant lived in a picturesque cottage in Brook, not so much a village as a hamlet, on the edge of the New Forest, close to the M27. Rick got out of the car and opened the gate to allow Sally to park in the driveway.

"Nice place," Sally remarked. She glanced wistfully at the stables in front of the house before marching up to the front door to ring the doorbell.

An attractive woman answered the door, her blond hair twisted into a long, thick plait, which reached nearly to her waist. Sally's gaze instantly alighted on the bump where the woman's waist used to be. She forced herself to look up. "DC Sally Gleeson and DS Richard Henderson, Hampshire police." She held up her warrant card. "Are you Lisa Grant?"

"That's right. Have you come about the break-in?"

Sally looked at Rick. "What break-in?"

"I reported it yesterday. The lock was broken on the back door. I was certain someone had been in here, but I've checked everything thoroughly and nothing was taken."

"If you reported it, I'm sure someone will deal with it," Rick said.

"We're here for something else." Sally didn't want to get sidetracked with anything that could be left to uniformed officers to deal with.

Lisa suddenly seemed panicked. "What's the matter? Has there been an accident?"

"Nothing to worry about," Sally reassured her. "We're making some routine enquiries. May we come in, please?"

"I suppose so. I could do with getting the weight off my feet."

Sally and Rick followed her into the large farmhouse-style kitchen. A black Labrador heaved itself out of a basket in the corner of the room and came over to sniff them. The greying hair around her muzzle made her look old.

"Don't mind Millie," Lisa said. "She's a sweetie. She wouldn't hurt anyone."

Millie quickly lost interest in her visitors and ambled back to her basket.

"How far along are you?" Sally asked. Lisa looked as if she might be about to pop. Sally hoped not.

"About six months. I can't wait to get this baby out." She pulled out a chair and flopped onto it. "I spent the first three months throwing up, and now I'm the size of a baby elephant, and my ankles are swollen." She gave a big sigh and kicked her shoes off. "Now, what did you want to ask me about?"

Sally sat opposite Lisa. "Do you know a man called Max Edmondson?"

"Yes, of course." She patted her stomach. "He's the baby's father."

Sally wasn't surprised. "Can you tell me where Max Edmondson was on Tuesday and Wednesday?"

"Yes, he was here with me, helping to decorate the baby's nursery. When I say helping, I mean Max did most of the work. I supervised and made tea."

"Was he with you the entire time? I mean, he must have had to go out for supplies."

"He walked Millie for me twice a day, and he drove to a DIY store in Cadnam to get some extra paint. But he stayed here most of the time. It makes a nice change having him around. He's so often away with work."

Sally wondered if Lisa actually knew about Max's wife. Firstly, that he had one, and secondly, that she was dead. Maybe she'd leave that bombshell for now. They might get more information out of her if she weren't on her guard or, more likely, in total shock.

"How long did he go out for?" She ran through the route in her head from Brook to Eastleigh. In the evening, if he took the M27, in light traffic he could easily drive it in fifteen minutes. Then he would have needed time to watch the house, gain access, and murder his wife before driving back again. At best, it would probably take at least an hour. He would need an incredible amount of luck, with all the stars aligned in his favour, to do it any quicker.

"In the morning, about half an hour. In the evening, I have no idea. I usually fall asleep in front of the TV these days. I'm knackered by eight p.m."

"What about Max's wife?" Rick asked.

Sally glared at him. She'd intended to leave that question a little longer.

Lisa looked confused. "Say that again."

"What about Max's wife? Have you met her?" Rick repeated.

"Max doesn't have a wife. At least he did. She died."

"Did you know her?"

"No, of course not. She died before I met Max. It's taken him a long time to get over losing her. That's why he wanted to take things slowly." She patted her bump. "This little monster has made us speed things up." She smiled.

Sally glanced over at Rick. He looked as confused as she was. "How long have you known Max?"

"Nearly two years."

Sally sympathised with the poor woman. Max Edmondson had clearly spun her a whole web of lies. Lisa deserved to know the facts. "Felicity Edmondson, Max's wife, died last Tuesday."

The expression on Lisa's face turned from horror to disbelief. She put both hands on her stomach as if to protect the baby from the truth about its father. "That's impossible."

"How often did Max stay over?" Sally asked softly.

Lisa coughed, clearing her throat. "He only stayed over occasionally when he didn't have to get up early the next morning for work, but I saw him a couple of evenings most weeks. Like I said, we were taking it slowly." She wiped a tear from her cheek, logic beginning to dispel the initial disbelief. "Do you think..." She burst into tears, violent sobs overwhelming her.

Sally put an arm on her shoulder and offered her a tissue. It was a miracle Lisa managed to get pregnant, given the short amount of time Max spent with her. "Can we make you a cup of tea?"

Lisa nodded. "There's a box of herbal teabags next to the kettle. I've given up caffeine because of the baby." The realisation that the baby's father might not be everything he'd claimed set off a fresh round of sobbing.

The kettle boiled quickly, and Rick placed a steaming mug of herbal tea on the table in front of Lisa. It smelled vile. For once, Sally was relieved that he hadn't made a cuppa for her.

Lisa's tears subsided, and she looked up at Sally. "How did Max's wife die?"

"We can't give any details yet, but we can tell you that she was murdered." Sally waited for another flood of tears from Lisa, but she was running through some deep breathing exercises. For a moment, Sally wondered if Lisa had heard what she said.

"Do you think Max killed her?" The question came out in a whisper as Lisa struggled to hold herself together.

"It's still early in the investigation, but we haven't ruled out the possibility." Sally wanted to be honest with her, but after yet another bombshell, Lisa was too vulnerable to leave on her own. "Is there someone who can come and sit with you for a while? This must be a terrible shock." The bottom had fallen out of the poor woman's perfect world. It might help her to have a shoulder to cry on.

"My neighbour might be home."

"Do you want me to go and ask her?" It might be useful to talk to the neighbour in case she'd seen Max leave the house last week.

Lisa nodded. "It's the house opposite with the Land Rover in the driveway. Her name's Georgina."

Georgina answered the door wearing jodhpurs and a fleecy top with pieces of hay stuck to it. "I was about to take a shower," she said.

Sally introduced herself, flashing her warrant card at the woman. "I've been visiting your neighbour, Lisa Grant. She's received some bad news, and I wondered whether you would mind sitting with her for a bit. I don't like to leave her on her own."

"It's not the baby, is it?"

"No, the baby is fine." Sally didn't elaborate on the bad news. It was up to Lisa how much she wanted to tell her neighbour about the piece of scum she was meant to be marrying.

"That's good. Tell her I'll be there in ten minutes. I need a quick shower first." Georgina began to close the door.

Sally put her hand on the doorknob quickly. "Before you go, can I ask one quick question?"

"Yes, what?"

"Last Tuesday, Max was staying with Lisa. Did you see him go out in the evening?"

Georgina responded instantly. "No, I didn't notice him leave, but his car was missing for well over an hour. I rent Lisa's stables and one of the horses got a touch of colic that evening. I had to call the vet out. Then Max came back well after ten and kicked up such a fuss because my vet parked in his space. It was an emergency, and it's not as if he even lives there, although I'm surprised he hasn't moved in by now, with the baby on the way."

"Thank you. You've been very helpful. I'll tell Lisa you won't be long."

They needed to speak to Max Edmondson again. He had motive and opportunity. If they could place him at the house in Eastleigh, it would be enough to arrest him.

Chapter 29

Danny Owen was a hard man to pin down. He'd been out of the office so many times this week that Charlie began to wonder if he was deliberately avoiding the police.

"Thank you for making time in your busy schedule to see us," Charlie said as she sat down in one of Tenurewise's few meeting rooms.

Danny appeared to have missed the sarcasm. "My pleasure." He beamed her a big smile.

Charlie imagined plenty of women must succumb to his charm and good looks, but his tactics wouldn't work on her. She sensed something false about him. It was obvious to her that the smile wasn't genuine.

"I need to ask you about the party again. What did you speak to Felicity Edmondson about?"

Danny leaned back in his chair. "How the hell should I remember?"

"The woman was murdered. I would have thought you'd remember everything you said to her, under the circumstances."

Danny crossed his arms defensively. "It was mostly idle chit-chat. None of it important enough to stick in my mind."

"Really? I got the impression the party was really a business meeting in disguise. Surely you must have talked about the contract with the council at some point."

"I left that to Alicia and Stephen. I was there to butter her up."

"And did *buttering her up* involve flirting with her?"

"Of course not. I prefer them younger." He grinned.

"Like Tracey Gulliver?"

"Not my type," he said flatly.

"I thought everyone was your type. I gather you were flirting with all the women. And you gave Tracey a lift home. Was that all you gave her?"

"Who told you that? I only gave Tracey a lift to the bus stop. She was frightened of walking back in the dark. Nothing happened. God, no."

"But you were flirting with Fliss. Did she turn you down?"

"I didn't flirt with anyone. If anything, it was the other way around. I can't help it if women find me attractive."

"So it must have upset you to find one who didn't. Did Felicity turn you down?"

Danny gave a big sigh. "You're barking up the wrong tree. Listen, this is just between us. No one else at the company knows, and it's none of their business. I'm gay."

Charlie wasn't too surprised at Danny's revelation. Something about his so-called flirting didn't ring true. She wondered what his father, the archdeacon, thought about that. Perhaps Archdeacon Owen was one of those more modern, progressive clergymen.

"Where did you go after you dropped Tracey Gulliver at the bus stop?"

"I drove straight home."

Charlie wondered if that statement was true. She watched him carefully, trying to read his face. "What time did you arrive home?"

"Ten p.m. The news started on the radio as I parked the car."

"Can anyone vouch for that?" It would rule him out instantly if he had an alibi.

"No, I live alone."

"I'll need your home address and your car registration number, please." Charlie pushed a piece of paper and a pen in front of him. She might be able to check his movements on ANPR to help verify his story. "Did you notice Felicity Edmondson argue with anyone at the party?" she asked as Danny jotted down his details for her.

He seemed about to say something, then abruptly changed his mind.

"Anything at all, even if it doesn't seem relevant," Charlie prompted.

Danny paused for a few seconds. "She did have a bit of a barney with the councillor woman."

"Diana Horn?"

"That's the one. Councillor Horn isn't a big supporter of our project. She voted against it. The only person who did."

"Then why did you invite her to the party?"

"It was Alicia's idea. She reckoned if we got Councillor Horn onside, we'd have less trouble in a couple of years if the council wanted to expand the contract and get us to purchase even more properties for them to lease."

"Did you hear what Felicity and Councillor Horn argued about?"

"Not really. Councillor Horn told Fliss she was making a big mistake, and at that point, Alicia and Stephen rushed in to do some damage limitation. They changed the subject and split them up. Councillor Horn left shortly after that."

Danny Owen had been much more helpful than he probably intended to be. Now, Charlie needed to track down Diana Horn and discuss what this big mistake might have been.

Chapter 30

Diana Horn lived on the outskirts of Southampton in a newly built cul-de-sac.

Charlie rang the doorbell. A dark blue Mercedes sat in the front driveway, indicating that Mrs Horn was probably at home. She rang the doorbell again.

Still no answer. Charlie stepped back to look up at the windows. There was no sign of anyone, even though Mrs Horn told her on the phone that she'd be in. She rang her number again.

"Yes?"

"This is Detective Inspector Steele. I'm at your front door. You said you'd be at home." Charlie tried to keep the annoyance out of her voice.

"Oh yes. I'm in the back garden. I'll be right there."

A couple of minutes later, the door opened. "I'm so sorry. I was tidying up the garden and forgot the time."

Charlie followed her into the kitchen, waiting as Mrs Horn pulled off her gardening gloves and washed her hands. She was an older lady, perhaps in her late sixties, although still looking pretty fit and well.

Mrs Horn dried her hands and turned towards Charlie. "What did you want to talk about?"

"You were at the party held by Tenurewise last week."

Mrs Horn snorted disdainfully. "I'd hardly call it a party. It was a small gathering."

"But you attended?"

"Yes, I specifically asked to be invited. I thought someone should represent the councillors, and as I'm chair of the housing committee, I wanted to know firsthand what was going on."

"I understand you weren't happy with the Tenurewise contract."

"No, I was not. The whole thing was an absolute shambles. I voted against it in the first place, you know, but I was the only one, so the proposal was passed."

"What was the problem?"

"What wasn't the problem? The company was supposed to deliver two hundred properties within two years. They buy them and lease them to the council, who can then sub-lease them to their tenants. I never believed those numbers were possible. They intended to buy individual properties on the open market. As soon as you start buying in large numbers, you simply push the prices up. And there's only so much supply in the first place, unless you move completely out of the area, and our tenants don't want to move. A lot of them have got children in school or relatives living nearby. They can't move a hundred miles away without completely disrupting their lives."

"How many properties are you expecting the company to purchase?"

"It depends on how long we give them. We're already one year past the original starting point. Every time there was another delay, they simply reset the clock and started counting from there. Now they've finally delivered one property, at least they can't keep resetting, but judging by the abysmal performance so far, I'd say we'll be lucky to get more than ten properties in two years."

"Is that really a problem?"

"I should say so. This contract was supposed to save the council a huge amount of money. We should have a hundred properties by now. That means we've had to house a hundred extra families in hotels. Do you have any idea how expensive that is compared to the cost of leasing a hundred houses? If they'd gone for a different option, it would have worked out much cheaper in the long run. That contract should never have been signed. The company has no track record. I'm not surprised they haven't performed."

"And you blame Felicity?"

"Absolutely. She was the one driving the project. And she didn't even check out the company properly. I'm sorry she's dead, but honestly, the council might be better off with a less reckless housing director at the helm."

Charlie shuddered at the lack of compassion. "What makes you believe Felicity didn't check out the company?"

"Because I did some research into it myself after things started to go wrong and nothing was delivered. It's a new company with no experience, and it's already got some hefty loans before they've even started buying two hundred new properties. I used to run a business with my husband. We owned a factory making high-end garden furniture, exported it all over the world, so I know what I'm talking about. We sold up last year and moved down here to be near our daughter, then Harry died of a heart attack. That's partly why I became a councillor. I needed something to do, and I wanted to put my skills to good use to help improve the local area."

"I'm sorry." Charlie assumed Harry was her husband. "What happens if Tenurewise goes bankrupt?"

"I expect the council will have to take their tenants out of those properties and put them in expensive hotel accommodation instead. But that's not the only issue. The worst of it is that the company's chief executive, Alicia Gardener, has links to organised crime. I expect you're aware of the Castle family."

"No. I'm new to this job. I only moved here last week."

"Oh dear. Well, the Castles are a big local crime family. They are into drugs, prostitution, possibly people trafficking, and an occasional murder thrown in. And Alicia Gardener is closely related to the family. Can you imagine the political fallout if it gets out that the council is dealing with a company that's funded from the proceeds of crime?"

Charlie made a note to find out more about the Castles as soon as possible.

"I have to ask. When you left the party on Tuesday, did you go straight home?"

"No. I went to drop off something to my daughter in the middle of Southampton."

"So she can confirm what time you arrived?"

"No, actually, she wasn't in. She took her son to A&E. He suffered a bad asthma attack."

"What did you and Felicity argue about at the party?"

Diana laughed. "The same thing we usually argue about. This infernal contract. I make a remark that we should have a hundred properties by now and could have saved a few hundred thousand pounds already. She told me to be more positive and start supporting the scheme. Two of the Tenurewise people butted in before we could finish the argument, so it was something and nothing. But Fliss wouldn't have taken it personally. I take my role in the council seriously, and she knew that."

Charlie went through the interview in her head as she drove back to base. Diana Horn had no alibi. And there was certainly no love lost between her and Felicity Edmondson. But Charlie couldn't imagine Horn choosing that specific murder method.

Chapter 31

Charlie went straight to find Zack when she returned to the station.

"Did you find out how Tenurewise was funded?" After Diana Horn's accusations regarding the Castle family, Charlie needed to know for sure if they were involved.

"Yes, Tenurewise is owned fifty-fifty by Alicia Gardner and a company called Palace Holdings. Palace Holdings is an offshore company registered in Jersey, but it's wholly owned by Ron Castle, Alicia's father."

"Did Palace Holdings put up any funding?"

"One hundred percent."

Charlie felt a tiny shiver rip through her. Did Ron Castle order a hit on Felicity Edmondson to protect his investment?

She refocused quickly. "What about Max Edmondson? Did his finances throw up anything?"

Zack shrugged. "Not that I can see. His business appears to be doing well. He pays a decent salary into the couple's joint account every month. There's no mortgage on the family home. No loans that I can find."

"So if he killed his wife, the motive isn't financial?" Max Edmondson was their number one suspect. Zack's findings didn't change that. Max had plenty of motive without worrying about money.

"No, I'd say not."

"Have you found anything else?"

Zack's face lit up. "I've been checking the ANPR system. Danny Owen's car was clocked on the motorway about five minutes from his home on Tuesday evening at six minutes past eleven. The journey from the house in Highfield Road to Owen's home in Winchester should take around twenty minutes at that time of night."

Charlie did a quick calculation. "So he lost over an hour." Danny had told her he got home at 10:00 p.m. She turned to the rest of the team. "Tyrone, can you visit Danny Owen tomorrow and get an explanation for that missing time period?"

Zack continued. "There's more. Max Edmondson's car was caught by a camera less than half a mile from Highfield Road at ten p.m., heading out of Eastleigh."

"That fits. Max could have done it, but it's circumstantial evidence. We need to find something more. What about the house-to-house interviews? Was there anyone you missed?" Charlie realised she was getting desperate, but if they could find an eyewitness that put Max Edmondson outside the house at the right time, that might be enough.

"No one saw him," Sally said. "But there were a couple of people in the flats who weren't at home when we called."

"We could do a reconstruction," Rick suggested. "Put Sal in a brown wig and give her a few wrinkles to make her look older."

Tyrone and Zack burst out laughing, immediately stopping as they noticed Charlie hadn't joined in.

"Seriously, that's a good idea." Charlie had used reconstructions before to jog people's memories. She would suggest it to the DCI and perhaps he would ask a TV crew to film it for the evening news.

Chapter 32

Sammie Broome was watching the evening news with her boyfriend, Mick Jones.

"Are you going to get dinner on, babe? I'm hungry."

She lay back in Mick's arms and groaned. "Give me five minutes, then I'll do something." Two of the grooms at the riding school where she worked had called in sick today, leaving them with twenty-eight horses between the two of them to muck out, groom, and get ready for lessons. She was exhausted. Maybe she could persuade Mick to go out for a Chinese takeaway, but he worked at Southampton docks on a zero-hours contract and work had been scarce this week, so money was tight. What a pity he couldn't cook, but, sadly, he could even burn water. Nothing edible would come out of their kitchen with him in charge.

Mick got up to go to the bathroom. Sammie lay back on the sofa and closed her eyes for a few seconds while he was gone. When she opened them again, the scene on the TV looked familiar. "That's our road," she exclaimed. "Hey, Mick," she called. "Come and look at this."

A woman with brown hair, wearing an expensive-looking blue coat, was walking along Highfield Road. Sammie immediately recognised the exact part of the road. It was right opposite their flat. She had a perfect view of that house out of their bedroom window.

Mick sat beside her. "What's up?"

"Look, that's the house opposite here." The woman walked up to the front door of number 17 and pushed it open, leaving the door ajar. Sammie continued to watch, fascinated. The woman appeared familiar. When had they filmed this? It must have been while she was at work.

A few seconds later, a man entered the house. The film clip ended, and the newscaster explained it was a reconstruction of a crime and gave a phone number to call if anyone had seen anything.

"What day did they say this was?" Sammie had missed half of what he said while she scrabbled for a pen and something to write on. She noted down the phone number on the cover of the TV guide.

"Tuesday, 31st March, around nine thirty p.m." Mick yawned.

Sammie didn't know why he was so tired. He'd been lazing around the flat all day today while she'd been working her arse off.

"When will dinner be ready?"

Sammie ignored him. She was too busy deciding what to do. Nine thirty was about the time she always went into the bedroom to draw the curtains before they went to bed. And their first-floor flat overlooked number 17. That's why the woman looked familiar. She was certain she'd seen her go into the house, and the man following her too. She wondered if there would be any reward money if she phoned the hotline and made a statement. She didn't have the energy to think about it now. Best to cook dinner and get some sleep. It would have to wait until tomorrow.

Chapter 33

Charlie got to work early and parked her car as close as possible to the building's staff entrance. They would probably have to waste most of today sifting through the statements that had come in after the reconstruction had been aired yesterday on both the six o'clock and the ten o'clock news. Ninety percent of them would be crank callers. The other ten percent would be mostly useless, with insufficient detail to be any good. They just needed one good one, that unicorn statement from a credible witness that gave enough information to be usable as evidence.

As soon as she got in, she went straight to the Organised Crime Unit.

Sergeant Bill Herbert was already at his desk.

Charlie introduced herself. "I need some information on the Castle family, especially Ron Castle."

Herbert nodded sagely. "Ron's the head of the family, but he doesn't usually get his hands dirty these days. What's your interest in him?"

Charlie explained about Tenurewise and Felicity Edmondson's murder. "Do you think he could have ordered a hit on Mrs Edmondson to protect his investment? We have reason to believe she may have been planning to advise the council to terminate the contract."

Herbert tapped his pen on the desk. "Slit wrists, you say. That doesn't sound like a professional hit. Far too messy. And risky to do it when there were other people in the house. That's not Ron's style at all."

"I did wonder about that, but I need to follow it up."

Herbert stared at her sternly. "Leave it."

Charlie opened her mouth to protest.

"OCU has an ongoing investigation into the Castles. If you start interfering for the sake of a very long shot suspicion, you could easily mess up months of work. I'm not asking, I'm telling you. Leave it."

"But—" Charlie didn't like being warned off, especially not by someone of a lower rank.

"I can pass that instruction up through your DCI if necessary. Leave the Castles alone."

Charlie gave in. She'd already had one telling-off from DCI Talbot. Another one so soon might prove terminal for her career. She decided to park the Castle connection for now.

She popped out to her car to fetch something she'd forgotten. On her way back in, the desk sergeant stopped her.

"There's someone waiting to see you. I saw you coming, so I put her in interview room one. She's in a hurry to get to work."

"Thanks. Did she say what it's about?"

"The Felicity Edmondson reconstruction."

Charlie groaned quietly. It would probably be a waste of time. The sooner she got it over with, the better.

Chapter 34

Sammie Broome sat in the interview room, nervously wringing her hands together.

"I'm DI Steele. Sorry to keep you waiting."

"I don't want to be late for work."

"Then why don't you tell me exactly what you saw." If Sammie came up with any details that hadn't been included in the reconstruction, Charlie would take her seriously. At the moment, she was simply looking to weed out another crackpot looking for her fifteen minutes of fame.

"I live opposite number 17, Highfield Road, the house they showed on the news last night. We're in a first-floor flat, me and my boyfriend."

"And what did you see?" Charlie encouraged her to stick to the point. She didn't want to waste the whole day.

"I saw that woman going into the house and a man following her. We get a really good view from the bedroom window. I went in there to draw the curtains at about nine thirty in the evening."

"Can you tell me anything about the woman?" Charlie wanted her to describe her.

"She looked a lot like the woman on the TV, except that she was wearing high-heeled black boots, not trainers like the TV woman."

Charlie's interest perked up. Sammie never would have known about the boots if she hadn't seen Felicity Edmondson. They'd tried to dress Sally in similar clothes, but at short notice, they didn't have any suitable boots to fit her.

"What about the man?" Charlie asked. "The one who followed her into the house."

"Tall, dark hair, medium build."

Charlie's hopes were immediately dashed. It was such a generic description, it could apply to hundreds of men.

"I've been thinking about it since yesterday," Sammie continued. "And I think I'd recognise him if I saw him again."

"Are you sure?" Charlie tried not to get her hopes up again.

"Yes, pretty sure."

"Would you mind looking at some photos?" Charlie pulled an iPad out of her bag. Zack had set up a gallery of photos for them to use for an online identity parade if they found a genuine witness.

"Sure." Sammie looked at her watch.

"We'll try not to keep you much longer." Charlie placed the iPad in front of her. "Take your time and look at each photo as many times as you need."

Sammie began to scroll through the images. Zack had provided ten photos: a random selection of local criminals, interspersed with photos of Max Edmondson, Danny Owen, and Stephen Pollock.

Sammie scrolled through them all three times, hesitating the second time on the photo of Edmondson. Finally, she settled on Edmondson's photo. "That's him."

"Are you sure?"

"Yes, that's definitely him."

"Did you see him come out of the house later?"

"No. Sorry. I shut the curtains, and we went to bed early. I have to be up before six for work."

Charlie arranged for someone to visit Sammie's flat later to confirm their bedroom gave a good view of number 17's front door, then let her go to work.

"We've got him," Charlie said when she went back to the incident room. The entire team was present. "An eyewitness has identified Max Edmondson."

"That's great," Rick said. "Can we arrest him now?"

"Not yet." There were still a few things she needed to do first so they would have a strong case against Edmondson. "Tyrone, I want you to visit the witness's flat." She handed him an address and phone number. "The boyfriend will be at home all morning. Check out the view from the bedroom window and how clearly you can see number 17's front door. Take some photos."

She turned to Sally. "I'd like you to set up an ID parade. Six should be enough. One of them needs to be Max Edmondson, and find five similar men. Take Tyrone when you go to pick up Edmondson. He should be free by then."

"What about me?" Rick asked.

"We're going to get a warrant to search Lisa Grant's house for the murder weapon."

Chapter 35

There was no sign of Max when Charlie and Rick showed up at Lisa Grant's home in Brook.

"Max is at work." Lisa had refused to leave the premises while they searched the house, protesting that she would have to stand out in the rain and she was pregnant. "He says working helps take his mind off things, and he needs to earn money, with the baby on the way."

Charlie said nothing. Max would more than likely need the extra money to pay for decent legal representation and, if he was convicted of Felicity's murder, he wouldn't inherit anything from her.

Charlie started in the kitchen. She made Lisa sit at the table, where she could keep a close eye on her. She didn't want Lisa removing any evidence while she wasn't looking.

The kitchen was the most obvious place to find a knife. Hidden in plain sight. She went directly to the knife block on the kitchen worktop and pulled out each of the seven knives in turn.

None of them matched the knife that Zoe Neale had lost. In addition, Tabitha had drawn her a detailed picture of the knife blade that would have been used on Felicity Edmondson. It would be small and very sharp to make those precision cuts on Felicity's wrists. The description tallied with Zoe's missing knife. Although the knife hadn't been used to stab anyone, which would have given a better idea of the size and shape of the blade, it still looked unlikely that any of these knives had been used.

"Max didn't do it, you know." Lisa stared at her as she searched.

Charlie moved on to the cutlery drawer.

"Then the evidence will show that." Charlie wasn't confident that Max would see his unborn child come into the world, or watch him or her grow up. The evidence was stacking up against him. She lifted out the cutlery tray and tipped it out onto the work surface.

Immediately, Charlie spotted a small, sharp knife. She picked it up, careful not to smudge any prints that might be on the handle. And held it up for Lisa to see. “How long have you owned this knife?”

Lisa stared at the knife. Finally, she spoke, her voice shaking. “I’ve never seen that knife before.”

Chapter 36

The DCI had come to Charlie's office for an update as soon as he heard that Max Edmondson was in custody.

"The knife has traces of Felicity Edmondson's blood on it, and it's the same brand as the knife Zoe Neale lost at the Tenurewise party, so it might be the same one. Lisa Grant, Max's girlfriend, denies ever seeing it before." It still worried her how Max got hold of the knife. The only explanation was that Zoe must have dropped it when she carried her equipment back to the van.

"And what about this eyewitness?" Talbot asked.

"Sammie Broome. She checks out. Her flat overlooks the front door of 17 Highfield Road. She claims she saw a man following Felicity Edmondson into the house at nine thirty p.m. on 31st March, and she picked out Max Edmondson in a line-up. Added to that, Max Edmondson lied about where he was that day. He claimed to be attending a conference in Edinburgh, but there's no sign of him ever having been there. Plus, his car was picked up on ANPR close to the murder scene at the right time, and Lisa Grant's neighbour said he went out and was gone for over an hour—again, around the time of the murder."

"I think we've got enough to charge him." Talbot stood up. "Well done, Charlotte. Good work."

Charlie was ready to interview Max as soon as his solicitor arrived.

"His solicitor's Terence Knott," Rick said. "He's brilliant. If he finds the slightest gap in our case, he'll drive a truck through it."

"Thanks, Rick." She wished he hadn't told her that. She would have preferred something that boosted her confidence instead of slamming it into the ground.

When Charlie finally walked into the interview room, Terence Knott appeared every bit as intimidating in real life as he had done in her head for the last twenty minutes. She sat down opposite Edmondson. Rick settled into the remaining chair next to her, facing Knott.

After everyone had stated their names, Charlie addressed Edmondson. "Do you understand that you have been charged with murdering your wife, Felicity Edmondson, on 31st of March this year?"

"Not guilty," Max said.

"You will get an opportunity to enter your plea at a later date. We just need to ask you some questions for now." Charlie was surprised that Knott hadn't told him to cooperate, given the amount of evidence against him.

"I didn't do it." Max stared at her, his blue eyes making him look alarmingly like a ferocious arctic tiger.

Charlie tried to ignore his stare, although his eyes constantly drew her back. She held up a clear plastic bag. "I'm showing the suspect exhibit G, a six-inch Sabatier kitchen knife. Max, when did you hide the knife in Lisa Grant's kitchen?"

Max made a big show of putting his head in his hands. "I've never seen it before."

"The knife has your wife's blood on it. How did it get into Lisa's kitchen?"

"I don't know."

"When did you put it there?"

Knott spoke up calmly. "DI Steele, my client says he's never seen the knife. Does it have his fingerprints on it?"

"No." Charlie couldn't tie it to him directly. Was he going to let Lisa, the mother of his unborn child, take the blame for something he did?

She changed the subject. "Tell me what happened after you followed your wife into number 17, Highfield Road."

"I wasn't there." Max sounded almost bored with the proceedings.

"Mr Edmondson, we have an eyewitness. They picked you out in a line-up."

Knott immediately jumped in. "I'll need the name and address of this witness."

"I can give you that when we finish the interview," Charlie said.

"I'd like it now, please, and then I'd like to request a break for my client."

Chapter 37

"Where is he?" Charlie had been waiting for nearly two hours for Terence Knott to return so they could continue with Max Edmondson's interview. Knott had left the station as soon as Charlie had given him Sammie Broome's details.

"He'll be checking out the witness," Rick said. "He knows we can't do anything until he gets back.

"Do you think he'll try intimidating her?" If Knott contacted her, Sammie might refuse to give evidence.

"No. Knott has his reputation to keep up. He wouldn't do anything that might backfire on him."

Terence Knott didn't return for over three hours. Then, as soon as he got back to the station, he asked to see DI Steele.

"I don't appreciate being kept waiting for so long with no explanation." Charlie didn't like the man. He was plain rude.

He smiled at her. "I'm very sorry, DI Steele. I needed to get something checked out."

"Well, now that you have checked it out, I'd like to get on with interviewing Max Edmondson." Charlie had looked in on Max half an hour ago. He wasn't coping well with being kept in the cells in limbo until his solicitor deigned to return. Max wanted to get this over with as much as she did. In his current frame of mind, he might be ready to confess.

"I really don't think that will be necessary." Knott straightened his tie. "What do you know about your eyewitness, Sammie Broome?"

Charlie eyed up Knott suspiciously. "She lives opposite the murder scene, works at a riding school in the New Forest. She picked Max out of a line-up. It's not about her. It's about your client."

"I'm afraid it's very much about Miss Broome," Knott said calmly. "Her name seemed familiar, so I did some digging in our old case files. Our Miss Broome has been an eyewitness before, a couple of years ago, on a case I handled."

"That's irrelevant." It was a coincidence. Not many people acted as witnesses twice unless they had criminal connections, but it happened.

"I'm afraid it's very relevant, DI Steele. You see, last time, Sammie Broome offered herself as a witness to collect the reward money that the victim's wife put up. She claimed to have seen a man running away from the murder scene, but she hadn't seen anyone. If we hadn't found out she was lying, her evidence would have sent an innocent man to prison. So, you see, by the time the defence lawyers have finished discrediting Sammie Broome, the jury won't believe a single syllable she utters."

Knott's revelation hit Charlie like a stampeding horse, knocking the wind out of her for a few moments. She'd been counting on Sammie Broome's witness statement. Losing it would leave a serious hole in their case. She'd need to discuss it with the Crown Prosecution Service to check if it was still viable to go ahead. She believed Sammie, but even if she was telling the truth this time, she would no longer be a credible witness. Her testimony might do the case more harm than good.

"I'll need the details of the old case." Charlie was still certain of Max Edmondson's guilt and hated to think he might get away with it because of insufficient evidence. If Sammie Broome was an unreliable witness, she needed to see it for herself.

Chapter 38

The CPS refused to support Charlie. The eyewitness account and her identification of Max Edmondson had been crucial evidence. And even though they could prove that Max had lied to them many times about his whereabouts when his wife was murdered, the CPS solicitor felt it might just as easily be motivated by wanting to keep his affair a secret.

Charlie felt deflated. With Max Edmondson now released from custody, they didn't even have a suspect for Felicity's murder. She glanced around at her team. None of them had taken a day off for nearly two weeks, and they all looked exhausted.

"Tomorrow's Sunday. I don't want to see anyone working." There was nothing productive they could do at the moment. "We'll rethink the case on Monday when we're fresh." She would be constantly rethinking it over the remainder of the weekend, trying to make sense of what, and who, and why.

"Thanks, ma'am." Sally smiled at her. "We'll find something to help us crack this case."

"Yes, we will," Tyrone agreed.

"If we all think about it tomorrow, one of us is sure to come up with an idea," Rick said.

"Just relax. Spend some time with your family." Charlie addressed the remark mainly to Rick. She was ashamed that she was completely unaware of whether the other members of the team even had any family. She wasn't much good at small talk or at making friends. Yet her team was still prepared to get behind her to help her get a result. It reminded her of the army. Her men would follow her anywhere, loyal to the end. She knew she would be thinking of much more than just the case tomorrow. She had a good team here, and she needed to show her appreciation more.

Charlie woke early on Sunday, immediately jumping out of bed, her mind on getting to work, before she remembered she was taking today off. A long day stretched ahead of her, and she wondered what to do with it. She would start by listing out the evidence to see if that would spark any ideas on where to investigate next. She might even sneak into the station for a few hours. No, she admonished herself. She needed a break as much as her team did, and she also needed to set them a good example.

She decided to clean her small rented flat, maybe watch some TV, then go for a walk and explore the area. That still left a lot of hours to fill.

The guilty part of her brain recalled Rick's chiding her to visit their mother. She supposed she ought to get it over with. Before she could change her mind, she dialled her mother's number.

The phone rang a few times before it was answered. "Hello."

Charlie hardly recognised the sleepy voice at the end of the phone. It was gone 8:00 a.m. Mum was always up well before this time, even on a Sunday, and yet it sounded as if she'd still been in bed. "It's Charlie."

"Yes."

Charlie had expected a bigger reaction than that, but she supposed if she'd just dragged Mum out of her bed, she must still be half asleep. Did Rick tell their mother about Charlie's move back to the area? He must have.

"I've got some free time today. I thought I might visit you."

"That would be lovely. Why don't you come for lunch? One o'clock."

Memories of Mum's mouthwatering Sunday roasts made Charlie realise she had barely any food in the flat. She readily agreed. Perhaps seeing her mother again wouldn't be as bad as she imagined. It had only built up into a big deal because she'd left it an embarrassingly long time. There were reasons for that. At least there were at first. Then, as always, work got in the way, and it had been difficult to fit in a whole day to make the journey to Hampshire to visit. She was a rubbish daughter.

Over breakfast, Charlie started to list the facts about the murder case. The location of the crime scene must be important. And if Max didn't do it, that led them back to one of the people who attended the party. Tomorrow, she would ask the team to do a deep dive into all seven of them. They might uncover a connection or a motive that way. They must have missed something. Perhaps they should also look at Felicity again. If she was murdered because of something that happened in her past, they needed to find it.

Chapter 39

Charlie tried to remember when she had last visited her mother's house. It had been too long. The closer she got, the more overwhelming the guilt became. She wouldn't blame her mum one bit if she launched into a huge telling-off as soon as she opened the front door. Whatever Charlie's reasons were for not visiting her mother, it didn't excuse her.

Her guilt only increased when the door opened. Her mother had aged. Her hair was streaked with grey, and an extra couple of stone gave her a more maternal and less glamourous appearance. Worry lines stood out on her forehead. She'd aged badly, even though she must be only sixty-seven. What had happened to her in the last few years to make her such a shadow of her former self?

"Charlotte?"

Charlie never liked the name. It was too formal. She occasionally used it at work, but at home the name made her feel like a Regency princess, and not in a good way. Even Mum had eventually been persuaded to call her Charlie, only using her full name when she'd done something wrong. She braced herself for the inevitable telling-off.

"Aren't you going to invite me in?" Charlie hesitated to hug her. It's what mothers and daughters did, but theirs had never been a particularly affectionate relationship. She sniffed the air, hoping she would smell Mum's famous roast beef, but disappointingly, no tantalising aromas floated out from the kitchen. Charlie conceded she'd given her rather short notice of her visit. Of course Mum wouldn't have planned on cooking a roast for herself. Charlie would be lucky if her mum made her a sandwich. She reminded herself that wasn't why she came.

Her mother looked embarrassed. "I'm really sorry. I've managed to double-book. I completely forgot my friend is taking me to the garden centre this afternoon. She'll be here any minute. I thought you were going to be her. Why don't you come back tomorrow?"

"I'll be working." She wouldn't take another day off until they solved Felicity Edmondson's murder.

"I'm really sorry, love."

"Don't worry." Her disappointment gave way to relief. This might be a good thing. Her mother would be especially pleased to see her next time, whenever that might be. The inevitable telling-off may not be so inevitable after all.

Chapter 40

Lisa Grant walked another lap of the kitchen. Where on earth was Max? He should be back by now. He'd gone out at eight thirty to give Millie her evening walk. It shouldn't take more than half an hour at the most, but it was already ten o'clock and still no sign of him.

She tried his phone again. She'd lost count of how many times she'd phoned him in the last half hour or so. The result was exactly the same. Straight to voicemail. She left yet another frantic message.

What if something had happened to Millie? Max might have let her off the lead, and she'd run off chasing a fox or some other nocturnal animal. George Brown's dog got stuck down a badger set last summer. What if something like that had befallen Millie? Or she might simply have run off and got lost, or been hit by a car. A black Labrador would be impossible to see in the dark.

Lisa's mind churned with dreadful possibilities. Perhaps Max, not Millie, had run off. She'd been beastly to him ever since that detective visited and told her the truth about Max's wife. Not that Max didn't deserve it. He absolutely did. But he'd also been immensely apologetic and more loving than ever, swearing that he cared more about her and the baby than anyone in the world. But his arrest opened up another great gulf between them. And even though the police released him and dropped the charges, Lisa still couldn't quite bring herself to trust him. If he had run off, it was because she'd driven him away. But however angry Max felt, he would never take Millie away from her. Never. Something bad must have happened.

She picked up her phone again, but this time, she didn't phone Max; she called the police.

The woman on the line spoke in a calm, sensible voice. "How may I help you?"

Lisa gripped the phone tightly. "My partner's missing. I'm sure something's happened to him." She was equally worried about Millie, perhaps even more so, but she suspected the police wouldn't go out of their way to search for a missing dog at this time of night.

"What's your partner's name?"

"Max. Max Edmondson." Would the woman recognise his name now that he probably had some sort of police record and place the case at the bottom of the pile?

"How old is Max?"

"Forty-one." He would be forty-two next week, and she hadn't given any consideration as to how they would celebrate or what present she would buy him. All this difficult business had put paid to those nice, real-life things. When he came home, she would give him more attention, reassure him she did still care, and organise a lovely surprise for his birthday.

"And when did you last see Max?"

Lisa took a deep breath, trying to stay as calm as the woman on the other end of the phone. All this stress wasn't good for the baby. "About half past eight."

"This morning?"

"No, this evening. He took my dog for a walk and hasn't come back yet."

"Let me get this straight. Max is a forty-one-year-old man, and he's been missing for an hour and a half. Is that correct?"

When she spelt it out like that, Lisa realised how ridiculous it sounded. But she knew something had happened to either Max or Millie, or perhaps even both of them. "Something's wrong," she insisted.

"Do you have any particular reason for being worried? Does Max have any history of mental illness?"

"No. Nothing like that." At least not that she knew of, not since she'd known him. Suddenly, she felt as if she didn't know Max at all.

"Have you tried phoning his friends and family? He probably popped in to visit someone on the way home."

"No." Lisa realised he'd never introduced her to any of his friends or family. It was one of the many signs she'd ignored during their relationship. She'd fallen in love and only let herself see what she wanted to see.

"You should try them first. Then call us again tomorrow if he doesn't come home by then. I'm sure there's a perfectly reasonable explanation."

"But I know something's wrong. I can sense it."

"I'm sure he'll soon be home." The voice on the phone remained as calm as ever. "If he doesn't show up within twenty-four hours, please phone us again." She hung up.

Lisa took some deep breaths. Perhaps the woman on the phone was right, but she couldn't stop herself from worrying, however hard she tried. She wished Millie were here. She really needed to give her a hug.

Chapter 41

Clarissa Canley urged her horse into a canter. A big log blocked the end of this track. The New Forest verderers often positioned logs across tracks like this to stop vehicle access. It was the perfect size to jump easily, about two feet in diameter. She and Hugo had jumped it the last time she'd ridden this way. The route made a good shortcut home, bypassing the tiny village of Brook with its nasty twisty road, and heading straight towards Bramshaw. They would be home in time for breakfast, then she would leave Hugo in his field and go to work.

She pushed Hugo on, approaching the jump on a perfect stride. "Come on, boy. Three, two..." She never got to one. As Clarissa counted down the strides, at the very last moment, Hugo slammed on the brakes, skidding to a halt before he reached the log.

Clarissa grabbed at Hugo's mane in an attempt to keep her balance, but the force throwing her forwards was too much to overcome. She tumbled over his shoulder, then hit the ground with a thud.

She scrambled to her feet, immediately looking for Hugo, who had backed up and was snorting loudly at the log, now several yards in front of him.

"What's the matter?" She walked towards him, holding out her hand. "It's all right. It's only a tree. There aren't any horse-eating monsters hiding behind it." What on earth had got into Hugo? This wasn't like him. He was normally such a reliable jumper, tackling any obstacle she pointed him at, and they'd jumped that same log perfectly before. She reached out and grabbed the reins, then caressed him on the neck, talking softly to him until he calmed down.

"It's all right, you silly sausage. Let's go and take a look. There's nothing to worry about." Her hip ached where she'd bashed it in the fall. She was going to have a massive bruise tomorrow.

Hugo would have to stand next to the log for her to use it as a mounting block because her painful hip simply wouldn't flex enough for her to get onto Hugo from the ground, and it was too far to walk home.

Clarissa found some mints in her pocket and used them to coax Hugo closer to the log. He still felt skittish, and she wondered if she would have to walk home after all. She rubbed his neck. He always enjoyed that. "Come on, just a little further." She finally persuaded him to stand close enough to the log for her to get on. She would have to be quick. In this mood, Hugo would shoot off like a rocket if a leaf so much as fluttered in the breeze. She scrambled up onto the log, her hip and thigh throbbing painfully from the effort. Still holding the reins and hoping that Hugo wouldn't spook and pull her off balance, she straightened up to her full height.

"Oh my God!" Clarissa froze. Was that what she thought it was? No wonder Hugo didn't want to come anywhere near here. Quickly, she slid off the log before Hugo pulled her off. Then she leaned over the top to get a better view. A man lay on the ground, tucked right up against the side of the log. She was immediately drawn to his eyes, icy blue, and veined with red. They stared at her as if pleading for help, but she could do nothing for him. She was absolutely certain the man was dead.

She wiggled further across the log, careful to keep hold of Hugo's reins. As she got closer to the dead man, a low growl sounded, making her jump. She'd been so fixated on the man's eyes, she hadn't noticed the black Labrador lying with its front paws and muzzle resting on the man's ankles.

"Good dog," she said softly. "I'm not going to hurt your master." She eased back slowly, although if the Labrador was any good at protecting his owner, the poor man wouldn't be in his current predicament. She shouldn't blame the dog. The man may have simply had a heart attack. She cast her eyes over his whole body until they alighted on the rope knotted around his neck. How did she miss that? He most definitely didn't die of a heart attack. The blue eyes stared at her as if pleading for help. But the only thing she could do for him now was to call the police.

Chapter 42

"What the hell happened?" Charlie had rushed out to the new murder scene with Tyrone and couldn't believe what she was seeing.

Max Edmondson's blue eyes stared up at Charlie. She wasn't sure if she felt worse for suspecting him of murdering his wife or for releasing him from custody. Because if she hadn't done the latter, he'd still be alive.

"It's only half a mile from his mistress's house," Tyrone pointed out.

Charlie wasn't sure if he was referring to Max or the dog lying at Max's feet. She assumed he meant Max. "That may not be significant. He was staying with Lisa Grant, so if anyone wanted to kill him, this would be the area where they'd find him."

"Is this connected to his wife's murder?"

"It's a huge coincidence if it isn't." The chances of the two deaths being connected were enormous. And that meant taking the investigation in a whole new direction.

"Who found the body?"

"A horse rider. Clarissa Canley. We had to let her go. Her horse was becoming difficult and wouldn't stand still." Tyrone shrugged his shoulders. "I've got her contact details."

"Good. Can you chase her up as soon as you finish here? We need to interview her while everything's fresh in her mind." Charlie looked around for the rest of her team. "Where are Rick and Sally?"

"They're on their way, ma'am."

Charlie was relieved to hear it. It shouldn't take them too long to get here. With the motorway clear, they could make the journey in about fifteen minutes. She addressed Tyrone again. "Can you chase up the pathologist, please? Then do something with that dog. It can't stay here. I'm pretty sure it belongs to Edmondson's girlfriend." Lisa

Grant definitely owned a black Labrador. "Her phone number may be on the collar."

While Tyrone was on the phone, Charlie looked critically at Max's body, trying to spot any detail that might be relevant. The body had been pushed right up against the fallen tree trunk, presumably in an attempt to hide it from view. The scuff marks in the dirt supported that theory. The first thing that jumped out, once she got past the piercing blue eyes staring at her, was the piece of rope knotted around Max's neck like a noose. That struck her as odd because it wasn't attached to anything. Had he been hanged, then cut down afterwards? She saw no sign of the rope having been cut. The pathologist might shed further light on it.

His face showed no bruising, and she noticed no marks on his knuckles and no sign of anything under his fingernails. As far as she could tell from the small amount of visible skin, he'd made no attempt to defend himself and suffered no obvious injuries. Did that mean the attacker approached from behind? Or did Max know his killer?

There wasn't much more to be gleaned from the body at this stage. She would have to wait for the pathologist. She moved well away, anxious not to contaminate the crime scene.

Tyrone must have read her mind. He called over to her. "The pathologist's on her way. She'll be about twenty minutes."

"Is it the same person who dealt with Felicity?" If the two deaths were related, it would be helpful to use the same pathologist for both of them.

"Yes, Tabitha Newbury." He turned his attention to the dog, approaching her from behind. The dog immediately got to her feet and growled at him threateningly.

"It's okay, doggy."

The dog started barking at Tyrone, making him jump back a couple of steps. He called over to Charlie. "We may have to call the RSPCA to deal with it."

Charlie laughed. She wondered how long Tyrone had worked in this area. He was a city boy, uncomfortable and inexperienced at dealing with a dog. How much worse must he have been when faced with a horse earlier? No wonder he allowed the witness to go home. "Don't be ridiculous." The old Labrador was more likely to lick him to death. "Let me try." She racked her brains to remember the dog's name. Millie, that was it. She approached her slowly, hoping her dog-whispering abilities exceeded Tyrone's because no way was she going to make Lisa Grant come out here to fetch her dog, certainly not while Max's body remained in situ.

"Hello, Millie," she said softly. "I'm going to take you home to your owner. You want to go home?" It occurred to her that Max must have spent a lot of time with Lisa for the dog to be protective of him. What a pity Millie didn't protect him earlier, when he needed it most.

Millie gave a small whimper and brushed her head against Charlie's leg.

"Good girl." Charlie grabbed her collar, using her other hand to give the dog's chest a good rub. "Come on. Let's take you home." She gave a little tug on Millie's collar.

At first, the dog resisted, but was persuaded to move with a gentle rub on her shoulder. "Is there a lead anywhere?"

"We could use a few leads to solve this case quickly," Tyrone said.

"Not funny." It occurred to Charlie that Millie's lead was probably in Max's pocket. She didn't want to disturb anything on the body. "See if you can find anything useful in the car. A piece of string or something."

She encouraged Millie to walk towards the car while Tyrone searched in the boot. The tag on her collar was engraved with a phone number. She didn't recognise the number, but Millie's name was also on the tag.

"There's nothing useful in here," he said.

"Are you wearing a belt?"

Tyrone looked puzzled. "Yes."

"Will your trousers fall down if you take it off?"

"Probably not."

"Let's have it, then. We can use it as a dog lead."

Tyrone made a face at her before reluctantly removing his belt. "I wouldn't mind, but the dog doesn't even like me."

Chapter 43

Tabitha showed up at the crime scene at the same time as Rick and Sally. Charlie noticed Tabitha had sensibly ditched the stilettos, but even the substitution zebra-print Wellington boots sported chunky three-inch wedge heels. A large matching black-and-white bow in her hair completed the ensemble.

Charlie held Millie's makeshift lead towards Rick as Tabitha pulled on her forensic suit. "This is Millie. She belongs to Max's girlfriend, Lisa Grant. Can you take care of her while I talk to Tabitha? Then we need to take her home and break the bad news to Lisa." Rick liked animals. Hopefully, he'd get on better with Millie than Tyrone had.

Rick took the lead. "I might have some dog treats in my coat pocket."

"You've got a dog?" He'd always said he wouldn't get one until he retired and could spend all day with it.

"Mia wanted one."

"Is someone going to show me this body?" Tabitha approached them.

"Follow me." Charlie led the way.

"His name is Max Edmondson, Felicity Edmondson's husband. He was found about forty-five minutes ago by a horse rider. His girlfriend's dog was with him."

"Was that the black lab you gave to Rick?" Tabitha pulled on some gloves as she walked.

"Yes. Edmondson is on the other side of this fallen tree."

"Does this rule him out as a suspect in his wife's murder?"

"He's pretty much ruled out, yes, but for other reasons." Charlie still felt sore about not being able to use their eyewitness.

"Let's take a look, then. You wait here. The fewer people tramping about the place, the better."

Tabitha assessed the body from the other side of the tree.

"Is it the same killer?" Charlie called out.

"Patience! I've only been here for ten seconds. I'll be able to tell you more when I've done the post-mortem, but my ten-second assessment says it's a completely different MO."

"It's got to be connected." Charlie had run through the case in her head while waiting for Tabitha to arrive. "They're both suicides that aren't suicides. Felicity with her slit wrists that weren't cut by her, and Max with a noose around his neck as if he'd hanged himself."

"He certainly hasn't hanged himself. Nor has anyone else. That noose isn't tight enough to do any damage, and it's the wrong kind of knot. However"—she pulled the rope down slightly—"he's got ligature marks and bruising around his neck, so he may well have been strangled."

"So you're saying the rope was added as an afterthought?" That gave credence to her fake suicide theory.

"It looks like it. And it may not have been premeditated, at least not the rope around the neck. That's a horse's lead rope, and unless I'm very much mistaken, the hairs stuck to it belong to that black Labrador. They must have been using it as a dog lead."

Chapter 44

Clarissa Canley worked as a sous chef at The Airfield, a pretty gastropub near Stoney Cross. Tyrone recognised the name but had never eaten there. The aromas wafting out from the kitchen made him hungry.

"Sorry to keep you waiting." Clarissa came out of the kitchen, wiping her hands on her apron, and led him to a table at the back of the pub. "I was in the middle of browning off some pork ribs to go in the pressure cooker. It would have ruined them if I left them half-cooked."

"That's okay. Can you tell me about this morning? What made you decide to ride your horse along that particular track today?"

"I often take that route. It cuts off the road, and you can have a decent canter on that long track up to where I found the body."

"And when did you notice the body?"

"After I fell off." She laughed. "I should have realised sooner. Hugo tried to tell me."

"Hugo?"

"Hugo's my horse. I was trying to jump the fallen tree. We've done it before, loads of times. But Hugo wasn't having any of it today. He obviously sensed something was wrong. That's why I fell off because he refused to go near it. Maybe he smelt it. Or he may have sensed the man's ghost. Animals can, you know."

Tyrone ignored the comment. Ghosts didn't exist. "Did you recognise the dead man?"

"No, I've never seen him before. Do you know who he is? It's a bit worrying someone being killed out in the forest. I ride around here on my own every day, although at least I can run away quickly on Hugo, if he doesn't dump me on the ground first."

"We can't say yet who the victim is." Tyrone realised his statement was ambiguous. He decided to keep it that way. "Did you notice anyone else in the vicinity? Anyone suspicious or anyone you didn't know?"

"A couple of dog walkers, but I meet them nearly every time I ride that route at that time of day. I don't know their names."

It didn't seem as if Clarissa was going to be too helpful, and he didn't know the time of death yet, so whatever she'd seen may not even be relevant.

"Have you nearly finished with me? Timing is always tight to prepare for lunch. I'm going to fall behind if I'm not careful."

Tyrone handed her his card. "Please don't discuss any details with other people. It sometimes helps with the case if the general public doesn't know exactly what happened. We use it to establish if they're telling us the truth."

Clarissa looked worried for a couple of seconds, then composed herself. "Yes, of course, I understand."

"Thank you." Tyrone guessed she'd already discussed it with some of her work colleagues. It wouldn't be normal if she hadn't. With luck, the shock of her discovery would have dulled her memory of the finer details.

Chapter 45

Millie recognised her home as soon as Sally pulled into Lisa Grant's driveway. She stood up on the back seat and started wagging her tail.

"Okay, girl. Let's reunite you with your mum." Rick opened the door and held on to Millie's collar as she jumped down to the ground.

The front door opened and Lisa Grant appeared wearing a fluffy pink dressing gown. As soon as she spotted Millie, all the worry left her face, replaced by a huge smile. She called out the dog's name. Rick let go of her, and Millie ran to her owner with a speed that belied her age.

For a few moments, the pair sat on the doorstep, Lisa hugging her dog, and Millie reciprocating by licking her face.

"Can we come in?" Rick asked, reluctant to break up the reunion.

Immediately, Lisa's face was struck with horror. "Where's Max? He should be with Millie. Have you found him?"

"Let's go inside and sit down." Sally put a hand on Lisa's shoulder and gently ushered her inside.

By the time she sat Lisa on her sofa, the poor woman's face was streaked with tears. Sally thought she may have guessed what was coming, but that wouldn't make it any easier. Millie jumped onto the sofa next to Lisa and snuggled into her as if she sensed that Lisa needed her.

"I'm afraid we have bad news." Sally noticed Lisa's hand move straight towards the dog. She hoped it would give her some comfort. "Max was found dead this morning."

Lisa stared up at Sally. "Dead?"

"I'm afraid so. About half a mile across the forest from here. We found Millie with him. She must have guarded him all night."

Lisa put both her arms around Millie and hugged her. The dog's muzzle rested gently on Lisa's bump. Tears streamed down Lisa's cheeks as she cried noiselessly.

Sally kept quiet, wanting to give Lisa time to take things in. She looked over at Rick and nodded towards the kitchen. A cup of tea wouldn't solve much, but at least it would help to return a tiny amount of normality to the situation.

"What happened?" Lisa asked after a few minutes.

"We don't know yet." Even if they did, Sally wasn't allowed to tell her everything at this stage. "But I can confirm he was murdered."

"Murdered? Why would anyone want to do that?"

"Do you know which route Max planned to take when he walked Millie?"

Lisa nodded. "He always takes the same one at that time of night to avoid the traffic. Up towards the golf course, then he does a circuit around the pond and back through the woods."

Sally wasn't sure how close that was to the crime scene. She would have to look it up on a map later. "Did Max take a torch with him?" He wouldn't be able to find his way through the trees without one, but they hadn't found a torch near the body.

"Yes. It's a big rubber one."

"Did Millie have a lead?" Another item that had been missing.

"Yes. Haven't you got it? It's not a proper dog lead. It's a blue rope with a clip on the end. It's one of Georgina's old horse lead ropes."

"Yes, we have it." Sally knew exactly where the dog lead was. Around Max Edmondson's neck. "But we can't let you have it back yet. It's evidence."

"It's okay. I don't really need it. Millie walks to heel for me and comes when she's called. But she doesn't know Max as well, so he has to keep her on a lead. Otherwise, she'd come straight back home to me."

"And last night, were you here all the time?"

"Of course. I was waiting for Max and Millie to come home. I even phoned the police to report Max missing, but they weren't interested. They said I should wait twenty-four hours in case he turned up." Her voice suddenly grew angry. "If you lot had done something when I asked, Max might still be alive."

"We can't be sure of that." It probably wouldn't have made any difference at all. If Max had been missing long enough for Lisa to report it, he was probably already dead by then. And by the time they mobilised enough police officers to comb the area in the dark, he almost certainly would have been dead.

"Have you got anyone who can come and stay with you?" Rick interrupted.

"Georgina might come over. She lives in the house opposite." Lisa glared at him as if everything was his fault. Everything had changed now that she blamed the police for allowing Max to be murdered.

"I'll go and find her," Rick said. "And I'll arrange for a family liaison officer to come over."

Sally took a sip of her tea, noticing Lisa hadn't touched hers. She was itching to get back to the crime scene and search for the torch because she wasn't much use here now. She hoped Lisa's neighbour showed up soon so they could leave.

Chapter 46

The crime scene was bustling with activity when Sally and Rick returned. The crime scene investigators were busy searching the area and taking samples and refused to allow anyone inside the cordon. One of them was stretching over to the far side of the fallen tree, but Sally couldn't tell whether the body was still in situ or not.

Charlie appeared from behind them. "The pathologist has taken the body already. She's keen to start the post-mortem immediately while she has a spare slot, so I'm going to watch."

"What do you want us to do, ma'am?" Sally looked at her expectantly.

"Can you please do a deep dive into Max Edmondson's life? His work, his family, friends, acquaintances, hobbies, addictions, club memberships, everything. Pay any relevant connections a visit as soon as possible."

"No problem, ma'am. Shall I start with the neighbours where the Edmondsons lived, seeing as we've already spoken to them about Mrs Edmondson?"

"What about Lisa Grant's neighbours?" Rick asked. "They may have seen something."

"I've already put Tyrone on that job."

"We have a rough route of where Max probably walked the dog last night." Sally looked up Google Maps on her phone. She held it in front of Charlie, her finger tracing the route Lisa had described earlier.

"That's great. Can you point out where the body was found?"

Sally scrolled the map across to the right and pointed at the spot. "It's nearly half a mile out of his way. He may have taken a different route last night, although Lisa said he always walked that way to avoid having to go on a road with no pavements or streetlights."

"Or he may have been murdered somewhere else," Rick added.

"That's possible, but it's a long way to carry him. More likely, he was lured in this direction, then killed," Charlie said. "We need the CSIs to confirm if this was the murder site."

Sally put her phone back in her pocket. "Lisa says he would have been carrying a big rubber torch."

"Can you ask the CSIs to look for it? And show them the map before you leave? They'll need to search the entire route."

"Yes, ma'am."

"And when you're investigating Max, flag up anyone who might be connected to both of the Edmondsons. Friends and family, obviously, but there may be less apparent connections with work colleagues and suchlike. There's a strong chance that the same killer is responsible for both deaths, and we're still looking for Felicity's killer. Let's meet back at the station, say six p.m., unless anything really important comes up." Charlie hurried toward her car.

"Shall we start by visiting Abi Hargreaves?" Rick asked after they finished explaining Max's dog walking route to Ollie Flanders.

"Good idea," Sally agreed. Abi had been helpful before. She may be able to tell them more about Max.

Chapter 47

Tabitha had already started Max Edmondson's post-mortem by the time Charlie arrived at the mortuary.

"Sorry, I haven't got time to wait around, so I cracked on with it."

"That's okay." The less time Charlie spent in this room, the better. "Have you found anything so far?"

"There's no sign of any defence wounds, so it's likely that someone took him by surprise and strangled him from behind. There's some minor bruising on his knees, consistent with falling forward onto them. And there are faint marks on his buttocks, similar on each side, but slightly irregular. He must have been sitting on that fallen tree when he was attacked. That would certainly have made it easier for the attacker."

"So the murderer wouldn't need to be tall?"

"Goodness, no. Even I could have done it."

That didn't rule out many people. Tabitha stood barely five feet tall.

"Could it have been a man or a woman?" Charlie's job would be easier if the pathologist narrowed down the options.

"I haven't removed the rope and examined the ligature marks properly yet, so I may revise my opinion later, but I'd say the element of surprise makes it perfectly possible for a woman to have done this."

Charlie's hopes of a fast resolution to this murder were falling faster than a brick in a river. She'd thought they were getting somewhere with Fliss Edmondson's case. But her husband's murder meant they were almost starting again from scratch. She tried to visualise the scenario. Max sitting down to take a rest. Someone creeping up on him from behind, strangling him to death, then pushing him forward onto his knees. There were plenty of trees for the attacker to hide behind. Was it someone random lurking in the woods? She ruled out the possibility. It was too much of a coincidence for this to happen so soon after his wife's murder. That meant someone must have been following him, perhaps all the way from Lisa Grant's house.

"I don't understand why the dog wouldn't have heard the attacker coming."

"Well, if this is the dog lead"—Tabitha pointed to the bright blue rope wrapped around Max's neck—"he must have let the dog loose, and it wandered off."

Charlie remembered Max's body was discovered a long way from his usual dog walking route. Could the attacker have been someone he knew, someone who persuaded him to go in a different direction? Then it would have been easy for them to walk up behind him while he was sitting down. They may even have suggested taking a rest for a few minutes. Or perhaps Tabitha's theory was correct, and Millie had strayed too far away to notice anyone strange.

"He probably deviated from his usual route looking for the dog," Tabitha said.

"Yes, that makes sense." It might be the most likely scenario.

"Why don't you get yourself a coffee while I work through all the standard stuff? I'm going to leave examining the neck and head until last." Tabitha nodded towards the door. "There's a kitchen, second door on the right. Help yourself."

Chapter 48

Abi was thinking about Fliss Edmondson again this morning. The woman she'd seen watching the house last week had been playing on her mind. She'd been looking out for her since the police visited a few days ago, but there'd been no further sign of the woman. Did that mean she might be the murderer? Abi shook the thought from her head. More likely, it meant nothing, and the whole thing was a total coincidence. If she told the police, they might spend ages following it up, trying to find the mystery woman, when they should be concentrating on hunting down Fliss's killer.

The doorbell rang, interrupting her thoughts.

Abi recognised Sally from when she visited last week. "Come in. I'm about to make a cuppa."

She led the way into the kitchen and filled the kettle.

"Why don't you sit down for a minute," Sally suggested.

Abi was fine standing up, but the way the detective said it sent an icy shiver through her. She did as she was told.

"I'm afraid I have more bad news." Sally sat at the table opposite Abi.

Abi wondered what was coming. It couldn't be as bad as Fliss's murder.

Sally's expression changed from compassionate to serious. "Max Edmondson was found dead in the New Forest this morning."

"What?" Abi was still having nightmares about Fliss being murdered. And now Max too? This couldn't be happening.

"Max Edmondson is dead," Sally repeated.

Abi's thoughts returned to the stranger loitering opposite the house a few days ago. What if it wasn't a coincidence? What if that woman murdered Fliss, then came back for Max? What if she realised Abi had seen her? She blurted it out without any further thought. "I saw a strange woman watching the Edmondsons' house last week."

For a moment, the room remained quiet until the hiss of the kettle boiling broke the silence. Abi got up quickly.

"Which day did you see this woman?" Sally pulled out a notebook and a pen.

"It must have been Monday because I'd just got back from my yoga class. So that would be about seven thirty in the evening." Abi turned her back on Sally while she busied herself making two cups of tea. If she'd told the police about this woman sooner, perhaps Max would still be alive. How could she ever forgive herself?

Sally jotted something in her notebook. "What was the woman doing?"

"She was standing under the tree, gazing at the Edmondsons' house."

"Can you point out exactly where she stood?"

Abi led Sally to the front door and opened it. She pointed to a spot across the road. "She was under that beech tree, as if she was trying to hide." The spring sunshine had burst the tree into life over the last few weeks, creating a canopy of new leaves that grew thicker every day. Last week, she had a better view of the woman than she would have now.

"Can you describe her?"

"Not really. It was dark. Pretty average. About my age and my size."

"And you'd never seen her before?" Sally jotted down some notes.

Abi glanced across at the notepad. *Late twenties, five-foot-seven, ten stone.* It was a fair assessment. She needed to lose weight. "I may have." Abi placed the mugs of tea on the table. "She admired Noah when I was out in the front garden a few days ago. I think she may have thought I was Fliss."

Sally wrote some more notes. "What about hair colour?"

"Brown." Doubts crept in. She certainly wouldn't be able to pinpoint the exact shade of brown. What if she'd remembered it completely wrong? She wished she'd paid more attention.

"And what was she wearing?" Sally looked up at her expectantly.

"Jeans. Sorry, I didn't really notice anything else."

"That's okay. We might find someone with CCTV or one of those Ring doorbells." Sally smiled reassuringly at her. "If you remember anything else, please call me." She handed Abi a business card.

Abi's worry about whether she had done the right thing escalated. "What if the woman found out she'd reported her to the police? Would she even recognise the stranger if she came for her next?

Chapter 49

When Charlie returned to the post-mortem, Tabitha was about to examine Max's head and neck.

"I've removed the rope," Tabitha said, "but we've got lots of photos. The knot on the noose is wrong, so it wouldn't have worked to hang him. There was one point where the murderer tied the rope left over right, instead of right over left, so it wouldn't have tightened properly."

"How do you know all this? Were you a Girl Scout?"

Tabitha laughed. "You must be joking. I looked it up on the internet. I've just spent the last ten minutes teaching myself to tie a hangman's noose."

Charlie smiled. "That might come in handy one day."

"It might. Anyway, the knot was just for show. There's no sign that the noose caused any strangulation. It simply wasn't tight enough. It makes me wonder why the murderer bothered with it."

Charlie had thought the same thing. "It was the same as Felicity Edmondson's murder. Either it was an amateurish attempt to make it look like suicide, or the murderer is making a point." Had the Edmondsons driven someone to suicide and this was payback? They needed to dig into the couple's past more thoroughly.

"There are ligature marks around his neck, consistent with the same rope. The killer must have tied it around Max's neck afterwards. There is also bruising towards the back of the neck, consistent with fingertips being used to increase the pressure of the ligature."

"Wouldn't he have fought it?" Charlie asked.

"I'm coming to that." Tabitha waited for Frank to take more photos. "The victim has a head wound, sufficient to render him unconscious. The object used was blunt and symmetrical."

"Could it have been a rubber torch?"

"I was about to suggest that," Tabitha said.

"So was he unconscious before he was strangled?" Charlie instantly compared it to Felicity's murder. She also had a head wound, which would have knocked her unconscious.

"Yes, I'm sure of it. Otherwise, his fingertips would show signs of trying to remove the ligature."

"Do you think it's the same killer?"

"Maybe. Maybe not. The similarities are superficial. The biggest similarity is the head injury, but different objects were used, and knocking out the victim to make killing easier isn't an unusual MO."

"But they're both set up to look like fake suicides." Charlie kept coming back to that. It was the biggest thing tying the two murders together. That, and the obvious connection that the victims were married to each other.

"Tenuous. It may mean nothing," Tabitha said flatly. "Let's stick to facts. By the way, those lovely blue eyes, they're contact lenses."

Charlie hid her surprise. She supposed the lovely bright blue colour was too good to be true.

"What I can also tell you is that Max Edmondson died between eight and ten p.m."

That fit the timeline they already had. "It must have been after eight thirty as that's when he left Lisa Grant's house."

"Between eight thirty and ten in the evening then." The timing was eerily similar to Felicity's murder. Was there something about the killer that made him or her available at that time in the evening? A job with a shift ending mid-evening, perhaps? That didn't fit with any of the possible suspects for Felicity's murder.

Charlie silently disagreed with Tabitha about the fake suicides. Someone had gone to the trouble of giving them these clues. She needed to follow them up.

Chapter 50

Rick hit the jackpot with John Langford, who lived three doors down from the Edmondsons and regularly drank in the local pub with Max.

"That's terrible news." Langford shook his head in disbelief. "Poor bugger. How did he die?"

"We can't give out any details yet, sir. May I ask, where were you last night after eight thirty p.m.?"

"In the pub, the Wagon and Horses. Ask anybody."

Rick thought it might be worth asking the bar staff in the pub about Max at the same time. "Did Max ever have any disagreements with anyone in the pub?"

"Not really. I mean, only heated debates, mostly about politics. Max held a lot of strong views about how badly the government is doing. He was always mouthing off about it."

"But he hadn't received any threats, as far as you're aware?"

Langford rubbed his hand across his stubbly beard. It looked as coarse as sandpaper. Rick half expected it to leave a rash on his hand.

"If he did, he certainly didn't tell me about it, and he didn't seem worried. He was pretty happy, and so he should be, with the wife and girlfriend on the go at the same time. I'd be happy with that."

"You knew about the girlfriend?"

"Caught them together one evening. I've got a mate who lives in the same area as lovely Lisa."

"Did anyone else know?" *Did Felicity know?* She obviously didn't kill Max, but maybe someone did it on her behalf, if she'd told them about the affair.

"If they did, I didn't tell them. Max swore me to secrecy."

"Where did Max work?" Rick remembered Max mentioning he was an architect. He wished he'd paid more attention. That was a glaring error in the investigation. They should have followed up with his employers before they arrested him. Maybe Charlie didn't have enough experience to investigate a murder, much less a double one, if she made a basic error like that. He immediately admonished himself. It wasn't his sister's fault he didn't get the DI job. He should support her more.

"He's a partner in a firm of architects in Southampton. Blowed if I can remember the name." He scratched his beard again. "Edmondson and some name beginning with D."

"Dunstan. It's Edmondson & Dunstan." Rick remembered where he'd seen that name before.

"That's the one."

"What about Max's family? Does he have any?" They should have asked Lisa Grant that question, but she was so upset, he'd backed off with the questions, assuming they might already have much of the information they needed.

"Not really. His parents are long gone. He has an older brother, but they fell out over something a few years ago. As far as I know, Max doesn't see him anymore."

"Do you remember the brother's name or where he lived?"

"Tom. I met him a couple of times when Max brought him to the pub. Didn't take to the man at all. No idea where he lives, but if you find him, I'd love to know what they fell out over. Max never told me."

"When did you last see Max?"

"It must be well over a week ago. He said he was moving out for a bit, so I guessed he must be moving in with the girlfriend. He didn't want to discuss it, so I didn't ask."

Rick sighed quietly. If Max Edmondson had any worries that his life might be in danger, they would probably never know. And any agitation he'd shown may simply be due to the split with his wife. At least now, they had one whopping big connection between the two murders. He checked his watch. It was too late to follow it up now.

He would head back to the station for Charlie's 6:00 p.m. meeting and visit Edmondson & Dunstan first thing tomorrow.

Along with Rick, Sally had spent the rest of the day interviewing as many people as possible who lived in the same road as the Edmondsons. No one else noticed the woman Abi claimed to have seen. And although a few people had CCTV installed, the cameras were all angled towards the houses, not into the road. She'd drawn a complete blank.

She called in to the CSI room on her way back to the office to check if Trina found anything from the grass verge opposite the Edmondsons' house.

"I didn't find much. A couple of footprints, but that's no use without something to match them to. One of them might belong to your woman. There can't be much foot traffic over that piece of ground. Most people would walk on the pavement."

"Well, at least that's something." Sally had worried about wasting police resources on such a long shot. Not that this piece of evidence would be of much help. It was still a long shot.

"There's something else." Trina held up an evidence bag containing two long brown hairs.

"I found them snagged on a branch at about head height. They may have come from your mystery woman, if she got her hair caught in a branch while she was hiding. I'll do a DNA test."

The knowledge that she would probably receive a bollocking from the new DI about spending her budget on something so tenuous tempered Sally's brief moment of excitement. Like the footprints, she would need a suspect to match the results against. And the mystery woman may turn out to be an innocent bystander, choosing the tree opposite the Edmondsons' house to shelter under while waiting for a friend to pick her up or making a phone call. She'd done everything possible regarding this line of enquiry.

Chapter 51

Charlie arrived back at the police station early. She wanted to sort out the murder board and make it as up to date as possible before the rest of the team arrived. She wasn't sure whether to start a new one for Max Edmondson's murder, or if she should cram everything together on the same board, given that the two murders were almost certainly connected.

Zack sat at his desk in the corner, staring at his computer screen.

"What are you working on?" Charlie asked.

"Rick asked me to trace Max Edmondson's brother, Tom."

"Any luck?" She hadn't realised Max had a brother. Technically, Tom Edmondson might be Max's next of kin. The brothers might also be close enough for Max to confide in him. Her hopes were immediately dashed.

"Dead end. Fatal car crash a year ago."

Charlie tried not to show her disappointment. "Any idea where I can find another murder board?"

"I'll get you one from the store cupboard." He immediately got up and hurried out of the room, before Charlie got a chance to question him further.

Charlie jotted down some notes before Zack returned. She waited while he set up the board next to the existing one. The two boards were neatly touching. Charlie considered whether she should move them a few inches apart, given that the couple had been contemplating divorce.

She took a marker pen and wrote Max's name at the top. "Can you find me a photo of Max Edmondson?" She asked Zack. "One of Lisa Grant, too." She was a notable omission from Felicity's board but probably belonged on both.

She wrote Lisa's name, leaving space to add photos. Then she wrote the date and the time of death. Tabitha's estimate was between

8:30 and 10:00 p.m., although Charlie guessed it would be nearer to 9:00, since Lisa had said he only ever walked the dog for half an hour in the evening. She finished it off with the word *strangled*. The board seemed remarkably bare. They didn't have any suspects yet.

Zack passed her two photos: Max and Lisa. Charlie added them to the board. It still looked bare.

Tyrone arrived, shortly followed by Rick and Sally. Charlie waited for them to sit down, then addressed them all. Despite not being religious, she found herself praying that her team had made more progress than she had.

"Okay, I'll go first. I attended Max's post-mortem. Time of death between eight thirty and ten p.m. He was strangled with the rope that he used as a dog lead. We believe the place where he was found was also the murder site. That leaves the question of how he got there. Did he deviate from his usual walking route and why? And was he followed? Or did someone lure him there?"

"How would they do that?" Rick asked.

"That's a good question. We need to find an answer." Charlie continued, "We think we've worked out what happened. He sat on the tree trunk. His attacker came up behind him, so the question is, did the attacker take him by surprise, or was the attack unexpected because it was someone Max already knew?" She needed a photo of the murder scene on the board. She made a note to ask the CSI team for one.

"So he's sitting on the tree trunk. That means the killer might have been any height. They hit him on the head, most likely with a big rubber torch. Edmondson was carrying one, but we haven't found it yet."

"Could the killer have been a woman?"

"Tabitha certainly thinks so. That means we haven't narrowed down the suspect list at all. It might be absolutely anybody."

"What suspect list?"

Charlie glared at Rick. She didn't need him questioning her or stating the obvious. Rick was family. He ought to be on her side, watching her back. "Rick, can you update us on anything you found out today?"

"I discovered a connection." Rick glared back at her as if he'd scored a point, which he had. "Max was a partner in a firm of architects, Edmondson & Dunstan. Their office is in Southampton, in the same block as the Tenurewise office. I'm going to check them out first thing in the morning. There's a good chance they've done some work for Tenurewise."

"Good work, Rick." Charlie forgave him for the point scoring. This might be the breakthrough they needed. "Anything else?" she asked as she wrote *Tenurewise* and *Edmondson & Dunstan* on the board.

"Yes, Max has an older brother, Tom. They fell out over something." He glanced across at Zack.

"Sorry, mate. Tom Edmondson died in a car accident last year." Zack shrugged his shoulders as if to apologise.

Rick looked slightly deflated, even though he had already come up with a potential breakthrough in the case. "I don't have anything else. Except the dog lead. That blue rope around Max's neck. That was the dog lead."

"That's exactly what Tabitha thought." Charlie moved on to the next person. "Tyrone, how about you?"

"I've interviewed most of Lisa Grant's neighbours, but none of them saw anything, and they all had alibis. Everyone was in the local pub for quiz night, and it didn't finish until chucking out time at eleven p.m." He looked apologetic at not being able to match Rick's discovery.

"Thank you, Tyrone. It's useful to rule people out. Then we can focus on who's left. Sally, did you find out anything useful?"

"Maybe. It's a bit vague, but Abi Hargreaves, the Edmondsons' next-door neighbour, saw a strange woman hanging around on Monday last week. She was loitering on the verge opposite and seemed to be watching the house. One of the CSIs went over there this afternoon to check the spot where the woman stood. I checked with all the neighbours in case any of them had CCTV, but it's all pointing at the houses, not the road."

"Do you have a description of this woman?" Charlie wished Sally had checked with her about sending a CSI to the scene. The chances of finding anything after so long were minimal. The scene must have been contaminated by now. And she didn't want the DCI haranguing her over wasting her budget. She decided to make the point to Sally privately another day.

"Not a particularly useful one. Brown hair, about five-foot-seven, ten stone. Could be anyone. But we may get something if any of the neighbours have CCTV."

"Okay. Phone me if you find anything." She turned to Rick. "Can I have a quick word in my office, please?"

Charlie had wanted to get Rick on his own to discuss something that had been on her mind for a while.

As soon as Rick shut the office door behind him, he started talking before Charlie had a chance to say a word.

"Have you visited Mum yet?" It sounded like an accusation.

"Yes, actually. I saw her on Sunday." Charlie was relieved she had made the effort.

"That's okay then."

Charlie sighed. "No, it's not okay. She invited me for lunch, then when I showed up a couple of hours later, she'd forgotten I was coming. Is she all right?"

"Of course she's all right," Rick said defensively. "She's sixty-seven. She's a bit forgetful sometimes. It's normal."

Charlie wasn't so sure. Was she being over-sensitive? Surely Mum wouldn't have forgotten so quickly that the daughter she hadn't seen for a few years was visiting. It wasn't normal. She shook the thought from her head. She didn't have time to worry about it, not with another murder to solve. And it wasn't what she had wanted to talk to Rick about.

"What's up with Zack? Is he always so nervous?" Zack's behaviour had been worrying her for a few days. This was no time for one of her team to have problems. She wanted to sort things out before they became an issue.

"I don't think it's him. It's you, Sis."

"Me? What have I done?"

"Nothing. It's just that..."

"What?" Charlie tried to remember if she'd said anything to Zack that he might have misconstrued.

"Our last DI recruited Zack. He's worried you might not want to keep him."

"Why wouldn't I? From what I've seen so far, he's brilliant." Zack, with his exceptional computer skills, was one of the biggest assets on her team. Why would she want to get rid of him?

Rick hesitated. "I suppose you're going to find out soon enough. Zack got kicked out of Southampton University for using the university computers for illegal hacking."

"What? And he's working for the police?"

"I wish I hadn't told you now. He didn't do anything. He simply enjoyed the challenge of proving he could get into any system he wanted. Your predecessor figured we should put his skills to better use. Call it rehabilitation if you like. Either way, Zack has been key to solving several major crimes, and you'd be an idiot to try to sack him."

"Yes, I agree with you," Charlie conceded. She'd seen how useful Zack could be. In any case, it wouldn't be easy to sack him. There would be all sorts of HR procedures to go through, and she didn't want the paperwork. "Can you reassure him his job's safe?" If she tried to talk to him herself, she'd probably scare him half to death.

"Sure."

"And tomorrow, take Tyrone with you to Edmondson & Dunstan and be tactful. Max's work colleagues may not even know he's dead." She hoped they wouldn't read it on the Internet before tomorrow. "When you've interviewed the architects, pay another visit to Tenurewise and ask the people who attended that party if they ever used that architect's practice and if they knew Max Edmondson. And find out where everyone from both businesses spent yesterday evening." At last, they were getting somewhere.

Chapter 52

Janette was in the kitchen when Rick arrived home late after he'd stayed at the station to catch up on some paperwork.

"Mia's in bed already. I've kept your dinner warm in the oven."

"Thanks, love." He hated it when he got home too late to see his daughter. He'd be out again early in the morning, too, so probably wouldn't set eyes on Mia until the weekend. It was always the same during a murder investigation, and Max Edmondson's death had only made things ten times worse. He gave Janette a peck on the cheek. "Shall I eat first before the food gets too dried up, then I can take a shower afterwards?"

Janette headed straight to the oven and, a couple of minutes later, a steaming hot steak pie with mashed potatoes and green beans was sitting on the kitchen table. It smelt delicious.

"Mia drew a picture of you at school today. They were learning how to draw faces in her art class." Janette sat at the table opposite him.

Rick laughed. "I hope she remembers what I look like." He joked about it, but inside, it wrenched his heart in two.

"I'm not saying it looks like you. She's no Van Gogh. Anyway, you'll have to wait to see it. She wants to show it to you herself."

Rick hoped she wouldn't have to wait too long. At this rate, he'd be working the weekend. "This pie's delicious."

Janette blushed. She always downplayed her cooking skills, but she was amazingly good.

"How's Charlie getting on?"

Rick finished his mouthful of pie before speaking. "She's doing well. I think she'll make a good DI." She'd made mistakes, but knowing Charlie, she'd work her socks off until she became the best DI in Hampshire. He felt a tinge of jealousy toward her single-mindedness. But Charlie didn't have any family responsibilities, so it was easy for her to put everything into the job. He glanced up at Janette. He wouldn't give up his wife and daughter for anything in the world.

"And you're managing to work together all right, with her being your boss? You know the DI job should have been yours."

Rick cringed inwardly. He passed his DI exam five months ago, and the DCI had all but promised the next available DI post to him. But he always knew they would have to advertise the post, which meant no guarantee he would be the best candidate on the day. He'd managed to hide his disappointment in front of his colleagues, but Janette knew him better than anyone. Failure had hurt.

"I'm sure there will be another DI post soon. I may have to look further afield."

"You know Mia won't cope well with moving schools or losing her friends. We're happy here."

Janette wanted the best of both worlds. She supported him one hundred percent in moving up in his career, but she also didn't want anything to change.

"Maybe Dorset or Wiltshire." Neither of those were too far away. "I could commute every day."

"And we'd see even less of you than we do now." Janette gave him a forced smile. "So, is it going all right, working for your sister?"

"It's going okay so far." He forked up the last piece of pie, savouring the tender meat and rich, delicious gravy. The idea of working for his sister had worried Rick. She'd spent most of her childhood trying to boss him around, and he'd spent most of his trying to resist. It was working out surprisingly well so far. He guessed they were both making an effort, knowing that one of them would be moved if they spent all their time disagreeing. He wondered how long that happy state would continue.

"You should invite Charlie to dinner. Mia wants to meet her auntie. So do I. It's been years since we last saw her."

"Maybe when this murder case is over." Rick picked up his plate and carried it to the dishwasher. "There's no chance of either of us finding time before then." Was there any chance of Charlie accepting the invitation, even when the double murder enquiry was wrapped up? If they hadn't been thrust into working together, would he have seen anything of his sister for another few years?

Chapter 53

The microwave pinged, and Charlie took out the hot dish containing yesterday's leftover Chinese takeaway, holding it by the edges so she didn't burn her fingers. She poured herself a glass of wine while the food cooled enough for her to carry the dish to the table without dropping it. She hadn't finished unpacking since the move to Hampshire, and much of her stuff was still in boxes, but she'd made sure to pack some special boxes marked *Essentials*, and one of those contained a set of wine glasses.

She sat down to eat. This case had really got to her. Felicity Edmondson had simply highlighted too many parallels with her own crappy life. The divorce had touched a nerve. In a way, she envied Felicity. Death had saved her from the pain of a protracted and bitter divorce.

Ian's request for a divorce had come as a shock to Charlie, much as she imagined the letter from Max's solicitor must have knocked Felicity sideways. But in reality, she should have seen it coming.

She and Ian had both been in the army, in the same regiment. But once Charlie left the army, they were frequently apart for six months at a time, while Ian was posted to some war-torn country on the other side of the world. Then, when he did come home, they no longer had that shared experience that had bonded them together for the last few years. They grew apart so gradually she didn't even notice. Of course, by then, she'd thrown herself into her new career with the police, and on some of Ian's visits home, if she was in the middle of an important case, it was impossible to give him the attention he needed.

The starkness of her flat, with its blank white walls and lack of furnishings, annoyed her. Ian would have called it minimalist and pointed out that it would be easier to keep clean. She resolved to find time to unpack the rest of her stuff, even if she did it one box at a time. It would lift her spirits if she had her things around her, making the flat feel more like home.

She still hadn't told Rick about the divorce. He liked Ian, so he was sure to be disappointed. In fact, she wouldn't be too surprised if Rick sided with her ex-husband. Perhaps that was why she hadn't plucked up the courage to tell him yet. That, and the fact that she felt like a failure because she'd had a wonderful husband who loved her, and somehow, she'd screwed it up. She tried to convince herself that Ian wasn't so wonderful. Ian Steele was good-looking and funny, a decorated hero who'd saved many lives. He was also a cheating bastard.

Charlie had kept Ian's name—about the only thing she did manage to keep of his. Rick probably assumed that Ian was away with the army and would stay with her next time he was back in the country.

At some point, she would have to visit Janette and Mia. Perhaps that would be the time to mention the divorce. She should be looking forward to seeing her only niece, but she was dreading it, knowing it would dig up some painful memories that she tried so hard to bury.

Charlie had been pregnant at the same time as Janette. That was the reason she'd left the army. It would have been impossible to care for a child with both parents being away at the same time for months on end and unfair to bring a child into the world when she and Ian both risked death on a daily basis. For the sake of their unborn child, Charlie had sacrificed the career she loved.

And it had all been for nothing. She went into labour at twenty-five weeks. The doctors had given baby Louise an eighty percent chance. For eleven days, Charlie barely left Louise's side in the neonatal unit. It was during one of her rare snoozes that Louise left her.

She wasn't ready to see her niece. It would rake up the memories that she'd tried so hard to bury, the ones she still hadn't got over. Rick had his daughter. She didn't have hers.

The Chinese wasn't nearly as enjoyable as it had been yesterday when it was fresh. Microwaving it made the prawns rubbery and the rice dry, although the lemon chicken remained passably edible.

Charlie tried to focus on the case. Perhaps if she went through the facts enough times, something would leap out at her. She was pinning her hopes on the proximity of the Tenurewise office to Max's architecture business. Rick and Tyrone were visiting the Edmondson & Dunstan offices tomorrow morning. Perhaps that would provide the breakthrough they needed.

Chapter 54

Rick and Tyrone arrived at the offices of Edmondson & Dunstan at eight thirty sharp.

"With a bit of luck, the boss will get in early, and we'll catch him before he gets sucked into meetings or site visits." Rick rang the bell for their office.

The intercom crackled slightly before someone spoke. "Do you have an appointment?"

"Detective Sergeant Richard Henderson and Detective Constable Tyrone Wilson. We'd like to see Mr Dunstan, please." Rick had already researched the firm online. There were only two partners, Max Edmondson and Keith Dunstan.

"Would you like to come on up? Someone will meet you at the top of the stairs." The door clicked open.

"Do you think they know about Max yet?" Tyrone asked as they walked up the narrow staircase.

"I haven't seen anything online yet, and I doubt if Lisa Grant is in any fit state to phone his office to tell them. So maybe not."

A middle-aged man in heavy black-framed glasses that overwhelmed his narrow face met them at the top of the stairs. He held out his hand.

"I'm Keith Dunstan."

They shook hands before Dunstan invited them into his office.

"We're here about Max Edmondson," Rick said as soon as Dunstan closed the office door.

"What about him? He didn't show up for work yesterday, and there's no sign of him yet today, either." Dunstan sounded annoyed. Something seemed to twig in his brain. "Has something happened to him?"

"I'm afraid so, Mr Dunstan. When did you last see Max?"

"Have you arrested him again? I understand he and his wife were having marital problems, but Max would have never murdered her."

"When did you last see him?" Rick repeated.

"Two days ago. He left here at about six. Said he'd be in early yesterday. We were supposed to visit a big client together first thing in the morning."

"I'm afraid Max was found dead early yesterday morning. I'm sorry." Rick glanced at Tyrone, who was taking notes.

"Oh my God! That's awful, and so soon after Fliss, too."

"How long have you known Max?"

Dunstan blew his nose, surreptitiously wiping a tear from his cheek. "We were at university together. Then, after we both gained a few years' experience, we talked about setting up in business together. When Max's father died, he used his inheritance to fund the initial start-up costs."

"What happens to the business now?" Rick wanted to know if Dunstan would benefit from Max's death.

"We set things up so that if anything happened to one of us, the other wouldn't lose the business. Effectively, Max's next of kin becomes a sleeping partner."

How appropriate. Rick instantly thought of Lisa Grant. But, of course, it wouldn't be her. He made a note to check out Max's next of kin. Probably some long-lost cousin, unless it went to his unborn child. He might need to get a legal opinion on that.

"Can you think of anyone who might have wanted him dead?"

Dunstan's face paled, rendering his skin deathly white against the sharp contrast of his black-framed glasses. "No. I don't know. Who would want to kill Max?"

"Please call me if you remember anything." Rick placed a business card on Dunstan's desk. "Where were you on Sunday evening between eight thirty and ten?"

"I must have been at home with my wife."

"Can you give me her contact details, please? And I'll need a list of all recent clients that Mr Edmondson worked with."

"Yes, of course. I'll get someone to dig that out."

"Did your business do any work for Tenurewise?" Rick asked.

"Yes. The company has one of the offices upstairs. We worked on a house for them recently. They wanted to change the layout from three bedrooms to four so they could charge a higher rent. Max worked on that one. It was only a small project, so we allocated one of our junior staff, but it proved to be a tricky layout and he struggled to work out how to fit everything in, so Max gave him some help."

"I'll need the address of that property." Rick wondered if it was the same house where Felicity Edmondson had been killed.

A total of seven people worked for Edmondson & Dunstan. Keith Dunstan found them two empty offices for Rick and Tyrone to interview everyone between them. Despite a few tears and a great deal of shock, no one else seemed particularly close to Max. It annoyed Rick that they gained no further useful information. They needed to make more progress.

Chapter 55

The Tenurewise office was a hive of activity this morning although Rick saw no sign of Stephen Pollock or Danny Owen. Given the latest information about Tenurewise's links to Max Edmondson, they would have to interview everyone who worked here, but Rick wanted to start with Alicia Gardner.

Alicia showed them into her office. Rick sat down and signalled to Tyrone to take notes.

"That's dreadful news," Alicia said when Rick told her about Max Edmondson's death.

"I understand Max did some work for Tenurewise on the property where Felicity died. Who would have dealt with him from here?"

"I don't know the specifics. Stephen Pollock would deal with that sort of thing. It made sense to use them as they're in the same office block as us. But I only found out the connection to Fliss Edmondson after she died."

"Did you meet Max?"

"He came to see me shortly after we moved into these offices, trying to sell his company's services. He gave a very professional presentation. That's why we decided to try them out. But after that, I only met him occasionally in passing in the lobby downstairs."

"Did anyone else in your company know Max?"

"You'd have to ask them that question, but only Stephen would have had business dealings with him."

"When will Stephen be back?" If he and Alicia were the only people at Tenurewise who had met Max Edmondson, Rick wanted to speak to him as soon as possible.

Alicia pulled up his diary on her computer screen. "He's out visiting properties for most of the day. We're under pressure to buy more houses for the council to use. You can catch him this morning in Burlington Road. That's not far from here. It's a new purchase. He's showing it to Tracey Gulliver at eleven a.m."

That sounded very useful indeed. Rick took the full address. They could drive there in ten minutes.

Chapter 56

The house belonging to Tenurewise was situated about halfway along the road. Scaffolding covered the front of the building, like a leg brace holding up an injured limb. Tyrone knocked loudly on the door.

The door opened immediately, as if Stephen Pollock was waiting on the other side for them to arrive. Rick guessed Alicia Gardener had phoned him.

"What do you want? I already told you everything I know," Pollock snapped.

"There have been some developments." Rick took a step forward, placing one foot in the doorway. "Can we come in?" He didn't intend to take no for an answer.

"I suppose so, if you must, but I'm expecting someone."

"Tracey Gulliver?"

Pollock looked at him questioningly.

Rick noted his surprise. "We just met with Alicia Gardener." Perhaps Alicia hadn't phoned him yet.

Pollock nodded. "What do you want to know?"

"You had some dealings with Max Edmondson. Can you explain what he did for the company and how much contact you had with him?"

"He drew up some plans for our Highfield Road house to convert it from a three-bedroom house to four bedrooms. Then he helped us get planning permission for the conversion. We met a couple of times, but most of the communication was done through email and virtual meetings on Teams."

"Did you have any complaints about his work?"

"No, not at all. The junior he sent originally seemed a bit out of his depth, but once Max took over, everything proceeded smoothly. He's really good at his job. We'll definitely use him again."

Pollock clearly wasn't aware of Max's death. Rick decided to keep it that way for a few minutes more. "Were you aware that Max was married to Felicity Edmondson, the council's housing director?"

"Not at first, but he told me once he realised what our plans were for leasing the house, in case we were concerned about a conflict of interest."

"And you didn't consider there might be a conflict?" Surely the relationship should have been flagged up.

"It's not easy to find good architects, and Max is exceptional."

"Max Edmondson was murdered on Sunday evening," Rick stated bluntly.

Pollock's jaw dropped. "What? You mean both of them?"

"Yes, and as Tenurewise had dealings with both Mr and Mrs Edmondson, that puts them front and centre of our investigation."

Pollock looked horrified. "Why would anyone at Tenurewise have killed them? We needed both of them for the company to survive and grow."

Rick silently agreed with him. He didn't think these murders were directly connected to the company. It felt personal. Somebody bore a major grudge against both of the Edmondsons for sure, but that didn't preclude it being one of the Tenurewise employees.

A knock on the front door interrupted them.

"That's probably Tracey Gulliver," Pollock said.

"Can you let her in?" Rick asked Tyrone.

"Please try not to frighten her away." Pollock appeared anxious. "We need the council's business."

"I would like to talk to her." Rick recalled Tracey had already told Charlie she'd never met Felicity's husband, but it didn't hurt to double-check.

Tyrone quickly returned with Tracey Gulliver.

"What's going on? Why are the police here?" Tracey fidgeted nervously. She put her hand up to her mouth. "There hasn't been a murder here as well, has there?"

"It's nothing to worry about," Rick reassured her. "We wanted a quick chat with Stephen, but seeing as you're here, would you mind if we ask you a couple of questions?"

Tracey nodded, fear still etched on her face.

"Why don't we go upstairs?" He didn't want to question her with Stephen Pollock present.

Tracey stepped back. "No. I'd rather stay down here."

Rick wondered if she was frightened of finding a dead body upstairs. The presence of him and Tyrone obviously worried her. He glanced over at Pollock.

Pollock picked up on Rick's wish for privacy. "I need to check something in the back garden." He left the room, and a few moments later, the back door clicked shut.

Rick looked around for a chair, preferring Tracey to be in a more relaxed state before he questioned her, but the house was still mid-renovation, giving them nowhere to sit unless they wanted to risk getting covered in dust and fresh paint.

"How are things at work?" Rick smiled benevolently, hoping she would shake off some of her tension before he mentioned the second murder.

"Without Fliss, you mean? It's difficult. I keep thinking about what happened to her. If only we hadn't gone to that stupid party. None of us wanted to go, but Fliss insisted that the council should demonstrate its commitment to the scheme."

Rick had expected her to complain about the increased workload now that they were a person down. The fact that she focused on the loss of her colleague may mean she was closer to Felicity Edmondson than she'd previously let on.

"Did you know Felicity's husband, Max?"

Tracey shook her head. "I never met him. Poor man. He must be devastated."

Why had no one found out about Max's death yet? The news of the murder had broken this morning in the media. Rick was constantly amazed at how out of touch some people were with the real world. Of course, so few people these days read a daily newspaper, but he would have thought most people would scan one of the news websites regularly to keep up to date with current affairs. Clearly, Tracey Gulliver hadn't even stumbled across the news on Facebook yet.

"Oh my God. You don't think Max killed Fliss, do you? You do, don't you? And he seemed like such a nice man."

Once again, Tracey Gulliver had added together two plus two to make a number far exceeding four.

"Max Edmondson was murdered on Sunday evening." Immediately, Rick regretted being so blunt as Tracey burst into tears. Considering she claimed never to have met the man, her reaction seemed rather extreme. Her nerves must be stretched to their limits, needing only a tiny amount of pressure to make them snap.

"Were you aware that Max Edmundson was the architect who planned the internal layout of the Highfield Road house? Did you have any dealings with him in that capacity?"

Tracey gazed up at him, her eyes still wide with fear. "I didn't even realise the internal layout had been rearranged. They must have made a good job of it. We didn't get to inspect the house until the renovations were nearly finished." She glanced towards the door, presumably checking in case Pollock came back. "I'm surprised they invited me to see this one so early. By the looks of it, they still have a lot of work to do. But with all the discussion about Tenurewise's poor performance, I suppose they're keen to show that they have another house to hand over to us soon."

"Where were you on Sunday evening, between eight thirty and ten p.m.?" Rick didn't seriously suspect Tracey Gulliver of killing Max, but the question still needed answering.

"I went out to dinner with my husband. There's a nice gastropub near Stoney Cross that we like. The Airfield."

Rick immediately recognised the name. Wasn't that where Clarissa Canley worked? "Do you know Clarissa Canley?" It was probably a coincidence.

"Of course I do. She's my husband's cousin. She's a sous chef at The Airfield. That's why we go there a lot."

Rick caught Tyrone's eye. Tyrone looked as surprised as he was. Rick wondered what his sister would make of this. Perhaps it wasn't a coincidence that Clarissa Canley found Max Edmondson's body.

Chapter 57

Charlie was in the office early on Monday morning when the phone rang.

"It's Trina Lucas. I'm in the CSI room. Could you please tell Sally I've got the results back on the DNA test for the mystery woman opposite Felicity Edmondson's house?"

Charlie hung up the phone. Sally hadn't arrived yet. Charlie wished Sally hadn't agreed to an expensive DNA test. The chances of getting a useful result were minimal because they had no idea how many people might have stood in the same place over the last few days. She decided to go and see Trina herself, then at least when Sally arrived, she would have all the facts, ready to give her a proper telling-off.

She was still seething with anger when she burst into the CSI room. "I've come for Sally's DNA results."

"Oh yes, the mystery woman. I ran it through the system."

"You know who she is?" Despite her anger, Charlie couldn't keep a small note of hope out of her voice. They needed a breakthrough in this case.

"Sorry, no. I didn't find an exact match. But the sample shows a familial match to one of your murder victims, Felicity Edmondson."

"When you say a familial match..."

"Mother or daughter."

It couldn't be Felicity's mother. Abi Hargreaves had described the mystery woman as being in her twenties. "And you're sure?" Was there a daughter? Tabitha had been certain that Felicity had given birth at some point in her life.

"DNA doesn't lie."

"What about Max Edmondson?" Max told them they had no children, but his track record of telling the truth was abysmal.

"If he's in the system, it didn't throw out a match."

"Okay, thanks." Charlie ran back to her office to fetch her coat. She would deal with Sally later. First, she needed to make an urgent visit to Felicity Edmondson's mother.

Chapter 58

Felicity's parents lived in a bungalow in Brockenhurst. Charlie drove at little more than walking pace through the village as a small herd of New Forest ponies meandered along the road in front of her. Several of them looked pregnant, no doubt waiting for slightly warmer weather before bringing their foals into the world.

The big wooden gate at the front of the property sported a large sign: *please shut the gate*. Charlie opened it, then took care to close it securely behind her. The small lawn in front of the house was pockmarked with holes the rough size and shape of a pony's hoof. Clearly, someone had neglected to read the sign on the gate.

Charlie introduced herself as soon as the front door opened. "DI Steele from the Hampshire and Isle of Wight Constabulary." It was a bit of a mouthful. She must remember to ask Rick if it was permissible to shorten it and simply say she was from Hampshire police.

"Have you found out who murdered my daughter?" Evelyn Lane-Smith gazed at Charlie with a mixture of hope and fear.

Charlie wished she could answer yes. Perhaps that might go some way towards lessening the pain on the poor woman's face. "We are following several lines of investigation. May I come in, please? I need to ask you a few questions."

The hopeful part of her expression disappeared from Mrs Lane-Smith's face as she opened the door wider. "If it will help." She left unsaid her doubt that the police hadn't got anywhere yet, so why would a few more questions make any difference?

Charlie sat in a green chintz armchair in a room that looked as if it hadn't been redecorated since the seventies. Evelyn Lane-Smith definitely liked green. Green walls, green swirly-patterned carpet, green curtains. It gave the room a cool atmosphere, instead of the warm, cosy vibe she'd expected from both the village and the property's owner.

"Now, what did you want to ask me, dear?"

Charlie came straight to the point. "Felicity had a baby. What happened to it?"

"I already told one of your colleagues, that's simply not true."

"We have irrefutable evidence."

Mrs Lane-Smith stared into space for a few moments. Her mind appeared to be in a different place.

Charlie remained silent, waiting for Evelyn Lane-Smith to speak.

Finally, she said, "How did you find out?"

Judging by the distress now crumpling the old woman's face, Charlie guessed the pregnancy was a well-kept family secret.

"The post-mortem." Tabitha had been absolutely correct. "The pathologist can tell from the size of the cervix, the presence of stretch marks, and—"

"Spare me the details, dear. Yes, Felicity had a baby. I persuaded her to give it up for adoption. She was only seventeen, and her teachers considered her clever enough to go to university. Keeping the baby would have ruined her whole life."

"Can you tell me the baby's date of birth?" If they were to stand any chance of tracing this child, they needed a starting point.

"Fourteenth of February, 1997. Valentine's Day. Fliss named her Valentine. I wish she hadn't given her a name. It made everything so much harder for her after social services took the baby away."

The name was unusual. If the baby had kept the same name, she would be much easier to find. But it was likely her new family would have completely changed her name.

"Who was the baby's father?"

"I can't help you with that. Fliss will take that piece of information to her grave. She was friendly with a few boys at school, but if she had a regular boyfriend, she never brought him home or even mentioned him."

"It wasn't Max, then?"

"Oh, goodness, no, dear. She hadn't even met Max back then."

"Did Max know that Felicity previously had a baby?"

"I really can't be sure. Some married couples share everything, don't they? But Fliss never liked to talk about it. Thankfully, she threw herself into her studies, then later put all her energies into her career. She would never admit as much, but it's classic behaviour if someone is trying to forget something traumatic."

"How long were Felicity and Max married?"

"About fifteen years. Fliss took her time getting married. She was too busy building up her career to find a husband."

Fifteen years was a long time. Charlie figured if Felicity hadn't told Max about the baby by now, she had never intended to tell him. They would never know now. "And they never wanted children of their own?"

"I know Max did. Perhaps if they'd discussed the subject more when they first met, they never would have got married. I got the impression they argued about it regularly. Max often used to drop hints or make snide remarks on the subject, even quite recently."

"What sort of remarks?"

"*I'm sure your mother would love some grandchildren.* That sort of thing. If Fliss hadn't agreed in fifteen years, she was hardly going to give in now. Stubborn, my daughter. It's a family trait. Besides, she was forty-six years old, and I'd already noticed her getting hot flushes, so Max was on a hiding to nothing."

Charlie thought of telling Felicity's mother that Max had been well on his way to becoming a father but bit her tongue. It would be a hurtful thing to share with her, although it would doubtless come out at the inquest.

"I always regretted making Fliss give up the baby," Mrs Lane-Smith said sadly. "I'm sure losing her child affected her more than she admitted. She used her career as an excuse for not wanting a child, but I suspect the real reason was that she worried something might happen to it and she didn't want to go through the pain of losing another child."

Charlie wondered if Mrs Lane-Smith empathised more with Felicity's loss now that she had lost a child herself, albeit a grown-up one.

The sound of a key in the front door made Charlie turn around quickly.

"That will be my husband. He popped out for a pint of milk." Evelyn lowered her voice. "Please don't mention Fliss's baby to him. He knows nothing about it. He was away with the army on a six-month tour during most of Fliss's pregnancy, so we decided not to tell him. I worried he might throw Fliss out on the streets if he found out. That's another reason why I considered it best to have the baby adopted. It was all done and dusted by the time he came home."

"Did the child ever try to get in touch with Felicity?"

"If she did, Fliss never told me. It's probably for the best. It hit her hard, trying to forget and press on with her life. Best not to rake up the past. It never does any good."

Chapter 59

Tyrone and Sally were in the office when Charlie arrived back at the station. Zack sat glued to his computer screen, as usual.

"Can we have a quick meeting in my office, please?" She would catch up with Rick later. "You too, Zack."

They squeezed into Charlie's small office, Tyrone standing while the other two took the chairs.

"There's been a development," Charlie said.

The team looked at her expectantly.

"Felicity Edmondson had a baby when she was seventeen. She gave it up for adoption. Her mother told me, and we already knew from the post-mortem she'd given birth. I should add that Felicity's father knows nothing about this, so please be discreet." She didn't want her team to inadvertently spark a family row when they were already grieving.

"This is all to do with what you discovered, Sally."

"Me?"

"Yes." She guessed Sally hadn't picked up the DNA results yet. "That woman that Abi Hargreaves saw watching the Edmondsons' house. The DNA results were a familial match to Felicity Edmondson. She must be the missing daughter."

Sally let out a small gasp. "Do you think she killed her real mother?"

"I don't know, but we need to find her."

"Was Max Edmondson her father? Is that why she killed them both, for giving her up?" Tyrone asked.

"No, Max isn't the father. Felicity and Max didn't meet until much later."

"So she's got no motive for killing him," Sally said.

"There's always a motive. But she may not have killed either of them. We need to stay open-minded on this. Let's concentrate on finding her first. The name on the birth certificate would have been Valentine Lane-Smith, and she was born on 14 February, 1997. Sally, I want you to get in touch with social services. Find out who adopted the baby. You may need to get a warrant before they give you that information. Tyrone, search the Edmondson house again. Look for any paperwork that might suggest the daughter has tried to get in touch. Letters, photos, anything. Remember, she'd be twenty-nine now. Go through Felicity's phone records for the last few months, too. See if you can match them to friends and family, then we'll investigate what's left."

"What about me, ma'am?" Zack asked quietly.

"Search on social media. We're looking for a woman with that date of birth. She may have moved away from the area."

"There may be hundreds or thousands. But if I can find photos, I've got some facial recognition software that would compare them to a picture of Felicity. It would be helpful to find a picture of her at the same age."

"I'll ask her mother." It would be like looking for a grain of wheat in a cornfield, but if anyone could do it, Zack could. Charlie already realised what a huge contribution he made to her team.

After three hours, Zack had drawn a blank, which was so unusual, it was making him quite stressed. There were simply too many possibilities. Charlie left him in peace to keep trying. If he couldn't narrow it down to single figures, there was no way they would be able to investigate them all further. Sally hadn't come back from her second visit to social services, after returning with a warrant for the information she needed. And Tyrone might take hours to search the Edmondsons' house thoroughly.

Half an hour later, Sally burst into the office in a state of excitement. "I've got it. The couple who adopted Felicity's baby lived in Southampton, Mr and Mrs West. Zack, can you track down a current address for them, please?" She passed him the old address.

"Well done," Charlie said. "Do you know what they named the baby?"

"Kylie."

"That should make her easier to find." Thank goodness Mr and Mrs West didn't name their baby Jane or Susan.

"Hopefully. But West is a common name, and the daughter may have got married by now and changed her surname again."

"So our best route is to track down the adoptive parents. Sally, can you focus on that? Zack, as soon as you find that address, search for Kylie West online."

Chapter 60

Sophia West lived in an expensive-looking house backing onto the river Solent. Charlie introduced herself and Rick.

"You'd better come in." Sophia ushered them inside quickly and closed the door behind them.

Charlie guessed she didn't want the neighbours to gossip about a visit from the police, although from what she'd seen of this neighbourhood in the few minutes she'd been here, the neighbours didn't seem to care much about anyone except themselves.

They sat in a large living room with glass patio doors on two sides, affording them a fabulous view of the river across the lawn, which must have stretched for at least 300 feet. A motorboat moored at the end of a small wooden jetty bobbed in the current. Rick stared at it enviously.

Charlie dragged her gaze away from the view to focus on Sophia West. "We're here about your daughter, Kylie."

Sophia's face lit up. "You found her?"

Charlie stared at her for a moment, confused. "We're hoping you can tell us where she is."

Sophia gave a hollow laugh. "I wish I knew. Kylie disappeared the day after her sixteenth birthday. That's thirteen years ago. Every month, I phone the officer in charge of the case to ask if they've made any progress, and I get fobbed off with some rubbish about them following various lines of enquiry. And now you show up, and *you* ask *me* where she is! That's really adding insult to injury. Don't you people talk to each other?"

Charlie kicked herself for not searching the name on the police system before they came here. She'd become so desperate for a lead on the case that she'd forgotten basic procedures.

"Please accept my apologises, Mrs West. We seem to have got our wires crossed. Can we start again? Perhaps you would tell me from the beginning what happened to Kylie?"

"And you'll reopen the case? I know it was closed, so don't tell me otherwise."

"Mrs West, I promise I will do everything I can to find your daughter." It was an easy promise to make, given that finding Kylie was her top priority at the moment, but not for the same reason Mrs West wanted her found.

"I'd better make some tea. This may take a while."

"What do you think of that boat?" Rick whispered as soon as Sophia West left the room. "I wouldn't mind taking that for a spin down the river. They must have serious money to afford a place like this."

"Rick! Shush!" Charlie didn't want Mrs West to come back and overhear them.

"Sorry. But how are we going to find Kylie now?"

"The same way as we find any missing person." They both knew that over one hundred and seventy thousand people went missing in the UK every year. Some of them were never found. Kylie might be dead. Except she had to be alive, otherwise who did that DNA come from?

Mrs West returned with a pot of tea and some bone china cups on a tray. "What did you want to ask me?" She poured the tea expertly.

"Tell me about the day Kylie went missing."

"She disappeared the day after her sixteenth birthday. My husband and I attended a function at the local golf club that evening and got home late. We thought she must be in bed when we came back. But then she didn't come down for breakfast in the morning, so I went to wake her. She'd stuffed pillows under the duvet to make it look like she was in her bed."

"So she ran away?" If she'd been abducted, she wouldn't have left the pillows in the bed. "Is there any reason why she would have done that?"

"Plenty of reasons, according to her. We gave her everything she could possibly want. A lovely home, an expensive education, plenty of love. We even bought her a pony, but she fell off in the first week, so we sent it back to the dealer. But she constantly complained about how awful everything was."

That didn't make any sense to Charlie, although it sounded like typical teenage behaviour. She remembered being pretty much the same at sixteen. She also remembered that teenage angst amplified every minor problem into a major drama. "Do you think there might have been problems at school that you weren't aware of? Was she being bullied? Did she have a boyfriend?" A breakup with a boyfriend at that age felt like the end of the world. With the hindsight of a difficult divorce behind her, Charlie knew that it wasn't. How lucky that teenagers couldn't see into the future and realise how much worse their world would become.

"I can tell you exactly what sparked off the bad behaviour." Mrs West sipped at her tea, clanking the cup down onto the saucer as her hand shook nervously. "Kylie was adopted. We couldn't have children, but we always treated her as if she were our own. We always loved her, possibly even more than if I'd given birth to her, because of how hard we had to work to get her. After Kylie's fifteenth birthday, we decided she was old enough to be told the truth. She practically screamed the place down, accused us of lying to her for years, and told us that as soon as she turned sixteen, she intended to find her real mother. It was hurtful."

"Do you think Kylie went looking for her birth mother?" Charlie would need to read the original case notes to check if the police followed up on that.

"Yes, I do. Maybe she's even living with her now, oblivious to the pain she's still causing me. I really hope she is. It's better than the alternative, isn't it?"

Charlie picked up on her use of the word *me*. "What does your husband think?"

"Henry says I should get over it because she's not coming back. But my husband is only Kylie's stepfather. Her father, my first husband, died when Kylie was twelve."

"Her adoptive father?"

"Yes. But the attitude of people like Henry was the reason we waited so long to tell Kylie she was adopted. People think about it differently. They keep reminding you, distinguishing an adopted child from a birth child. But if you'd ever adopted a child, you'd know there is no distinction. To us, she was always our real child."

"How did she get on with her stepfather?"

"They had a good relationship until we told Kylie about the adoption. She turned on me and said a lot of hateful things. But she totally rejected Henry. She said he was twice as far removed from being her real parent as I was. I wish we'd never told her, but then she'd have to find out eventually. She would need her birth certificate or adoption certificate to apply for a passport."

"That must have been awful for you, going through all that." It didn't sound as if Kylie ever intended to come back. Charlie hoped Mrs West didn't realise that. She didn't want to take away her one small grain of hope.

"I can't begin to explain how dreadful. After the police wound down their efforts, we hired a private detective, but even he couldn't track down Kylie."

Charlie felt sorry for Mrs West. It must be awful not knowing what had happened to their daughter for all these years. It made her even more determined to find Kylie. "Do you have any photos of Kylie?" Charlie would ask Zack to run them through his facial recognition software to find out if Kylie bore any similarity to Felicity.

"I'll find some for you. I will get them back, won't I?"

"Yes, of course." She would get them copied and give them back quickly. "Did Kylie have any distinguishing marks? Birthmarks or scars?"

"Not birthmarks, no. She did have a scar, but it may have faded by now."

"Where was the scar?" Charlie hoped it was somewhere visible. It would make things much easier.

"It was on her left wrist, just below her watch strap. She fell off a swing and broke her wrist badly. The surgeon had to pin it."

Charlie tried to picture the wrists of their main suspects but couldn't recall noticing any scars. Maybe it had faded, or maybe their wrists had been covered. "Do you have anything of Kylie's we can use for DNA testing? A hairbrush, perhaps." It was a long shot. Anything like that may have been washed, or the DNA may have deteriorated too much to be of use after so long.

Mrs West froze. She stared at Charlie suspiciously. "Does this mean you found her body?" She started to tremble.

"No. No, nothing like that. We simply have some DNA we'd like to compare it to."

"Is Kylie in trouble?"

"No." It wasn't exactly a lie. Kylie West may be in a tremendous amount of trouble. They wouldn't know until they found her.

"I kept all of Kylie's baby teeth," Mrs West said. "Are they any good for DNA?"

"It might work to get partial DNA, but they would be over twenty years old now, so the DNA may have degraded too much. Do you have anything else?" It wouldn't hurt to have as many options as possible.

"I put all of her stuff in boxes in the attic after we moved house." A tear streaked down Mrs West's cheek. "I didn't want to move, in case she came back, but my husband insisted we needed a fresh start. He didn't want to continue living in the house I'd shared with my first husband. We left our forwarding details with the people who bought our old house, but we never heard from them. Anyway, you're welcome to search through the boxes."

Chapter 61

"Who is Kylie West?" Charlie asked as soon as they got into the car. They hadn't found anything in the boxes of Kylie's stuff that pointed them to where she might have gone. They would have to track her down the hard way. With no other suspects, Felicity Edmondson's long-lost daughter appeared to be the most likely candidate for one or both of the murders.

"Do you think she's responsible for the murders?" Rick stared at her doubtfully. "If she was keen to find her real mother, why would she want to kill her? We might be wasting our time."

Charlie also didn't know why Kylie would want to kill her birth mother. They would have to find her first and ask her. "Rick! Sophia West has lost her daughter. Do you want to tell her we're wasting our time? Or that we don't give a damn. Even if it turns out Kylie has nothing to do with these murders, finding her won't be a waste of effort."

"But if she ran away, surely she won't want anything to do with her adoptive mother."

"And we can't make her. But at least it will give Mrs West peace of mind to know that Kylie isn't dead." Charlie understood the pain of losing a child. She would certainly try to persuade Kylie to meet with Sophia West, at least once. Rick's lack of empathy upset her. It made her feel less guilty about her long estrangement from her family.

"What if she is dead? Then you're raking up a whole load of pain for the poor woman."

"If she is dead, then we'll have to find out who killed her. At least Mrs West will get some closure." Charlie didn't like Rick questioning her authority. If he continued to do it, she would need to have a word with him in private.

"Janette wants you to come to dinner one evening," Rick said, changing the subject. "Mia wants to meet her auntie."

Charlie noted that Rick hadn't said *he* wanted her to come. "I doubt if I'll get time while this investigation is going on."

"Yeah, that's what I told Janette. But when it's finished..." He let the words trail off.

"I'll think about it."

"So how are we going to find Kylie West?" Sally had joined the rest of the team back in the office. "She might be anywhere in the country."

"Zack has identified three possibilities. Sally, I want you and Tyrone to follow them up." His facial recognition program had identified three women on Facebook, with the right date of birth and the right facial features. The odds against any of them being Kylie West were huge, but they had little to lose by trying.

Charlie had a second plan. "Rick, you're with me." Perhaps she would get a chance to talk to him in the car later. She needed to knock his insubordinate attitude on the head.

"What are we doing?"

"We're going to take a good look at everyone we've already spoken to. The most likely scenario is that the killer is someone who had access to the Tenurewise house. We need to consider them all carefully. One of them may be a similar age to Kylie. Let's make sure she's not hiding in plain sight. But we can't discount any of the others either. One of them may have a partner or a friend who might be Kylie West. If she's changed her name, she's out there somewhere, and we don't know who she is. So let's find out if anyone else in the picture has a close connection with a twenty-nine-year-old woman." She turned to Zack. "I need you to check the three women you've already identified. See if any of them are connected to anyone from Tenurewise, the council, or Edmondson & Dunstan."

"One other thing," Charlie said. "According to her mother, Kylie West may have a scar on her left wrist. It may have faded by now, but it's worth checking."

Chapter 62

Charlie didn't like the frown on DCI Talbot's face. She'd been summoned to his office at the end of the day.

"Give me an update on the Edmondson murders. Do we have a suspect?"

Charlie relaxed slightly. At least she had something positive to report. "We're looking for Felicity Edmondson's daughter. She was given up at birth for adoption. We think she came looking for her parents."

"Has she been in touch with the Edmondsons before?"

"No, sir."

"I assume Max Edmondson is the father."

"No, sir. Felicity didn't meet Max until much later. We don't know the identity of the father."

"Then it's a bit of a long shot, isn't it?"

Charlie didn't like his instant dismissal of her line of enquiry. Even if Max Edmondson wasn't Kylie's father, she might not know that, which made it irrelevant. "The Edmondsons' neighbour saw a woman who seemed to be watching the house. We found DNA evidence that clearly shows a mother-daughter link to Felicity Edmondson."

"But surely if the daughter wanted to find her birth parents, it wouldn't be to kill them."

"We won't know that until we find her, sir."

"It's still a long shot. Are you anywhere close to locating her?"

"Not yet, sir."

"Then I would focus on the people who were in the house prior to Mrs Edmondson's murder. I gather you discovered a connection to Mr Edmondson via his architecture business."

"Yes, some of them did know both of the Edmondsons, but no one has a clear motive."

"Perhaps you should concentrate on finding one instead of wasting resources on a wild goose chase. What did you plan to tell this poor girl if you did find her? *We know who your parents are, and by the way, they're both dead.* Wouldn't that be a kick in the teeth for her?"

Charlie had already considered that, mulling it over every which way in her head for most of the night, until she finally drifted off to sleep a few minutes before she had to get up. Just because it was difficult, it didn't mean they shouldn't do it. "But what if Felicity's daughter really did kill both of the Edmondsons?"

"Focus on the most likely suspects first. Look, I know you're doing your best, but this is your first DI post, isn't it? A double murder isn't the easiest case for you to start with. I've got an experienced DI who is just finishing up a case. DI Simon Russell. He should be free in a couple of days. I think he should take over this case as soon as he finishes the one he's working on. You can assist him and learn from his experience."

"With all due respect, sir, I've been assisting an experienced DI for the last few years." She didn't want Talbot bringing in someone to take over the case. However he dressed it up, it would be a retrograde step for her.

"Then you should have learnt more. No arguments. I'll tell DI Russell to take over the case on Monday." DCI Talbot stood up.

As she left the DCI's office, Charlie felt absolutely flattened. She'd been so sure about Kylie. She was much closer to the case than the DCI, having met all the people involved. Perhaps she should have explained things better. But he should also have supported her more. He might consider that bringing in someone to take over *was* supporting her, but it wasn't. All it would do was give her doubts about her ability. Already, she was questioning her own gut instinct. She needed to turn this case around. Failing in her first case would be unthinkable.

Chapter 63

Reject52: *I don't want to do it anymore.*

ChessDevil501: *You promised. I did what you asked.*

Reject52: *I'll help you if you still want to.*

She shut down her laptop. ChessDevil was worrying her. She'd never planned to keep her side of their agreement. It wasn't as if ChessDevil had even done everything she wanted him to, just some of it. She still wasn't sure how he'd react now that she'd refused to go through with the final step in the plan, his plan, not hers. Thank God he didn't know where she lived, but he could soon find out if he wanted to. She didn't honestly believe he had the balls to come after her. She would help him with his plan. That would get him off her case for good. But she wouldn't go with him. She only hoped she could persuade him that would be enough.

Chapter 64

Charlie arrived at the station on Friday morning, having had hardly any sleep. She'd hoped her restless night might have borne fruit. But instead of providing her with answers, all it achieved was to give her bags under her eyes. While she waited for the others to arrive, she set the coffee machine going, making it stronger than usual, and jotted down some notes.

Yesterday's meeting with the DCI had knocked her back. But she'd faced worse situations and survived. She would do what she always did, pick herself up and fight for what she wanted. She had until Monday to solve this case. It was possible, but she would need her team to get behind her. The trouble with that was she hadn't known them long, apart from Rick, and she wasn't sure how much support she'd earned in that short time.

She broke the news to the team as soon as they got in, explaining that the DCI wanted to bring in another DI if they didn't solve the case before Monday. "We've only got one day." She couldn't ask them to work yet another weekend.

"We've got three days, ma'am," Sally said. "Friday, Saturday, and Sunday."

"She's right, Charlie. Three days give us a chance," Rick added.

"I can't authorise any overtime for this." If they were volunteering in the hope of earning some extra money, they needed to be put straight.

Tyrone put his hand up. "I haven't made any plans for the weekend, ma'am. Count me in."

"Me too," Zack said.

Sally promised her support and, lastly, Rick pledged to work all weekend if need be.

Charlie looked at her team, touched at the way they were rallying behind her. She started to smile. The smile broadened until it took over her entire face. Three days gave them a fighting chance. "Okay, let's all get a coffee while I make a plan." They needed to attack this. Her biggest worry was how to keep the investigation on track, her track, while still keeping the DCI happy. If he thought she was disobeying orders and continuing to chase after Felicity's long-lost daughter, she probably wouldn't even make it to her three-month review. She'd be out of a job long before then.

Ten minutes later, the team crammed into Charlie's office. Rick had popped out for some doughnuts, and the smell of freshly brewed coffee filled the room.

Charlie glanced at her notes, which she'd hastily written while she waited. "I've made a plan. But I want everyone's input on this. Let's brainstorm it. No one's ideas are too trivial to be heard." She glanced at Rick, who was chomping a mouthful of doughnut. She didn't need his approval, but she wanted it. He nodded.

"The DCI wants us to concentrate on people who were at the party."

Sally put her hand up. "I thought we were looking for Kylie West."

Charlie smiled at her. "That's exactly what we're doing. There were four women at that party, not counting Felicity. Alicia Gardner, Kate Lovell, Tracey Gulliver, and Zoe Neale."

"What about Councillor Horn?" Tyrone asked.

"Let's leave her for now. I want a deep dive into the lives of the other four women. How old are they? Where did they come from? Trace their entire life history back to when they were sixteen."

"You think one of them is Kylie?" Rick said.

"It's possible. That's why I've ruled out Diana Horn. She's sixty-eight years old." Charlie took a deep breath. "We've been looking at this backwards. Kylie West ran away from home at the age of sixteen." She hoped to God that Kylie ran away and hadn't been abducted or murdered, either immediately or at a later date. "She almost certainly would have been homeless. I've checked the original misper files. The police interviewed all known contacts at the time, and it didn't appear that anyone assisted her in getting away."

"So she may have gravitated towards wanting to work with homeless people if she empathises with them," Sally suggested.

"It's a theory." Charlie had no idea if the theory would hold water, but someone must have had access to the Tenurewise house and have known that Felicity Edmondson would be there that night.

"It's a good theory." Tyrone reached for a second doughnut and took a massive bite out of it.

"Perhaps she took a job with the council deliberately to get close to her mother. Tyrone, check the employment histories of Kate and Tracey. See how long they've worked at the council. And wipe the jam off your chin."

Sally passed Tyrone a tissue.

"She might have come across her by accident, as they were both working in the same field," Rick said. "That doesn't rule out Alysia or even Zoe."

"Good point." Charlie took a mouthful of coffee. She'd been talking so much, it was growing cold.

"We can probably disregard Tracey Gulliver," Zack said. "She's thirty-eight years old."

"Let's not discount anyone too soon. If she's changed her identity, she might have completely changed her age as well. She could pass for twenty-nine, especially a twenty-nine-year-old who may have spent a couple of years sleeping rough." As she said it, she racked her brains to think of any woman she knew who would adjust their age upwards instead of downwards. Certainly not her. Perhaps they would be able to exclude Tracey quickly and concentrate their resources on the others.

"Zack, take what you've already researched on all four women and dig deeper. We need to go back and build a timeline of at least the last thirteen years for all of them. Go back to when they were sixteen. One of them might lead to the West family." If her theory was correct, one of them would lead to a dead end when they changed their identity, then they could focus on that person. She turned to the others. "You three, start by interviewing their work colleagues. Find out how long they've been there and who their previous employers were. Check with HR. They may have a CV for them. And ask about their friends and family and hobbies—anything that might reveal any information about them. We can work on friends and family at the weekend, but we've only got today to garner any information from their place of work."

"Yes, ma'am."

"One more thing." Charlie didn't want to get any of her team into trouble. "If the DCI asks, we're re-investigating people who attended the party. Don't mention Kylie West."

Chapter 65

Zack was in the office on his own when Charlie came back.

"We can rule out Zoe Neale." Zack looked up from his computer screen. "I've traced her back to school age. Tyrone got a positive ID on her photo from one of her old school friends. They've been best friends since they were ten, and they're still regularly in touch."

"That's good." One down, three to go. "Any progress from the others?" They agreed earlier that the team would report to Zack regularly and Zack would help them with any internet searches.

"Rick is on his way to the Tenurewise offices."

"Tell him to contact the Organised Crime unit. They might be able to give him more about Alicia's connection to the Castle family. What about Sally?"

"She's at the council offices. Tyrone was with her, but Tracey Gulliver is off sick, so he's gone to visit her at home."

"How far have you got with the timelines?" If they managed to verify the women's identities back to the age of sixteen, that would rule them out. She would like to narrow the field of suspects as soon as possible so they could focus resources. The Monday deadline would creep up all too fast.

"Tracey Gulliver might be the easiest. She got married eight years ago. Her wedding anniversary photos are on Facebook. I asked Tyrone to find out her maiden name and the name of the school she attended."

"Surely you can work out her maiden name from her family contacts on Facebook." Zack was supposed to be brilliant. She would have expected him to find Tracey's entire life history within a few minutes.

"You'd think so, wouldn't you, but there's no trace of her any earlier than eight years ago. There's definitely something suspicious going on there."

"Okay, keep on it, and make sure you update Tyrone." Hopefully, Tyrone would come up with more information when he spoke to Tracey. "What about Kate Lovell?"

"There's very little on her. I've got a few databases I can check, but it will take some time."

"That's something we don't have," Charlie reminded him.

"Don't worry. I'm talking a couple of hours, not days. I'd best get on with it." He focused on his computer screens.

"Tell me as soon as you get a result."

Tyrone knocked on Tracey Gulliver's front door.

She answered it quickly. "I wasn't expecting you."

Tyrone wondered if she'd been expecting somebody else. "Can I come in?"

Tracey hesitated, then reluctantly opened the door wider.

"What do you want?" she asked as soon as they sat in her living room.

Tyrone was busy trying to take in his surroundings, looking for anything that might help him, such as family photos. There was only one, Tracey and, he assumed, her husband. It looked recent. "I just need some background information."

"Can we make it quick?" Tracey seemed nervous.

"How long have you worked for the council?" Tyrone started with an easy question to get Tracey relaxed.

"About seven years."

"And before that? Who did you work for previously?"

"I was with a small homeless charity, A Place To Live. They ran a hostel in Southampton, but they were forced to close down when they lost their funding."

"And you got married eight years ago, right?"

"How did you know that?" Tracey sounded defensive.

"Just answer the question."

"Yes. We did."

"What was your name before that?"

"Tracey Brown."

Damn. Brown was such a common surname. How was he ever supposed to track her down? "Have you always lived in this area?"

Tracey shook her head. "I moved around a lot when I was young and before I got married. What's this got to do with Fliss's murder? I assume that's why you're here."

Tyrone decided the best policy was to be at least partially honest. "We think the motive for Felicity's murder goes back a long time. We're trying to track people back over the last twenty years or more, to see if there's a previous connection."

"Well, there isn't."

"Can you prove that? I can't just take your word for it."

"How do you prove you don't know someone?"

"You can't. But if you give us the full facts, we can check things out." Tyrone was sure that Tracey was holding something back. "The sooner we can rule you out, the sooner we can find who actually did kill Felicity. Her killer is still out there somewhere."

Tracey flinched visibly. "You won't find anything. I didn't meet Fliss until she came to work for the council about five years ago."

"Then give me something I can use to check that out. Where did you go to school?"

"You won't find me. I changed my name."

Tyrone's heart began to beat faster. He stared at Tracey Gulliver. Was she really Kylie West? "What's your real name?" He looked at her left wrist, seeing no sign of a scar. It didn't prove anything. Like the DI said, it may have faded by now.

"My first husband beat me up badly. He nearly killed me."

Tyrone understood her reluctance. "If you tell me your real name, I promise he won't find out where you are now."

"Oh no, it's not that. He died a few years ago in a car accident. It's just that Nigel, my current husband, doesn't know anything about that. He thinks my real name was Tracey Brown."

"All I want to do is verify who you really are. We don't need to involve your husband."

Tracey hesitated, then shrugged her shoulders. "My real name is Cindy Cameron. I went to Royal Oak School in Cheltenham. There should still be a few teachers there who remember me. They always remember the naughty ones, don't they?"

"Thank you. Just one more thing."

Tracey, or whoever she was, looked at him suspiciously.

"Can we take a DNA sample to help verify your real identity?" He knew they wouldn't have time to get the results back before Monday, but if they didn't have the tight time limit, it would be the obvious thing to do.

"No. I don't want to do that. I've already said too much. I'd like you to leave now, please."

Tyrone got up. It worried him that Tracey refused to give him a DNA sample, but perhaps they wouldn't need it. He would ask Zack to check out Cindy Cameron. If Tracey was telling the truth, they should hit a dead end on Cindy about the time that Tracey Brown came into existence. Meanwhile, he would chase up the Royal Oak School on the phone.

Chapter 66

Rick hadn't gone straight to the Tenurewise offices. Instead, he visited the organised crime unit to do some digging into the Castle family.

"Yes, I know Alicia Gardner." Sergeant Bill Herbert had worked in the OCU for almost twenty years. He knew the Castle family better than anyone in the Hampshire police force. "She's Ron Castle's daughter. They still see each other regularly, but as far as we know, she's clean. We've got no evidence of her involvement in any crime, although we know Ron is helping to fund her business."

That tallied with what Zack had dug up, but that wasn't Rick's biggest concern at the moment. "How long have you known Alicia?"

Bill laughed. "Since she was a little girl with pigtails."

"And she's definitely Ron's daughter?"

"Don't ever say that to Ron. He'll kill you." Bill sounded serious. "Yes, Alicia is his daughter. She even looks like him. He dotes on her."

Rick's hopes were dashed for a moment. Alicia wasn't Kylie West. But with that confirmed, they were one step closer to finding out Kylie's real identity. He hoped his sister was on the right track, for all their sakes.

Sally didn't have much luck at the council offices. Kate Lovell hadn't come in today, and no one had heard from her. She'd spoken to some of Kate's colleagues, but she got the same thing from all of them. Kate Lovell kept to herself. She focused on her work and didn't chat much. No one knew anything about her family, where she worked previously, or what she did in her leisure time.

As Kate was a contractor working through an agency, Sally decided to visit the agency, Public People. She smiled at the irony of the agency name, which referred to the agency supplying personnel to the public sector. Kate wasn't a public person at all. She seemed to be extremely private.

Public People worked out of a small office in the cheaper part of Southampton.

"DC Sally Gleeson." She showed her warrant card to the receptionist, a bored middle-aged woman. "Can I speak to the manager, please?"

"Take a seat." The receptionist picked up the phone.

Sally remained standing until a tall woman in a navy-blue business suit came out to meet her. The woman ushered her into a small office.

"I need to talk about Kate Lovell. You placed her with the council in the housing department."

"Yes, I know Kate. The council thinks highly of her. And she's been working via us for several years, gaining experience in a variety of different placements. What's the problem?"

"I need her home address, and I'd like a copy of her CV, please."

"I'm not sure I can give you that information. Do you have a warrant?"

Sally stared at the woman. "She's gone missing." Technically, it wasn't a lie, although, as far as she knew, Kate's absence was entirely voluntary.

"I see. Well, I suppose if it will help Kate, and seeing as you're the police, I'll make an exception." She tapped on her keyboard a few times, and a printer behind her whirred into action. She stretched over to snatch a piece of paper from the printer's out-tray and handed it to Sally. "Here's her CV. I'll get her address."

Sally scanned the CV. Kate appeared to have held plenty of short-term positions over the last few years. Most of them were in the North of England. She wondered if they would all check out, or whether some of them were made up in order to get her current job. Would anyone from her previous jobs have got closer to her than her Southampton colleagues? She may have kept her guard up working in close proximity to Felicity Edmondson, but been more forthcoming in previous jobs. It was too late in the day to contact any of Kate's former employers and tomorrow was the weekend. If they hadn't got anywhere with the case by Monday, she would start contacting them, even if she had to go behind DI Russell's back.

"Do you have a picture of Kate?" Zack hadn't been able to find any pictures of her on the Internet. "Can you send it to my phone?"

"Sure." The manager took Sally's business card with her phone number on it. Then she handed her a piece of paper with a handwritten address on it. Cadnam. It wasn't far from Southampton. Sally thanked the woman. She would go there first.

Chapter 67

Zack was busy playing with his latest toy. He downloaded some software that aged people's photos or gave them different hairstyles and colour. He was morphing Kylie West's photo into a twenty-nine-year-old version, then playing with different hair, adding a little more weight to her face, and experimenting with glasses. When he was happy with the results, he printed out ten different versions of twenty-nine-year-old Kylie. He picked them up and took them to Charlie's office.

"I think you should look at these." He started to spread them out on Charlie's desk. "I've got a new program that changes people's faces. These are different versions of Kylie West, how she might look aged twenty-nine." He pointed at a couple of them excitedly. "They're similar to Kate Lovell and Tracey Gulliver, but I can't work out which one. Both women have similarly shaped faces."

Charlie stared at the pictures. "I can't be sure either. But this is good work. It certainly takes Alicia Gardner out of the equation. None of these pictures remotely resemble her."

Sally parked her car in the last available space on Cornwall Road and walked the final hundred yards. Cornwall Road was part of a large council estate, built in the nineteen eighties. The planners had obviously been idiots, allocating one parking space per house. In reality, many of them were family homes, with two adults and children in their late teens or early twenties. Consequently, cars were crammed into every available space.

Number ninety-eight was fronted by an overgrown hedge. The gravel path was covered with weeds, and peeling paint on the front door completed the un-cared for appearance. Sally immediately noticed that the front window was broken, and no curtains hung in any of the windows.

She kicked aside some brambles and peered through the broken window.

The grime-encrusted glass made it difficult to see clearly, but the room appeared empty of furniture. A few old magazines tossed haphazardly across the floor were probably the only thing keeping any part of the floor clean. She jumped backwards as a large spider crawled right in front of her face, before realising it was on the other side of the glass.

Sally checked the address the employment agency had given her. It definitely matched.

There seemed to be signs of people at number ninety-six. Sally marched over and rang the doorbell.

She held out her warrant card to the scruffy man who answered the door. "I'm looking for your neighbour Kate Lovell." She pointed to the house next door.

The man took the cigarette out of his mouth. "Ain't nobody lives there, love. Been empty for about three years. The old bloke who owned the house died, and the relatives are fighting over who inherits."

"Are you sure you haven't seen anybody there?"

"Some bird shows up once a week to check the house. But there's definitely no one living there. Have you seen the place? It's a dump."

"Can you describe the woman who visits?"

"Brunette."

"Is she young or old? Tall? Short?"

The man shrugged his shoulders. "Youngish, tallish, skinny. She always comes on a Saturday evening. You'd think at her age, she'd be out with a boyfriend at that time."

Sally took out her phone and scrolled to the picture of Kate Lovell that the employment agency sent her. It wasn't the best photo.

Kate's hair flopped across her face, hiding some of her features, and one side of the picture was in shadow. She showed it to the man. "Is that her?"

"Yes, that's definitely her."

As soon as Sally was back in the car, she phoned Zack.

"Can you check out ninety-eight Cornwall Road, Cadnam, on the Land Registry. Who owns the house and is there any connection to Kate Lovell?"

Zack phoned her back within ten minutes. "It's currently registered to an Arthur Jones, who died nearly three years ago. I can't find any obvious connection to Lovell."

Sally's suspicion immediately increased. Was Kate using the house as a postal address, dropping in once a week to pick up her post? If that was the case, she clearly didn't want anyone to find her. She headed back to the office. She needed to talk to the DI. They might be able to pick up Kate Lovell when she called at the house tomorrow evening.

Chapter 68

It was nearly six o'clock when the team met back at the office. Charlie had checked earlier that the DCI had left for the day, so without fear of him dropping in unexpectedly, she held the briefing in the incident room where there was more space.

"Okay, guys, any progress? Who wants to go first?"

Zack put his hand up.

"What have you got, Zack?"

"The real Kate Lovell is a twenty-year-old nurse who died in a car accident twelve years ago. Our Kate Lovell is using her National Insurance number. She appears to have stolen the nurse's identity."

"That explains why she is officially thirty-two years old, and we almost discounted her as being Kylie. Is there anything that ties her to the Wests?"

"I haven't found anything yet, ma'am. But the other interesting thing is that she was admitted to hospital six years ago following a suicide attempt. Paracetamol overdose."

Charlie wondered where he got that information. She would have a quiet word with him later in case he was hacking into confidential medical records. She didn't want him to get into trouble when he was only trying to help. Best to set some boundaries now, before he went too far.

Zack continued, "That might explain the feeble attempt to make both murders look like suicide. Maybe she's making a point that her birth parents drove her to it."

"But Max isn't her birth father," Rick interrupted.

"We don't know what she knows or doesn't know. She may have assumed he's the father," Sally reminded him.

"We need to find Kate Lovell. So where is she?"

"I know where she'll be tomorrow evening, ma'am." Sally stepped forward. "She gave a false address to her employment agency.

It's a house in Cadnam that has been empty for three years. The neighbours say she checks the property every Saturday evening, regularly as clockwork. I think she must be collecting her mail. There's no other reason for her to go there."

"Okay, organise a team to watch the house from tomorrow afternoon and pick her up. But we need to try to find her before then. She's already murdered two people. It's possible she may have other targets, or she may abscond from the area." Charlie was also mindful of the DCI's deadline. They couldn't afford to waste a whole day doing nothing, particularly as they still didn't have irrefutable proof that Kate Lovell was their murderer.

Charlie updated the murder board, which now had extra sheets of paper stuck onto it with bits of tape, which could be removed easily, to keep the DCI in the dark about the direction in which the investigation was proceeding.

"Rick, what do you have on Alicia Gardner?"

"I spoke to Bill in organised crime. He's known her since she was a young girl. There's no way she's Kylie West."

Charlie nodded. It backed up the lack of resemblance in Zack's computer-generated photos. "Well done." Rick might feel as if he'd come up with nothing solid, but ruling out someone would enable them to focus their resources more. "What about you, Tyrone?"

"Tracey Gulliver isn't who she says she is, but I don't believe she's Kylie West either."

"Go on."

"She changed her name when she fled from an abusive husband. She was helpful eventually. I managed to trace her back to her school in Cheltenham. They confirmed that she was suspended because of a butterfly tattoo on her ankle. She showed me the tattoo."

"Did you check for a scar on her wrist?" Charlie asked, wanting to be certain they hadn't missed anything.

"Yes. There's no sign of any scar."

"So it looks as if Kylie West must be Kate Lovell," Charlie summed up. That was assuming her theory was correct and Kylie West was responsible for these murders. For a moment, she wondered if the DCI might be right. She might be wasting time focusing on this. She quickly pulled herself together. She needed to find the courage of her convictions and follow her gut feeling. "Let's go home and get some rest, then we'll come back at seven o'clock tomorrow morning, hopefully with some ideas of where to find our suspect." Kate must live somewhere in the area. Even if she wasn't at home when they visited, a search of her house might help them find her, if they could get a warrant without irrefutable evidence.

The team picked up their coats and filed out of the office. Zack was still at his computer.

"Go home, Zack."

"I'd rather stay a bit longer. I want to check the ANPR system for Lovell's car. We might be able to narrow down the area where she lives if I can track her recent journeys. Then I can move on to CCTV to narrow it further."

"Okay, but don't stay too late." Charlie hoped Kate Lovell lived in a built-up area with plenty of cameras. If Zack came up with something, it would give the team a much-needed head start in the morning.

Chapter 69

Charlie drove into the police station car park at six forty-five on Saturday morning. She wanted to set an example by getting in before her team arrived and also make a plan while it was quiet. A smattering of cars dotted the car park, probably people on the night shift. She envied their being able to go home to bed soon. She'd hardly got any sleep last night for worrying about the case. Things like that never used to affect her. Was it the added pressure of being the senior investigating officer, or the fact that the DCI had threatened to bring in someone to take over from her? However well-meaning he was, in her eyes, it would spell failure.

She was surprised when she entered the main office to find Zack sprawled over his computer keyboard, asleep. For a moment, she thought he might be dead. The computer was bleeping, no doubt caused by whatever keys his weight was leaning on. How he could sleep with that noise going on, she had no idea, but he was definitely asleep. As she moved closer, the regular beats of Zack's snoring reassured her.

"Wake up, Zack," she said loudly, reluctant to touch him in case he was startled, but if he could sleep through the loud beeping, she could shout like a foghorn and he wouldn't hear her. She gave his shoulder a gentle shake.

Immediately, Zack lifted his head and groaned.

To Charlie's relief, the beeping noise stopped, although the beat continued to pulse inside her head. "Have you been here all night?"

"What? No. I mean, maybe." Zack rubbed his eyes and yawned.

"Go home. Get some rest." He was no use to the team if he was tired. Besides, he needed a shower.

"I found something." Zack seemed wide awake already. "I tracked Kate Lovell's car. The cameras pick it up every morning on

Forest Road in Cadnam, then again coming past the Western Docks in Southampton. She makes the return journey later in the day."

"That's the journey to work. Is there anything to help us with where she lives?"

Zack had already woken up his computer, which was still logged in, and pulled up a map. "The car shows up here on the A31." He pointed his pen at the spot. "But there's another camera not much further along the same road. Here." He used his finger to indicate the position. "There's no sign of her on that camera."

"So she must turn off down this road." Charlie placed her finger on the screen halfway between the two spots Zack was indicating.

"Yes. And that's a dead end." Zack converted the map to the Google Maps Street View. "I reckon at most, you've got thirty houses to search."

A shot of adrenaline raced through Charlie's veins. They could do this. She would ask for some uniformed officers to help do a house-to-house search of the area. Immediately, doubt rose inside her. What if nothing came of it and it got back to the DCI that she'd ignored his instructions? She couldn't risk involving anyone else. Still, there were four of them. They had to try.

"You've done a great job. Now you really must go home, Zack. No arguing. Come back when you've had a few hours' sleep and a shower."

Chapter 70

Charlie turned onto Forest Road, slowing her speed so that Rick could keep an eye out for Kate Lovell's car. She checked the rearview mirror. Sally and Tyrone were getting into position. They agreed to park at the end of the road and Tyrone would stay in the car, in case Lovell made a run for it and they needed to go after her.

The houses in Forest Road were a mixed bunch, starting with smaller, cheaper-looking properties nearest to the main road, then gradually increasing in opulence until they arrived at the final property, which boasted a huge garden, electric gates, and a house big enough to accommodate a football team.

"We should probably start at the cheap end." Charlie didn't see how Kate Lovell would be able to afford to either buy or to rent at the far end of the road.

"She might have a rich boyfriend."

"She might, but let's work with the most probable scenario first." Charlie turned the car around. In her experience, rich boyfriends weren't as easy to find as some people seemed to think. "Any sign of her car?"

"I haven't seen it yet."

"Let's double-check on the way back."

Charlie pulled out to pass a long row of parked cars.

"There it is, Sis." Rick pointed at the line of cars. The blue Renault Clio was tucked into the middle of the line, easily missed from the other direction.

Charlie quickly found a parking space. She was disappointed that the car wasn't parked directly outside one of the houses. It would have made their job much easier. "Get Sally down here. We'll focus on this part of the road. Lovell won't have parked too far away from where she lives."

Rick made the phone call while Charlie reversed into the empty parking space.

"Sally's going to start at number thirty-six and work towards us. How about if you start at the house with the camper van parked outside and meet up with Sally in the middle? I'll do the other side of the road. She's got to be in one of these twelve houses."

Charlie agreed. On one side of the road, a field of ponies separated this block of properties from the next one, and the opposite side of the road had been sparsely built on with only four houses nearby and large gaps of open space between their nearest neighbours.

"Let's be discreet. We don't want her to see us coming." She wondered if she should get Tyrone to help. It would speed things up. But if Kate ran for her car, he would be in a better position to follow her if he stayed where he was.

Charlie hit pay dirt at the first house she visited. A young woman wearing a fluffy pink dressing gown answered the door. Charlie showed her the photo of Kate.

"Yes, I know her. She lives in the white house at the end of this row. Is she in any trouble?"

"We just need to speak to her." Charlie thanked her for her help.

She walked towards the house. A thin layer of dirt on the walls made the house look more pale beige than white. It was well overdue for repainting or even a good clean. She dialled Rick's number. It diverted to voicemail. Before Charlie got time to leave a message, the door of the white house opened. Even from this distance, she recognised Kate.

Kate spotted her and started running towards the Renault Clio. Charlie sprinted down the road. With a bit of luck, she could head her off. If Kate reached her car, she would be out on the A31 in a few seconds. She hoped Tyrone was paying attention. He may have to follow her or try to block the road to prevent her from leaving.

Charlie ran across the road towards the blue Renault, lengthening her stride so her long legs ate up the distance faster. She was so focused on reaching the car before Kate, she only noticed her veer off in the opposite direction at the last moment. Kate threw herself onto the grass verge and rolled under the fence into the horses' field. Immediately, she jumped to her feet and took off across the grass.

Charlie started back across the road, stopping in her tracks as a black Range Rover blared its horn at her. She lost valuable seconds, and Kate was well ahead of her as she hurled herself towards the post and rail fence. She saw Rick out of the corner of her eye and pointed in Kate's direction, too out of breath to shout. Rick must have seen her because he darted after her.

Charlie scrambled over the fence and set off in pursuit of Kate, who was now well ahead. Kate had the advantage of knowing where she was going, whereas Charlie had no idea what lay on the other side of this field. If she lost her, she wouldn't have a clue where to look.

She heard Rick running up behind her. They were both fit, but Kate flew across the field like a frightened deer, increasing the distance between them. She shouted to Rick, her breathless voice firing out the words in staccato puffs. "Where does this go?"

"God knows."

Not helpful. Traffic noises buzzed through the air, the sounds of a road up ahead. She focused on the disappearing figure in front of them. Kate was dressed in jeans and a brown coat, the sort of clothes that would blend into the background. It would be easy to lose her. Charlie made a final effort to speed up as Kate vanished into the hedge.

"Where did she go?" Rick gasped.

"There must be a way through." As she got closer, she noticed a small gap with a stile set into the thick hedge.

They quickly climbed the stile and found themselves on a road opposite a row of small shops.

"Where is she?" Charlie looked up and down the deserted road. The only movement came from a bus pulling away from the bus stop just beyond the shops.

"She must be on the bus." Charlie realised it too late to do anything about it.

"Yes, I think that's her sitting in the back seat." Rick pointed.

Charlie quickly phoned Tyrone. "Find out where the number seventy-six bus goes. It's headed away from Cadnam, possibly towards Southampton." She gave him the registration number. "Kate Lovell is a passenger. Try to intercept the bus before she gets off."

"What now, Sis?" Rick looked despondent.

"We go back to her house."

"Do you think she'll return there?" He sounded sceptical.

"I think the neighbour who told me where she lives phoned her to warn her I was coming. She only had a few seconds to make a run for it. If she was quick-thinking, she might have picked up her phone and her purse. Or she may have left with nothing."

"She'll get kicked off the bus pretty quickly if she can't pay her fare."

"Let's hope Tyrone finds her before that happens."

As they walked back towards the house, at least Charlie felt vindicated. Kate Lovell wouldn't have run like that if she wasn't guilty of something. She was out there somewhere, but they were running out of time to find her.

Chapter 71

As they neared Lovell's house, they both spotted it at the same time.

"She left the door open."

Kate had fled in such a hurry, she hadn't even shut her front door, let alone locked it.

"That gives us an excuse to go in without a warrant," Charlie pointed out. She took two pairs of nitrile gloves out of her pocket and passed a pair to Rick, then pushed the door wide open. "Let's see what we can find. We may have to get the CSIs out here." If nothing else, they could find some DNA and test for a match to Felicity Edmondson, and also the baby teeth that Mrs West had given them.

Before they started searching, Charlie phoned Sally to update her. She sent her to get some background information from the neighbour who pointed out Kate's house earlier. Sally promised to come to Kate's house when she finished.

"I feel like we shouldn't be here," Rick said. "Are you sure we don't need a warrant?"

"The door was open. We're worried someone might have broken in." She was thankful they had that excuse because if they needed a warrant, it would waste valuable time, and they probably wouldn't be granted one because the biggest piece of hard evidence they had was the fact that Kate had run away and that wouldn't cut it with a magistrate. Everything else was simply evidence of motive. They still had nothing that tied her to Max Edmondson's murder, and the only thing tying her to Felicity's murder was the fact that she was at the party with her. It was Charlie's gut instinct that tied everything together. Nothing else made sense. But gut instincts didn't go down well as evidence. She could see why Rick was concerned. It would be their word against Kate's that the door was open. "Look, Rick, if you want to go back to the station and leave me to do this on my own, I'll understand. There's no point in us both getting into trouble."

"Or we could search in half the time with me helping. If we don't find anything, we can pretend we were never here."

Charlie doubted if that would be possible, but she appreciated Rick's loyalty. "We'd better not make too much mess, then."

The house was sparsely furnished. Charlie guessed Kate rented it and, if she didn't plan to stay for the long term, she wouldn't want to spend much money on furnishings.

"I'll start upstairs. You search down here." Charlie headed for the stairs.

Two bedrooms and a bathroom. It shouldn't take long. The main bedroom was furnished with a double bed, a small wardrobe, and a large chest of drawers. Charlie started with the drawers.

They mostly contained underwear and T-shirts. Everything was neatly folded—a sharp contrast to her own bedroom. A couple of handbags and some belts were squashed into one end of the top drawer. Charlie opened the handbags, but both were empty. She moved on to the wardrobe.

Everything was arranged by colour, mostly browns, oranges, and reds. Charlie checked the pockets, then the floor of the wardrobe, where several pairs of shoes were neatly arranged. The room was unrealistically tidy, with no trace of dust anywhere. It felt sterile. If Kate Lovell was hiding anything, it wasn't in here.

She quickly lifted up the mattress on the bed, in case anything was hidden underneath. Again, she drew a blank.

The second bedroom was unfurnished and obviously used for storage. Some cardboard boxes were lined up against one wall. Charlie opened up the nearest box. It contained several pairs of shoes. The second box was more interesting. A photo album and a few books. Charlie flipped through the photo album. Most of the photos were of landscapes, some with ponies in the background, so Charlie guessed they were taken in the New Forest, although she didn't recognise any of the locations. There were no people in any of the photos, as if Kate had no friends and no family. Even though it added to Charlie's gut feeling about the woman, the absence of people in her life didn't count as hard evidence of murder.

The other boxes were uninteresting: some old clothes and more books, mostly paperback classics like Dickens, Austen, Tolkien, and the first Harry Potter book.

The bathroom cabinet contained a variety of hair products, as well as a packet of paracetamol and some contraceptive pills. Did Kate have a partner? She checked for an extra toothbrush or razor but found nothing. Charlie bagged Kate's toothbrush. She could get a DNA sample from it. Apart from that, she felt like she'd wasted her time. She hoped Rick's search had been more productive.

Rick called Charlie over as she came downstairs. "I found her passport. If it's a fake, it's a good one. And there's a laptop. Zack is on his way. He should be here in a few minutes."

Charlie checked her watch. Zack might have got about three hours' sleep if he was lucky. She should have told Rick about Zack staying in the office all night. "Does it have a password?"

"Yes. I didn't want to try guessing in case it locked me out. Zack will get into it," he said confidently.

Zack arrived a few minutes later, bringing his own laptop with him. To Charlie's annoyance, he looked as if he'd enjoyed a full night's sleep.

"Where's the laptop?"

Rick handed him a spare pair of gloves. "Put these on first." He pointed to a glass coffee table next to the sofa, where he'd set up the laptop and plugged it in to charge.

Zack knelt on the floor and powered up Kate's laptop. Rick watched him carefully to see how he managed to unlock the password, but Zack was much too quick, accessing the machine in seconds. He took a flash drive out of his pocket, then logged into his own laptop. "I'll get some programs opened up, ready to analyse what's on there, but I want it backed up onto the flash drive first, in case anything goes wrong. It's not a powerful machine, so it will probably take ages. You may as well do something else while you're waiting, or you'll be bored stiff."

"I'll catch up with Sally and talk to more of the neighbours," Rick said.

Rick spotted Sally coming out of one of the houses opposite. "Any luck?"

"She doesn't socialise much with the neighbours. They think she's a bit stuck-up."

"How many more houses do we need to visit? I'm free to help while Zach is searching Kate's laptop."

Sally counted on her fingers. "Six or seven. If you finish this side of the road, I'll do the remaining houses on the other side. Tyrone is still chasing that bus. If he hasn't caught up with Kate, I'll put him on surveillance duty as soon as he returns in case she comes back."

"Do you think she's likely to return home now that she knows we're after her?" Rick wouldn't come anywhere near the place if it were him.

"She might be desperate. Don't forget, she left in a hurry without taking anything with her."

Chapter 72

Casey Summers at number seventy-eight seemed to dislike Kate Lovell less than any of her other neighbours.

"She's not sociable. This group of houses held a barbecue a while back, and she refused to come. But I've chatted to her a lot as she comes and goes. I'm often outside weeding the front garden." Mrs Summers nodded towards a large lawn surrounded by immaculate flower beds. "She's friendly enough when she wants to be."

"What do you talk about?" Rick hoped it might shed some light on where to find her.

"All sorts of things. The weather, my rose bushes, the cost of petrol."

"What about her family? Does she ever say anything about them?"

Mrs Summers shook her head slowly. "No. Come to think of it, she never talks about herself. Even if I ask questions, she avoids them. Maybe she's just shy."

"Have you noticed any visitors going to her house?" Their houses were almost opposite each other, giving Casey Summers a perfect view of Kate's front door.

"I haven't seen any, but maybe her friends show up later in the evening, if they're working. What's she done? She must have done something if the police are asking about her."

"We simply want her to help with our inquiries." He wouldn't get anything else out of this woman, so he thanked her and moved on to her neighbour before she asked any more questions.

Chapter 73

Charlie came back downstairs, where Zack was still working on Kate's laptop. She'd searched the whole house again in case they'd missed something the first time, but found nothing new.

Zack looked up. "She's put some serious encryption on this machine. She must have something to hide."

"Does that mean you can't get into it?" Charlie's hopes fell.

Zack glared at her disdainfully. "It took me less than twenty seconds to get in."

Charlie relaxed, reminding herself to have more faith in Zack. "Have you found anything?" She was pinning her hopes on that laptop.

"Plenty so far. She accessed a suicide site on the dark web. According to her browser history, which she tried to delete, but I recovered, she's a regular visitor. She browsed pages on hanging and slitting wrists."

"That's interesting." Charlie knew it wouldn't be enough evidence on its own, but it would certainly help them to build a bigger picture.

"She also visited a page about jumping off tall buildings. Do you think she might have another victim in mind?"

"It's possible." Charlie was already worried that might be the case. She mentally ran through a list of people Kate might have a grudge against: her adoptive parents, social workers who helped facilitate the adoption, Fliss's mother, and that was only the start.

"She's been active on the chat page on the same website for several months. She mentioned her birth parents a few times. It's not pretty. And she obviously thinks that Max Edmondson is her father. I can print out everything back in the office, but you should read some of it now."

Charlie peered over Zack's shoulder, scanning down the page. Some of the opinions on the chat were frightening. "Are you sure Kate is definitely *Reject52*?"

"Yes, I've traced it back to this IP address."

"Who is *ChessDevil501*?"

"I'm still trying to trace him or her. Over the last few weeks, she almost exclusively chatted to ChessDevil, whereas before that, she used to join in a lot of other conversations. Also, some of these conversations are open-ended, as if they might have finished them off somewhere else. I'm trying to find their private chats. They may be a lot more revealing."

"I think you should prioritise finding ChessDevil. If we find him or her, we may find Kate."

"I'm on it." Zack went back to tapping at his keyboard.

Charlie stepped outside. There wasn't much in the front garden. Unlike some of the neighbouring properties, Kate's front garden wasn't paved for parking. The lawn, overgrown by several inches and sprouting dandelions and buttercups, was in dire need of some TLC. There was nowhere to hide anything. She was about to go back into the house when Tyrone showed up.

"Sorry, ma'am, Kate Lovell wasn't on the bus. The woman you saw in the back seat wasn't her."

She must have gone into one of the shops. Charlie cursed herself for not searching more thoroughly. "Don't worry. Can you stay in the house in case Kate comes back? She didn't have time to take anything with her, so she might sneak back to collect some things if she thinks everyone's gone."

"If she shows up, do I arrest her or what?"

"Yes. We've got enough to arrest her on suspicion of Felicity Edmondson's murder, if she won't come in for questioning willingly. We can't risk her getting away again." They may have enough to arrest her, but Charlie knew they didn't have sufficient evidence yet to make the charge stick. "I'm going back to the office with Zack. He found a lot of stuff on her laptop. She's been active on a suicide website. She may have only been researching her murder methods, but remember, she apparently tried to commit suicide a few years ago, so she may be vulnerable." Kate hadn't seemed vulnerable when she'd been racing across the field ahead of Charlie, but it would be negligent of her not to bring up the point. She may not even come back here. Tyrone might be in for a long wait.

Chapter 74

Zack burst into Charlie's office without knocking and waved some pieces of paper at her. "I found the private messaging between Reject and ChessDevil," he said excitedly. "They're a really messed-up pair."

Charlie took the sheets of paper and began to read through them quickly.

Zack summarised them as she read to speed things up. "I've got an address for ChessDevil. I tracked it from his IP address. It's in Southampton. They planned the two murders together, but it's not clear which one of them actually did them."

"Could they have done one each?" Charlie flipped over the page. It was harrowing reading.

"Maybe. But there's another thing too. It looks like they've made a suicide pact."

"Does it say where or when?"

"No, but I think they may have met in person recently."

Charlie put down the pieces of paper to finish reading later. "Give me ChessDevil's address. Then phone Rick and tell him to meet me there urgently. Bring him up to date on what's happened. And get me some uniform backup." She needed to find Kate Lovell and ChessDevil before they killed anyone else or killed themselves.

Chapter 75

Charlie got out of the car and looked up. Fairview was a high-rise block of flats at least ten stories high, maybe twelve. ChessDevil lived at number twenty-four. There were forty-seven flats in total, making number twenty-four about halfway up.

Charlie pressed the button for number one.

"Who is it?" an elderly female voice answered.

"It's the police. DI Charlotte Steele from Hampshire Constabulary. I'm here to see one of your neighbours. Please can you open the front door?"

The door clicked, and Charlie pushed it open quickly.

A large out-of-order sign was taped to the lift door. Quickly, Charlie found the stairs and started running.

By the time she reached the sixth floor, she was puffing heavily. She slowed to a walk and recovered her breath enough to listen at the door of number twenty-four. No sounds came from inside. She knocked at the door. Still no noise from inside the flat. Charlie stepped away and phoned Zack.

"Can you get on to uniform and tell them whoever's coming to back me up needs to bring the enforcer to the sixth floor and get access to flat twenty-four?"

"Will do, ma'am. Have you found ChessDevil?"

"If he's in there, he's not answering the door." She hung up the call and headed back out to the stairwell. With the lift out of order, anyone coming or going would have to come this way. She would also spot the uniformed officers coming up the stairs.

Charlie went through a few facts in her head as she waited. ChessDevil might be the only person Kate could turn to now that the police were after her. The suicide pact worried her. Kate had already tried to commit suicide a few years ago. It wouldn't be much of a stretch for her to be tipped over the edge by a like-minded person. To her horror, she recalled Kate had been looking at the webpage showing details of suicide by jumping off tall buildings. She glanced up. Another six floors towered above her. Twelve floors were plenty high enough for a fatal leap. Did the tenants in this block of flats have access to the roof? It should be secure. The old building was covered by the same safety legislation as any modern building, but judging by the state of repair of the stairwell, standards were slack.

Charlie was torn between watching ChessDevil's flat and investigating access to the roof. She looked at her watch. Rick and the uniformed officers should both be here soon.

A faint scream echoed down the stairwell, leaving her with no choice.

Chapter 76

Charlie raced up the stairs two at a time, her long legs eating up the steps. Her heart thumped loudly as she ran, which, combined with her heavy breathing, made it impossible to hear if anything was going on above her. She pressed on, only slowing for the final flight of stairs, to get her breath back before she reached the top.

The door in front of her was open, a chilly wind confirming it must lead to the roof. She crept through it slowly. Whatever was going on out there, she didn't want to startle anyone.

At first, she saw nothing, then the sound of heavy sobbing floated across the large roof area. "Please stop. I don't want to do it anymore. I don't want to die."

Kate Lovell stood at the edge of the roof, a single iron bar between her and a fatal fall to the road beneath them. An arm gripped her from behind, but whoever was holding Kate, they were hidden by a concrete pillar. Charlie leaned forward to get a better view.

Before Charlie could see anything, Kate was pulled sideways out of sight. Charlie gasped, bracing herself for the blood-curdling scream that must surely follow.

"Who's there?" The voice sounded familiar but tautly wound up as if it might snap at any moment. "Come out so I can see you."

Charlie put her hands in the air and walked slowly out into the open. "I only want to talk." She stifled another gasp as she saw the man who was holding Kate Lovell, taking a moment to recognise him with his faded red baseball cap pulled down over his eyes. "It's okay, Danny. Come away from the edge and let's talk about this."

Danny Owen didn't move. He must have gripped Kate tighter because she started to cry again.

"There's nothing to talk about. It's all going to end in a few minutes, and there's nothing you can do to stop us."

Kate's sobbing grew louder.

"Come away from the edge, Danny. It doesn't need to end." Charlie crept forward a few paces as she spoke calmly. "Whatever's troubling you, there's always a better answer. Let me help you."

"We made a pact, me and Kate. I helped her. Now she's helping me. We're going to jump together."

"I don't want to, Danny. I don't want to die." Kate trembled visibly, despite Danny holding her in a firm grip.

"Danny, why don't you let Kate come over here? I can take care of her." Charlie edged closer, still too far away to grab Kate. She would be of no use in that split second of opportunity if Danny made the jump and pulled Kate with him.

"She promised we would do it together."

"She's scared, Danny. Why don't you both step away from the edge? We can talk about this."

"I don't want to talk. I just want everything to stop."

Charlie thought she heard a noise behind her. She looked around, but there was no one there. Where was Rick? Where was her uniformed backup? Even if she persuaded Danny to step away from the edge of the roof, there was little she could do on her own. And Rick might not even find her up here.

"What would your father say if he saw you here?" Charlie had reservations about mentioning the archdeacon, but she was desperate. If this got into a conversation about the finer points of religion, she'd be floundering. The last time she'd stepped into a church was on her wedding day. A church wedding hadn't helped to avoid a painful divorce.

Danny gave a hollow laugh. "He'd say suicide is a sin. The same as being gay is a sin. He couldn't care less about what I want. He cares only about how it affects his career."

"But can't you see, if you jump now, he's going to win. You need to stay and fight it until he accepts you as you are."

"He'll never accept me."

"He will. But if he doesn't, you can embarrass the hell out of him. It's your life. Don't lose it because of him. You can make it what you want it to be."

"Of course I can't. I'll go to prison, won't I?"

Charlie hesitated before speaking. "I understand why you did it, how unhappy you are. If you explain that, the judge will be lenient with you." It would make no difference at all, but Charlie wasn't going to tell him that now. "You'll be out in a few years, then you can start a new life, on your terms. And a prison sentence will embarrass the hell out of your father." Perhaps the archdeacon would pray for Danny. She doubted if that would do any good either.

Danny remained silent. Even Kate had stopped sobbing. The silence was eerie, as if something monumental was about to happen. Charlie hoped this wouldn't end with them both jumping.

Charlie waited, and a couple of minutes later, Kate slowly came into view, followed by Danny Owen. Danny's left arm was wrapped around Kate's neck in a chokehold. Both of them still stood worryingly close to the edge of the roof.

"Danny, why don't you let Kate come over to me, then we can talk?" Charlie's heart beat almost hard enough to burst through her chest. One wrong word and Danny could still throw himself backwards over the metal rail, taking Kate with him.

Danny removed his arm and pushed Kate forwards. She stumbled before regaining her balance and ran towards Charlie.

"Go and wait over there." Charlie pointed to the door that led back inside the building. "You're safe now." Kate Lovell would go to prison for her part in the murders, but they'd deal with that later, when she got over the shock of almost plummeting to her death.

Charlie turned her attention back to Danny. He was climbing over the railing. She lunged towards him and grabbed his arm to pull him back.

"Danny, this isn't the answer. Please, let's talk about it."

For a split second, Charlie thought he had changed his mind. He started to climb back over the railing towards her. She kept hold of his arm, wrapping her leg around the metal post at the bottom of the rail to anchor herself.

As he tried to heave himself back over the rail, Danny's foot slipped. He screamed as he fell several inches. Charlie clung onto his arm, reaching out with her other hand and gripping the sleeve of his coat. A stiff gust of wind lifted the baseball cap from Danny's head. It floated towards the ground.

"Grab my arm, then see if you can reach the railing with your other hand." Charlie braced herself against the metal railing. She hoped the rail was strong enough to withstand their combined weight. She glanced down at the ground, quickly looking away before she was overcome with dizziness. The adrenaline pumping through her made her stronger, but she couldn't hold on for much longer. One foot began to slip. She braced herself against the metal railing. It had better not give. She was at serious risk of being dragged over the edge. Danny might get his suicide partner after all.

"Charlie?"

Charlie's heart leapt in her chest at the sound of Rick's voice. "Over here. Hurry." She couldn't cling on to Danny for much longer.

Rick ran to her, followed by two uniformed officers.

"Get hold of him!" Charlie felt a pair of strong arms wrap around her, anchoring her to the rooftop as Rick and the other uniformed officer took hold of Danny Owen and heaved him back up over the rail.

Charlie took some deep breaths, trying to hold herself together as she was led away from the edge of the roof. "Thanks," she gasped.

"That was a close call. I thought we were both going to fall." The breeze on the rooftop sent an icy chill through her. She needed to get off this roof. She turned around when they reached the door back into the building. Danny Owen was in handcuffs and was being helped along by one of the constables.

Rick ran over to Charlie and put an arm around her shoulders. "Are you okay, Sis?"

"I'm fine. Where's Kate?" She'd completely forgotten about Kate Lovell.

"I don't know."

"She was here. Danny helped her with the murders, and they made a suicide pact. They were going to jump together, but Kate bottled out at the last minute." Charlie wondered if Kate ever intended to follow through with the pact. "Danny was going to take her with him anyway, but I persuaded him to let her go. She was waiting by the doorway."

"We didn't see her when we came up the stairs."

"We need to find her." They seemed to spend too much of their time searching for Kate Lovell. Charlie cursed herself for letting her get away.

Chapter 77

It seemed as if they were back to square one. They still didn't have Kate Lovell in custody. She may not have murdered either of the Edmondsons, but she was certainly wrapped up in the plan up to her neck.

"Perhaps when we interview Danny Owen, he'll tell us where to find Lovell," Rick suggested.

"That might take too long. She'll be gone by then, even assuming Danny is willing and able to talk." The police doctor insisted on a psychiatric examination to ascertain whether Owen was fit to be interviewed.

It dawned on Charlie that perhaps they did know where to find Kate Lovell. "What about that house? The empty one she keeps going back to every Saturday."

"Cornwall Road? Do you really think she'll go there now?"

"It's worth a try. She might not have anywhere else, and she doesn't realise we know about that address. Let's get over there now. If she's using it as a bolthole while she works out what to do, we can arrest her. Otherwise, we can leave Tyrone and Sally to watch the place in case she shows up later."

"Tyrone's still keeping watch on Kate's house."

Charlie had forgotten. "Okay, let's leave him there." Someone would have to take over from him soon. "Where's Sally?"

"She's gone to see Kate's adoptive mother, just in case Kate shows up there."

"Let's leave her there." If Kate decided to visit Mrs West, Charlie doubted it would be a happy family reunion. More likely, her adoptive mother was on Kate's wish list for another murder now that Kate had nothing to lose.

"It's just you and me then, Sis."

"Looks like it." They needed to stop wasting time and get over there. Fast.

Chapter 78

Zack phoned as they were driving to the empty house. Charlie put him on speakerphone.

"Tyrone called me. Kate Lovell returned to her house. She took her car and Tyrone couldn't reach her quickly enough to stop her."

Charlie cursed under her breath. They should have thought of that. Kate must have taken the car keys with her. After all, she'd been heading towards it when she first left the house. They should have clamped the car.

"Ma'am, I've been tracking the car on ANPR. It looks like she might be heading towards the empty house in Cornwall Road."

"We're on our way there now. How far out is she?"

"About ten minutes, maybe less."

"Damn." Rick thumped his fist on the steering wheel. "It's going to take us at least fifteen. She might be gone by then."

"Step on the gas. We can't afford to miss her. This may be our only chance."

Rick accelerated, overtaking the car in front of them, barely squeezing back into the gap in time to avoid the oncoming lorry bearing down on them.

Charlie phoned Tyrone and asked him to go to the empty house. He was no use now staying at Kate's house, and they might need an extra person if Kate tried to give them the slip again. She called Zack back.

"Where's Kate now?"

"Still headed in the same direction. There aren't any more cameras on that road, but I'll keep checking, in case her car reappears somewhere else."

"Thanks, Zack. Let me know as soon as you pick her up again. If we don't catch her at the house, it's the only way we can trace her." She hung up the call.

Rick had made up some ground while she'd been on the phone. With luck, they wouldn't be too far behind Kate Lovell.

Rick swung the car right-handed onto a side road. Charlie didn't recognise the route, but Rick had lived and worked in this area for a long time, so she didn't question him. He knew shortcuts that she didn't.

"Good of Zack to work all day Saturday for nothing," Rick remarked.

Charlie laughed for the first time that day. "Did you hear the excitement in his voice? He's taking part in a real live car chase, with none of the risk. He's loving this."

Rick laughed. "Still good of him."

Charlie agreed. She would have to show her appreciation to the whole team when this was over. They'd potentially put their jobs on the line for her. She was immensely relieved that it was paying off. Her job was on the line, too, more than anyone's. "How much further is it?"

The tyres screeched on the tarmac as Rick took the corner a touch too fast. He gunned the car back up to speed, shifting through the gears expertly. "Almost there."

"If she's inside the house, I'll take the front, and you go around the back." She wished now that she'd left some surveillance on the empty house, but she'd had Kate so close, keeping watch here seemed an unnecessary waste of resources, and with only the four of them, it would have been impossible. She cursed DCI Talbot for tying her hands on this.

Rick slowed down.

"It's the house with the overgrown hedge at the front." Charlie pointed ahead.

The house was still some distance away, and Charlie couldn't see it properly yet. "Is Kate's car in the driveway? We can block it in." She didn't intend to let Kate Lovell get away a third time.

"I can't see it."

"Then let's not park directly outside the house. We don't want to give her any warning that we're coming."

Charlie spotted movement up ahead. A car poked its nose out of the driveway of the empty house.

"That's her. That's Kate's car." She must have parked it behind the hedge.

The car pulled out onto the road.

"We have to make it stop."

Rick accelerated towards the car before Kate got the chance to pick up much speed. He moved to the opposite side of the road and headed straight towards her. Immediately, Kate swerved to try to avoid him, but Rick was ready for her, gliding across the road in front of her.

"Hold tight," he said.

Charlie braced herself. What the hell was Rick doing? There was no time to argue with him. He accelerated towards Kate's car, then jerked on the handbrake, yanking the steering wheel hard left to spin the car.

Charlie swore. The impact wasn't as forceful as expected, but it still delivered a hefty wallop, setting off the airbags as it caught the Renault Clio on the front wing and rotated it sideways. Rick braked, controlling their vehicle expertly. He threw open his door.

"Let's get her while she's still in shock." He ran towards Kate's car.

Charlie followed, her ribs sore where the airbag had punched into them, and reached the car shortly after Rick. He pulled open the driver's door. Charlie leaned in to grab Kate's hands and cuff her.

"Kate Lovell, I'm arresting you for conspiracy to murder Felicity Edmondson and Max Edmondson. You do not have to say anything. But it may harm your defence if you do not mention when questioned something which you later rely on in court. Anything you do say may be given in evidence." She reached across Kate and unclicked the seatbelt.

Chapter 79

The doctor wouldn't let them interview Danny Owen until the following morning.

He declined a solicitor. "I'm a qualified solicitor, and I can represent myself better than some inexperienced duty solicitor that I'm likely to get on a Sunday."

Charlie considered reminding him that his areas of expertise were property law and company law, neither of which properly equipped him to deal with criminal law and a double murder charge. However, if he was foolish enough to represent himself, he would probably talk more, which would make her job easier.

"Are you sure?"

"Of course I'm sure. I'd rather get on with it."

"Present are Detective Inspector Charlotte Steele and Detective Sergeant Richard Henderson." Charlie addressed the suspect. "Can you please state your full name for the tape?"

"Daniel Owen."

"Danny. Do you mind if I call you Danny?"

"I prefer Danny."

Charlie smiled at him, trying to put him at ease. The more relaxed he was, the more he might open up. "So, Danny, can you tell us in your own words how you met Kate Lovell?"

"We met online."

"Was that on the *End It All* website?"

"Yes. I didn't know who she was then. She was just *Reject52*. She sounded as screwed up as I was, so I started chatting to her on the site."

"And you were *Chess Devil*? Is that right?"

"Yes."

"Do you play chess?"

Danny laughed. "No. My father's a bishop, or very nearly anyway. And he thinks I'm the devil, so I thought the name fitted."

Charlie remembered the background checks into Danny revealed his father was being lined up to replace the Bishop of Leeds when he retired. She didn't suppose that would happen once the news of Danny's arrest became public.

"When did you decide to meet in person?"

"It was only a couple of weeks ago. When Kate showed up and I recognised her, I nearly made a run for it, but she knew who I was by then. I'd told her what I would be wearing, so I couldn't deny it."

"Did Kate tell you she was adopted?"

"That was almost the first thing she told me. We bonded over a hatred of our respective parents. Hers because they rejected her, and mine because my father won't accept that I'm gay. He thinks I'm an evil sinner." Danny laughed. "I'm probably going to ruin his career now, and I'm really glad."

Charlie shuffled her notes. Was that what this had all been about, payback for Danny's father for putting his religious beliefs before his son?

"Did Kate give you the names of her birth parents?" She wanted Danny to say the names, without her putting words into his mouth.

"Yes, her real mother was Fliss Edmondson. I'd already had a few run-ins with Fliss while we were negotiating the Tenurewise contract. She got very bolshy when she didn't get her own way."

"Is that when you decided to kill her?"

"I decided no such thing," he said defensively.

"Tell me what happened after you left the Tenurewise party."

"I dropped Tracey off at the bus stop and drove home."

"Tracey Gulliver?"

"Yes. She didn't want to walk to the bus stop in the dark. I dropped her off."

"And what time did you get home?"

"About ten p.m." Danny gave a little smile. He seemed overconfident, considering he had just lied to her.

"We have your car on the ANPR system heading into Winchester after eleven p.m." She'd asked Tyrone yesterday to check the time discrepancy with Danny, but he hadn't managed to catch up with him, then they had both forgotten. Charlie had been beating herself up about her mistake in not following it up immediately.

The smile fell from Danny's face for a second, but he recovered quickly. "Oh yes, I remember now. I went to the supermarket to do a food shop. They're open twenty-four hours and it's quiet at that time in the evening."

"Which supermarket?" Charlie fired her questions at him quickly to give him as little time as possible to think.

"Sainsbury's. It's near my house."

That didn't fit at all. Danny's house was near the centre of Winchester. She glanced at her notes. "You were still on the motorway at six minutes past eleven. And we can check the supermarket CCTV. Will we find any evidence of you shopping that evening?"

Danny lowered his head despondently.

"Why don't we start again? Where did you go after you dropped Tracey Gulliver at the bus stop?"

"I went back and parked near the Highfield Road house, waiting for Fliss to leave. I was going to confront her, tell her about Kate and get them to talk. But Fliss must have already left because when I saw her, she was walking towards the house. I was planning to wait outside until she came back out, but she left the front door wide-open and headed straight up the stairs, so I followed her."

"Then what happened?"

"I told her Kate was her daughter."

"How did she take the news?" It must have come as a shock to the poor woman to learn that someone she'd been working with for months was her long-lost daughter. Charlie sympathised with her.

"She laughed. And then she denied having a daughter."

"But that was no reason to kill her." Charlie was struggling to make the leap. She could understand how Kate might react so strongly to an outright rejection like that, but why would Danny react so violently on Kate's behalf?

"I had to. Kate would have killed me for giving up her secret. She'd already asked me to kill Fliss. Admitting failure would be bad enough in her eyes, but when she found out I'd told Fliss about her... I didn't know what else to do." Danny was becoming more and more distressed.

"What happened next?" Charlie asked gently.

"She had her back towards me in the bathroom. It was a perfect opportunity, especially as I'd already given myself an alibi by leaving. I thought the police would probably blame it on one of the people left in the house."

"Wasn't that risky? One of them might have come upstairs and seen you."

Danny grunted. "The kitchen door was shut, and I could hear Alicia and Stephen shouting at each other. Once those two get into an argument, it can go on for hours."

"How did you kill Felicity?"

"I banged her head against the wall to knock her unconscious, then popped her in the bath and slit her wrists."

Charlie allowed herself a moment of inner elation. He'd confessed on tape. They were home free, at least as far as Fliss's murder was concerned.

Danny continued, "I thought slitting Fliss's wrists would be a nice homage to Kate, and she'd know that I'd done it. Did you know she tried to slit her wrists when she was younger? She's still got a very faint scar."

Charlie stopped herself from gasping. Kate had to be Kylie. Sophia West said Kylie got the scar when she broke her wrist. Kate had clearly used it to manipulate Danny. She would leave that bombshell for later, if she needed it.

"Why would you do that for Kate?" There was obviously no romantic attachment, not with Danny being gay. Charlie couldn't work it out.

"Because I wanted to kill myself, and I couldn't do it on my own. I didn't have the guts. I thought it would be easier if we could do it together. And I wanted to jump because there's no going back, no chance to change my mind and phone for an ambulance. I needed that finality."

"And Kate agreed to this?"

"It was her idea. She promised that if I killed her birth mother, she would do this for me. She didn't think she could kill her own flesh and blood, even though she hated the woman."

"What about the murder weapon? The knife you used to slit Felicity's wrists? Where is it?" Had Danny planted it in Lisa Grant's kitchen?

"I'm not sure. I gave it to Kate. She asked for it."

Charlie wondered how stupid Danny could be. Giving Kate evidence that might tie him to Felicity's murder wasn't clever. Then again, if he was planning on suicide, he probably hadn't cared. "Where did you get the knife?"

"It belonged to the caterer. I took it while everyone was upstairs having a tour of the house. The caterer was busy putting something in the oven, so I pushed it up my sleeve and left the room before she noticed."

That made the murder premeditated. Danny's story about it being a spur-of-the-moment reaction was complete rubbish. He'd stolen the knife and taken it with him.

"What about Max Edmondson? How did you kill him?"

Danny's face turned white, and his eyes flashed with fear. "I didn't kill Max."

Charlie half believed him, especially as he'd finally opened up about Felicity's murder. "Why didn't you and Kate commit suicide as you'd agreed? After all, you killed Felicity. That was your part of the bargain. Did she refuse and ask you to do one more little favour for her first? Did she ask you to kill Max Edmondson?"

"No, yes, I mean..." Danny looked confused. "I'd like that lawyer now, please."

Chapter 80

Kate Lovell sat in interview room three, staring into space. DC Sally Gleeson was seated opposite her, with Kate's solicitor, Avril Vance, next to her client.

Charlie watched her through the one-way glass in the viewing room. Danny Owen was back in the cells until his solicitor showed up, and Rick had gone to make coffee.

"Did you ask Danny Owen to kill Felicity and Max Edmondson for you?" It was the third time Sally had asked that question. But whereas Owen had eventually spilled his guts, Kate Lovell remained stoically silent.

Avril Vance interrupted before Kate could speak. "We're here to talk about Danny Owen trying to throw my client off the roof of a twelve-story building."

"Mrs Vance, the question pertains to Danny Owen's motive, which makes it highly relevant. Would you please instruct your client to answer?"

A DC wouldn't normally lead on an important interview, but with Sally's former experience as a DS, it was a no-brainer, and it certainly looked to Charlie as if she could handle things. She'd left her to it because of the time constraints on how long they could hold both suspects, and the fact that it seemed Kate would only be charged with conspiracy to murder, although that frequently carried a life sentence. Danny's denial of murdering Max Edmondson might change everything. It certainly pointed the finger at Lovell.

The tantalising aroma of freshly brewed coffee entered the viewing room before Rick appeared. He placed a steaming mug in front of Charlie. "How is Sally doing?"

"Kate isn't nearly as cooperative as Danny has been."

"Looks like they're taking a break." Rick pointed at the one-way glass.

Damn. Charlie's craving for coffee had made her lose concentration. It looked as if the solicitor wanted to talk to her client alone. "Can you fetch Sally in here, please?" They needed to compare notes to see if the accounts of the two suspects tied up. Maybe this would be a good time for Charlie to step in and help with Kate's interview.

Sally joined them in the viewing room. "She's not saying much, ma'am. Her solicitor isn't helping by making her out to be a victim, who Danny was trying to push off the roof."

"Danny confessed to murdering Felicity Edmondson, but he swears he didn't kill Max." Charlie took a sip of her coffee. It burnt her lip.

"Do you think Kate might have done it?"

"It seems likely. Do you mind if I come in with you and ask a few questions?" They had more than enough to charge Danny Owen, putting no pressure on them to finish interviewing him, whereas they would have to let Kate go in a few hours if they didn't get anywhere with her. Danny's accusation might not be enough to make the conspiracy charge stick.

"That would be great. I'm not making any progress with her."

"They look as if they've nearly finished." Kate and her solicitor were no longer talking, and the solicitor was tidying up her notes.

"Let's get on with it then."

Chapter 81

"DI Steele, my client has been severely traumatised by that madman who threatened to throw her off a high-rise block of flats. She really shouldn't be here." Avril Vance glared angrily at Charlie.

"We can ask the doctor to examine her if you think she's not fit to be interviewed." That was the last thing Charlie wanted. She'd end up having to apply for an extension to hold Kate for another twelve hours. And there was never any guarantee that the judge would agree to it.

"She doesn't need a medical examination. She needs to go home."

"I have to ask a few more questions. The sooner they get answered, the sooner your client may be allowed to leave, so I suggest she starts cooperating and talking to us." Charlie had no intention of letting Kate go home yet. She needed to talk to the CPS to see if there was enough evidence to charge her. There was no one in the CPS office on a Sunday, but they must have an on-call number to phone.

Avril Vance leaned over and whispered something to Kate.

Charlie addressed Kate directly. "Do you know who your real father is?"

From the look on Kate's face, she hadn't been expecting that question. And while Kate showed signs of shock, Mrs Vance looked puzzled.

"Is this relevant?" Vance protested.

"It's very relevant. Kate, who is your real father?"

Kate stared at Charlie for a few moments. Charlie waited patiently for her to fill the silence, hoping that Avril Vance wouldn't butt in instead.

"It's Max, Max Edmondson," Kate said quietly.

Charlie smiled. "I'm afraid that's incorrect. Max Edmondson didn't even know your mother when you were born. In fact, they didn't meet until at least ten years later. DNA testing will prove he's not your real father. Did you follow him across the New Forest in Bramshaw?"

"He was leaving Fliss for another woman. The other woman was pregnant, and he seemed really happy about that. I saw him through the window, kissing her bump. He loved that baby, and it wasn't even born yet. But he didn't want anything to do with me. You don't know what it's like being rejected all your life."

"So you killed him?"

"I followed him. I just wanted to ask him why. Why didn't he want me when I was born?"

"But he couldn't tell you because he didn't know what you were talking about."

"I didn't know. I swear I didn't know. I never would have..." Kate started to sob.

"What happened?" Charlie asked softly.

"He kept telling me to go away. Then he sat down on a fallen tree trunk and let the dog off the lead. He turned his back to me, and the piece of rope he used as a dog lead was lying on the tree trunk next to him." Kate paused, shutting her eyes and taking deep breaths.

Charlie wondered if Kate wished she'd jumped off that roof yesterday. The enormity of what she'd done seemed to be sinking in. "Take your time," she encouraged gently. "What happened next?"

"I hit him over the head with a big stone, then I grabbed the rope and pulled it around his neck as tightly as I could."

"And the noose?"

"I thought that might implicate Danny. He tried to hang himself when he was younger."

"Did you intend to go through with the suicide pact?"

Kate shook her head. "No. If I wanted to kill myself, I would never jump off a building. It must be terrifying and so painful when you hit the ground. I hoped Danny would pluck up the courage to do it by himself, but he became obsessed with us doing it together. He would have killed me if you hadn't shown up."

Charlie decided she would still put a suicide watch on Kate. She was facing a long time in prison. That prospect would surely bring out any suicidal tendencies.

Chapter 82

Charlie switched on the recorder, and they listed the names of everyone present, which now included Michael Ingram, Danny Owen's solicitor.

Danny looked tired and frightened. Perhaps he was just beginning to realise the trouble he was in.

"Danny, did Kate Lovell ask you to kill Max Edmondson?"

Danny locked eyes with his solicitor for a moment. "Yes, but I didn't do it."

"Why not?"

"Because I don't think he's Kate's father. I was in a meeting with him, and he said his fifteenth wedding anniversary was coming up soon. So I congratulated him and asked him how long he'd known his wife. It didn't add up, you see. No one has a fourteen-year engagement. He hadn't even met Fliss when Kate was born."

"So you didn't want to kill him?"

"No."

"And yet, he's dead. How do you explain that?"

"I don't know. Perhaps Kate did it."

Charlie had hoped he might implicate Kate, but even though Kate had already confessed, she wanted proof, not simply a vague inkling. "Did you explain to Kate that Max wasn't her real father?"

"I tried, but she accused me of lying." Danny looked hurt. He was embracing his new role now, victim instead of perpetrator.

"Were you surprised when Max Edmondson was killed?"

"I was shocked."

"Did you confront Kate about it?"

"No. I thought she'd be happy. I thought she would think that I did it, then she would go through with the suicide pact. That's all I wanted."

"So you were happy to take the blame for something you didn't do?"

"I didn't care by then. It didn't matter because I knew I'd be dead soon."

Charlie made a note to arrange a suicide watch for Danny Owen as well. She didn't want him to kill himself while she was responsible for him.

"Interview suspended, a quarter past ten a.m."

Chapter 83

The DCI made a surprise visit to the incident room first thing on Monday morning. Charlie had been about to go up to his office to update him on the case.

"I hear congratulations are in order." The DCI glanced at Charlie as he addressed the whole team.

Charlie wondered who had told him the news. They had only finished sewing up the case late last night. She hadn't even had a chance to run it past the CPS yet, although she was confident they would have enough evidence to prosecute.

"Yes, sir. We have Danny Owen in custody for Felicity Edmondson's murder, and Kate Lovell for the murder of Max Edmondson."

"Well done. It's a good result."

"It was a team effort, sir. Everyone worked all weekend on the case." She wondered if she should ask him if they could claim overtime. Perhaps she would bring up the subject in private. No point in getting everyone's hopes up in case the DCI said no.

"Yes, well done, everyone." He turned back to Charlie. "DI Steele, may I have a word in private?"

Charlie followed him into the corridor.

"Good result for your first case. Well done for sticking to your guns. If it wasn't for your bloody-mindedness, we wouldn't have cracked the case."

Charlie couldn't stop a big, beaming smile from lighting up her face.

The DCI continued, "But if you ever disobey my orders again, I'll make sure you end up back in uniform directing traffic. Do you understand?"

Charlie's smile faded quicker than it had appeared. "Yes, sir. Sorry, sir." She guessed now wasn't the time to ask if she could pay her team for working the weekend.

"Good. Carry on, DI Steele." Talbot walked towards the lift.

Charlie watched him go. Her first case as SIO and she'd solved a double murder. She hated the DCI for taking the shine off her celebration. Despondently, she went back into the incident room.

"I'm going to my office to sort out the paperwork for the case," she said. "We should go out to the pub later in the week to celebrate." She forced a smile. "I'm buying."

"Thanks, ma'am."

"Yes, thanks."

Rick came up to her. "Don't forget it's Mia's birthday today. We're having a party for her friends, but they'll go home at six. You will come over later, won't you? Janette's cooking dinner and Mia's looking forward to seeing you."

Charlie nodded.

"Seven p.m.," Rick said. "Don't be late."

Chapter 84

Ollie Flanders had summoned Charlie to the CSI lab. He beckoned her over to his desk as soon as she entered the room.

Flanders didn't wait for her to sit. "We found Felicity Edmondson's glasses in Owen's flat."

"Are you sure they're hers?" She'd specifically asked them to search for the missing glasses.

Flanders stared at her with disdain. His tense face muscles made his scar stand out more than usual, giving him a slightly scary appearance. "We got an optician to check the lenses. They match her prescription. And DNA on the glasses matches to Mrs Edmondson."

Charlie regretted questioning him, but it was important to tie up every bit of evidence. They already had Danny's laptop, which proved he really was ChessDevil, tying him to Kate. "Sorry, we haven't really got off on the right foot, have we?"

A flicker of a smile appeared on Ollie's face. "I guess you could say that."

Charlie waited for some sort of apology from him, but none came, so she turned around and walked towards the exit.

"DI Steele."

Charlie stopped. What did Flanders want now?

"You did a great job with that case."

Charlie glanced around, trying to prevent the corners of her lips from turning up. To her surprise, a proper smile was plastered all over Ollie Flanders's face.

"Thank you," she said.

At lunchtime, Charlie took a break to find a gift for Mia's birthday.

Eastleigh was too small to have a large selection of shops. Whatever did a ten-year-old girl want for her birthday, anyway? Charlie hadn't a clue. If Louise had lived, she would know the answer to that. Or maybe she would have never made a good mother.

She pulled out her purse and drew out a small, well-worn photo. Baby Louise still stabbed at her heart every time she looked at her picture. She closed her eyes for a few seconds, blinking back the tears. This case had affected her in so many ways: the Edmondsons' impending divorce, the baby Felicity was forced to give away. If only Felicity's mother had allowed her to keep her baby girl, things would have worked out very differently.

She slid the photo back into its hiding place. She still needed to find Mia's birthday present.

She found a small jeweller's and chose a pretty gold necklace. It was probably too expensive for a ten-year-old, but maybe that would help to make up for all the birthdays she'd missed. She got the shop assistant to gift-wrap the necklace and slipped it into her bag.

Mia said goodbye to the last of her friends. "I've had the best birthday ever." She picked up Duke and carried him over to the sofa. She looked exhausted, despite the huge smile.

"Why don't you and Duke watch TV for a bit while I help Mummy clear up." Rick felt pretty tired himself, even though he'd only arrived home from work halfway through the proceedings. A houseful of ten-year-olds wasn't something he could cope with every day.

Janette was loading the dishwasher.

"I don't know how you do it." Rick gave her a hug. "Put your feet up for a few minutes and let me help."

"Thanks, love."

Rick put the dishwasher on and started tidying things into the cupboards. A delicious smell came from the oven and he wondered what she was cooking. He knew his wife would have gone to a lot of trouble for Charlie.

"You didn't tell Mia that Charlie was coming, did you?" He still wasn't convinced she would show up, and he didn't want Mia's birthday to end in disappointment.

"No, of course not. But I'm sure she'll come. It's her niece's birthday, and she hasn't got the excuse of a murder investigation now."

Rick laid the table. He'd been relieved the murders had been tied up before Mia's birthday. His daughter would have been so disappointed if he hadn't been able to make it to the party. "Charlie did a good job." No, not a good job, a great job. He was proud of his sister. He just couldn't quite bring himself to tell her that, not yet.

Chapter 85

Charlie sat outside in the car. After the intense pressure of a double-murder investigation and the adrenaline rush of solving the crimes and closing the case, she should feel more relaxed. But the truth was, she never found it easy to switch off. Her mind was still buzzing, and her body wracked with tension as she relived and reanalysed each part of the investigation, singling out what had gone wrong and what she could do better next time. She should be unwinding and enjoying the victory.

The light in Rick's front window made his house look warm and cosy. Rick was lucky to have a loving family. She didn't belong there. And she wasn't in the right frame of mind to smile and be sociable. Not today.

She reached into her purse and pulled out Louise's photo. Louise would be ten now if she'd lived. What would she look like now? What would she like doing? Charlie knew she should let go of the past, should have done that long ago, but how did she do that without feeling disloyal to her beautiful daughter? She promised herself she would work on the problem in the near future. Perhaps there was a support group she could join, although she didn't relish the thought of telling a bunch of strangers about Louise.

Charlie took a deep breath and got out of the car. She could hear the muffled sound of the TV as she walked up to the front door. She fumbled in her bag for the gift-wrapped necklace. The slim box was just the right size. Without hesitating, she pushed it through the letterbox and walked quickly back to the car. There was a hot bath and a glass of wine back at her flat with her name on it.

DRIVEN TO MURDER

Hampshire Crime: DI Charlotte Steele book 2

A rising star. A deadly secret. A race against time.

When a top stock-car driver is found murdered at a Hampshire race meeting, Detective Inspector Charlie Steele is thrust into the high-octane world of motorsport. The serious beating of the victim points to a frenzied rage.

The case takes a darker turn when Summer Darby, the sport's brightest female driver, becomes the target of a chilling attack. Someone wants her out of the race. And the closer Charlie gets to the truth, the more she realises Summer is hiding something that could make her the killer's next victim.

With suspects closing ranks on and off the racetrack, Charlie's investigation hits a dead end. When another attempt is made on Summer's life, the case becomes more than a murder inquiry. It becomes a desperate fight to stop a killer before they strike again.

Now it's a race Charlie can't afford to lose.

ROCK BOTTOM

Download the prequel to The Murder Mile series **FREE** when you sign up to my author newsletter.

The locals call it the Murder Mile because of the rising number of murders, but she didn't expect her own mother to be one of the victims.

When Rose Marsden receives the devastating news of her mother's death, she rushes to London to find out what's going on. At first, it looks like a burglary gone wrong.

As she struggles to come to terms with her tragic loss, the shocking revelation that her mother died of a drug overdose rocks her world still further. The police have labelled her mother as a junkie and closed the case, but Rose is certain her mother would never touch drugs. She is desperate to find out the truth and get justice for her mum.

Despite her efforts, Rose is frustrated by lack of proof, and her own safety is put at risk during a frightening encounter with a local gang member. Now, fear of reprisal means the only way to survive is to find evidence to convict the murderer.

The Hale Hill estate is a dangerous place. Will Rose's stubborn persistence turn her into the next victim?

Be the first to find out about new releases, special offers, book recommendations and interesting snippets about my books, and about me. Download the free book and sign up on this link https://dl.bookfunnel.com/vbr1ef83yq, or visit my website at https://www.christinepattleauthor.com/

Other Books by Christine Pattle

The Murder Mile Series

Book 1 INTO THE RED
Book 2 STONE COLD
Book 3 DARK SHADOW
Book 4 KNIFE EDGE
Book 5 WHEEL SPIN
Book 6 GUN SHOT
Book 7 FATAL SUBSTITUTE
Book 8 FINAL RETRIBUTION

The Clarke Pettis Series

Book 1 THE FRAUD
Book 2 THE COVER-UP
Book 3 THE PAYBACK

Standalone books

SECRETS NEVER DIE
All books are available on Amazon and are in Kindle Unlimited.

About The Author

Christine Pattle writes thrillers. Countless hours spent watching every high-octane film available in her youth instilled a permanent love of edge-of-your-seat suspense. She soon moved from film to books, devouring all things thriller, crime and mystery.

Most of Christine's books are set in the fictional towns of Brackford and Hale Hill, which are based on Romford and Harold Hill in north-east London, where she worked for several years. Harold Hill is the location of the real 'murder mile'.

When she's not writing, she's busy scaring herself silly riding big, feisty horses, or walking around the countryside dreaming up exciting new plots. As if that wasn't enough, she still manages to squeeze in the day job, trying to make small budgets do great things in the fight against homelessness.

You can contact Christine by email:
christine@christinepattleauthor
Visit Christine's website
https://www.christinepattleauthor.com/
Or visit her Facebook page
https://www.facebook.com/ChristinePattleAuthor

Acknowledgments

A HUGE thank you:

To you, the reader. Readers are by far the most important people in an author's world. Of all the millions of books you could have chosen to read, a massive THANK YOU for giving my book a chance. I really hope you enjoyed it. If you can spare a few minutes to leave a review for the book on Amazon, or even a couple of seconds to give it a star rating, I would be very grateful. It helps other readers to discover my books and inspires me to keep on writing.

To my brilliant editor, Emily at Laurence Editing.

To my cover artist, Get Covers.

And, finally, to all the authors who have ever inspired me. I love reading.

COPYRIGHT

www.ingramcontent.com/pod-product-compliance
Ingram Content Group UK Ltd.
Pitfield, Milton Keynes, MK11 3LW, UK
UKHW040634150726
13770UKWH00023B/161

9 798233 018985